The Murder of Grace Bryant

by

Suzanne Rossi

The Murder of Grace Bryant

Cover Art by *Kim Mendoza*

The Wild Rose Press, Inc.
PO Box 708
Adams Basin, NY 14410-0708
Visit us at www.thewildrosepress.com

Publishing History
First Crimson Rose Edition, 2017
Print ISBN 978-1-5092-1368-9
Digital ISBN 978-1-5092-1369-6

Published in the United States of America

"Is that what this is all about?
Proving your father innocent?"

I squeezed my folded hands together harder. "Yes."

The man took a moment to gaze out of the window. "To be honest, I was never sure. He was grief-stricken over the loss of his wife and bewildered that anyone would think he could have done it. He had an air of honesty—of openness—about him I liked."

"And yet, the evidence was there," Josh added.

"The evidence was there. The blood, the fingerprints, the time gap, the argument, it was all just too much to ignore."

Josh rose and extended his hand. "Thanks, Dan, we appreciate your input."

I also stood. "And thank you for taking the time to answer my questions."

"Miss Bryant, are you thinking of trying to get the case re-opened?"

"Well, in order to do that, I'd have to find the real killer, wouldn't I? Goodbye, Mr. Harper."

We left the room with him staring at us, a surprised expression on his face. I wondered if he'd start digging again, too.

I may be opening one hell of a can of worms.

Praise for Suzanne Rossi

"Suzanne Rossi has cemented her spot on my must read list with this romantic suspense [*A NOVEL DEATH*]."

~Night Owl Reviews

~*~

"…the author did a wonderful job of pulling me into the storyline [of *THROUGH MY EYES*]."

~Night Owl Reviews

~*~

"Overall, this author has again proven [in *THROUGH MY EYES*] how good she is at writing a novel in the paranormal genre."

~The Romance Studio

~*~

RENDEZVOUS WITH DEATH: "I have never been let down by this author when looking for a fabulous suspense story."

~Night Owl Reviews

Dedication

I often try to set my stories in familiar locations. The more I know the area, the more realistic I can make it sound to the readers.

For this novel, I used my husband's family farm in Northwest Iowa. It was first homesteaded in the late 1880s and has been in the family ever since. I had the privilege of visiting twice and fell in love with the old farmhouse, so when I wrote this book, Paullina, Iowa, became the small farming community of Wellington, and the farm played a central role in the story. I tried to keep everything as close to reality as my memory allowed.

As a result, I'd like to dedicate this book to the Peek family. Uncle Chet, who grew up on the farm, and his sons, Stan and Tom, along with my husband, Bruce, and his brothers, Brent and Brian, who were all frequent visitors during holidays and the summer months.

I hope all of them will read this story, remember, and smile.

Prologue

I sat at my kitchen table clutching a glass of wine in trembling fingers. The clock on the wall read three in the morning. I'd heard it again—the sound that had awoken me for the fourth night in a row. There was no accompanying dream this time, only the long, mournful moan of a train whistle.

The sound took me back to my childhood. Long ago, it had rolled across the Iowa cornfields to creep through my open window and tickle my seven-year-old imagination. Where was the train going? New York? Chicago? Or the most exotic of places like Hollywood, where movie stars lived? The train tracks and depot had been located south of town in what Mother had always called the warehouse district. Sometimes, I'd force myself to stay awake until the lowing cry of that midnight locomotive dissipated into the darkness.

That had all taken place long ago before the incident that had erased so much of my memory.

I raised the glass to my lips with shaking hands and took a long sip. Over the past few months, bits and pieces of dreams drifted through my mind—dreams about my mother, my father, and the days leading up to the tragedy. Sometimes, the dreams were bright and carefree, not unlike my life before that night. At other times, they bordered on nightmares—disjointed and making no sense.

Until the train whistle that is. No longer able to ignore it, I knew what I had to do—return to Wellington, Iowa, a town I'd left soon after the murder.

I was being summoned home.

Chapter One

I stood on the back stoop of the farmhouse—a house I hadn't entered in twenty-five years—and stared at the key clutched in my hand. It would be so easy to turn around and drive back to Chicago. Forget this crazy idea and resume my life. That's all I had to do—turn around and leave. But I couldn't do that. I had a plan, and it was a plan I had to carry out.

I inserted the key into the lock and twisted. The door opened on slightly squeaky hinges. Taking a deep breath, I hefted my suitcase and walked inside the enclosed back porch.

Four days ago, I'd phoned the family attorney, John Casey, here in Wellington and asked him to make sure the place was ready for occupancy.

"Occupancy? By whom?" he'd questioned.

"By me. I'm coming home."

Silence had greeted my words.

"Why?" Did I read alarm in his tone?

"Why not? It's my home. Just have someone get it ready. I'm sure that after all these years, the place can use some sprucing up. I'll be there on Thursday afternoon."

"How long are you staying, Callie?"

My sudden announcement had caught him unawares. Not even his lawyer skills erased the surprise in his voice.

"Permanently, Mr. Casey."

I waited as he paused. "Very well. I'll contact a cleaning crew over in Jasper right away. I was out there a few months ago. The house appeared in fair condition. It didn't need any major repairs."

"Excellent, but then I expected no less. My aunt paid you quite well to oversee the upkeep," I reminded him in a cool tone. I could be snotty at times.

"I agreed to look after the place because your father was a good friend. Money had nothing to do with it."

The rebuke was clear. While not sincere, I apologized anyway. "I'm sorry, I didn't mean to suggest otherwise."

I had to tread lightly. John Casey was a question mark in my forgotten past, which meant he could be either friend or foe.

"Will you stop by the office for the key?"

"No need unless you've changed the locks. I have my late aunt's."

"The locks are the same. No reason to change them. No one steals anything in Wellington."

No, they just commit murder.

That was then. This was now. I stood on the back porch willing myself to continue on. I reached for the doorknob, twisted, and then pushed. It stuck slightly, just like always.

I sat my bag on the beige patterned linoleum floor in the kitchen. Memories, good ones, flooded my mind as I entered. I saw it through the eyes of a seven-year-old again: my mother making breakfast at the stove, my father enjoying a cup of coffee at the table by the window, me sitting next to him watching Mother try to flip pancakes.

My throat tightened and tears prickled behind my eyes. I closed them and swallowed.

Not now. Maybe later.

I walked through the café doors and into the dining room. Nothing had changed. The table and chairs, sideboard, and china cupboard—empty now of my grandmother's "company" china and crystal—still stood where I remembered.

Turning to the right, I paused in the archway to the living room. It, too, was unchanged. The TV, a bulky console, was nestled in the corner. The full-sized sofa was on one side of the room while the matching loveseat was opposite it. My father's recliner sat angled so he could watch TV without having to turn his head. He'd been a great Minnesota Twins fan.

The cleaners had done a good job. The rooms smelled of pine and the hardwood floors gleamed along with the matching woodwork. Not a spec of dust marred the furniture surfaces. Even though old and hopelessly out of fashion, the lace curtains hung bright with recent washing. I'd replace them at a later date. For now, they worked.

Try as I might, I couldn't keep my eyes from the matching archway leading to the spacious foyer. My heartbeat accelerated, and I wanted to run. For the first time, I doubted my decision to come home.

It's just a room, Callie. Just another room.

Lifting my chin, I heaved a deep breath, and strode toward the scene of the crime. The grandfather clock in the corner opposite the staircase no longer worked, its hands forever frozen at one-fifty-four. The large Oriental rug was no longer on the floor. I was sure it had been seized as evidence for Daddy's trial, and afterward, I assumed my aunt had had it destroyed.

The oak floors stretched naked. My gaze was drawn to a slight discoloration in the middle of the room. Like a lightning bolt crashing through the roof to incinerate me on the spot, I realized what I saw.

Bloodstains. Mother's blood. I whirled on shaking legs and walked back into the living room, my stomach boiling with nausea. I inhaled several deep breaths and fought for control. After a few minutes, my stomach settled and I returned, defiantly staring at the floor. The bloodstains would never be erased from neither the floor nor my mind. I needed a new rug.

I clenched my jaw and crossed the bare oak boards, then mounted the stairs. Four steps up, I paused on the landing. The sun, shining through the stained glass window, cast a multi-hued pattern on the ancient and threadbare runner. I ignored the bright colors and stared toward the second floor. A flash of memory zipped through my head—a small child crouched near the top step, hands clutching the spindles of the railing, and seeing... What? The vision retreated. Had I remembered or just imagined it?

Remember what Doctor Halloran said. Don't push it. Let the memories come gradually at their own pace.

I licked my lips and ignoring the image in my mind, climbed the rest of the way turning left in the wide hallway. I passed the door to my brother, Denny's, room. I didn't look in. I couldn't. Not yet. I still missed him.

My room lay at the back corner of the house. More memories choked me as I entered. The antique four-poster bed with the patchwork quilt, the dresser, and chest of drawers hadn't moved. It was as if I'd left yesterday. I dropped my suitcase on the rag rug by the bed and walked to the window. Shoving the curtains aside, I threw the latch and pushed on the sash. It opened smoothly. The curtains rippled in the light April breeze, bringing with it the light scents of lilac along with newly plowed and planted soil.

I turned and caught my reflection in the dresser mirror. A woman with a blonde, chin-length bob and blue eyes stared back. I'd half expected to see the image of a child.

With a sigh, I quickly unpacked the suitcase and put the clothing in the drawers, hesitating over the last item—a .38 caliber snub-nosed Smith & Wesson revolver. I'd bought it a few months ago and repeated trips to the firing range had made me, if not a marksman, at least able to hit what I aimed at. I opened the nightstand drawer and dropped it in.

I had more luggage in the car, but would get it later. The moving van with my things was scheduled to arrive within the next couple of days.

I sat on the edge of the bed, kicked off my shoes, laid down, and closed my eyes, pushing my mission to the back of my mind for now. I needed to rest, to rejuvenate. Using imagery suggested by my psychiatrist, I visualized a tranquil meadow with a burbling creek, and then sighed when my tight muscles relaxed.

Regardless of whatever would come, I was home.

****

An hour later, I stood in front of the refrigerator. It was empty, of course. The ice-maker, however, was working. Somebody had thought to activate it. I was surprised to find a full array of dishes and utensils in the cupboards. I remembered none of it and the shine on the silverware suggested someone had bought it recently. John Casey?

I finally found the glasses, selected one, scooped several cubes in, and filled a glass from the tap. The cold well water tasted good. It needed no purification like in the city.

A car pulled into the driveway and parked behind mine. I didn't recognize either woman emerging.

So, it's begun.

In true country fashion, they came into the enclosed porch, and then knocked on the kitchen door. I opened immediately.

"Callie? Oh my goodness, you look just like you did as a child," the first woman gushed.

"Please come in." I stepped back and offered them access to the kitchen.

"We heard in town that you were coming home, and when we saw your car in the drive, just had to drop by. Hope we're not intruding," the second lady chimed in.

"Not at all. Although I have to admit, I don't recognize either of you."

The first woman laughed lightly. "Oh good heavens, of course you don't. I'm June Simpson. My husband and I own a farm just north of town."

"And I'm Lorna Bell. My late husband, Rich, and I owned the secondhand store in town. I run it now."

I vaguely remembered Lorna Bell, but had no memory of June Simpson. And the comment about just passing by was a crock. I was sure our farm was nowhere near either of their homes. I remembered neighbors' names.

"Please, have a seat," I said indicating the kitchen table. I needed to maintain a calm, slightly timid demeanor. "May I offer you some iced water? I'm afraid that's all I have at the moment. I just got here and haven't been to the store yet."

The women glanced at each other, no doubt surprised I hadn't led them into the living room. They sat anyway.

"Water is fine," June said.

"The house looks to be in good shape," Lorna commented as I plunked ice cubes into glasses and ran the water.

I ignored the subtle suggestion to show them the rest of the house.

"Yes, I had John Casey make sure it was livable before I came." I handed them the drinks and took a chair. "I take it you knew my parents."

Lorna sipped and shot a glance at June.

June smiled. "Oh, yes, indeed. Your father and I graduated from high school together. Knew him all my life. He and your mother used to throw the best parties and barbeques."

I shifted my gaze to Lorna. "And did you know my father as well?"

She lowered her eyes and sipped the water again. "Yes. I was a townie and had to help out a lot at my father's hardware store, but your daddy often came in. He was so good-looking, even as a boy. Just about broke every female heart in Wellington when he married your mother."

A snippet of forgotten conversation from long ago popped into my head. As usual, Mom and Dad were arguing.

"And just how many times do you have to go to the secondhand store in a week?" Mother had said, in a raised voice.

"I told you, Rich and I are old friends. We lunch together whenever I'm in town." Daddy's voice had held a patient tone.

"And of course, you never *see Lorna."*

"Naturally, I see her if she's there."

"She makes cow eyes at you every Sunday in church."

My attention centered on Lorna. Had she been infatuated with my father in spite of having a husband?

"Yes, my mother was beautiful and so full of life—until…" I deliberately let the words "the murder" remain unspoken.

Both women stared. June recovered first.

"Yes, such a tragedy. And I want you to know that never for a moment did I believe your father did it."

"Me, neither," Lorna added.

"I'm glad you feel that way, because I agree." I wondered how much these women knew about my parents' relationship. They both had known Daddy all their lives. But Mother? How did they get along with her?

Lorna shifted in her chair and stared at the table top, not meeting my eyes.

June wiped the condensation from the glass, and took a long drink before looking at me. "Have you been living with your mother's sister all these years?"

The abrupt change of subject told me both women had something to say but weren't. My psychiatrist, Dr. Halloran claimed I was a champ at changing the subject.

"Yes. In Chicago. Aunt Dee died several months ago."

One of the last conversations I'd had with my late aunt popped into my head. She was dying and apparently felt the need to cleanse her soul.

"I lied, Callie. I wanted revenge. I was angry and wanted to punish your father for what he did. It was wrong, and I'm so sorry. Please forgive me."

I forgave her to ease her mind. Those were the last words she'd spoken. She lapsed into a coma and died a few hours later. Deep down, I didn't really forgive her. She had lied about way too many things, and those lies were the catalyst for me being here—along with a promise to my brother, Denny.

No reason to tell these women that I'd never met my aunt until that horrible week, but Mother had talked about her older sister and the big house they'd grown up in near Lake Michigan. She'd made Chicago sound like paradise.

"And your brother, Dennis, is he still in Chicago, too?"

Pain and sorrow slashed at my heart. "No, Denny was in the army. He died in Afghanistan two years ago."

"Oh dear, I'm so sorry," June said, her hand pressed to her chest.

"And so you decided to return to Wellington? I'd think Chicago would be more your style," Lorna blurted, and then recovered. "I mean, having grown up there, a small Iowa farm town must seem boring. Goodness knows, your mother thought so."

At last, an honest remark. June sent her friend a

11

furious look.

I didn't answer, but rose and reached for their glasses. "Can I get you a refill?"

June glanced at her watch. "Heavens! Would you look at the time? We have to get going."

Both women stood with Lorna echoing June's words. "Yes, I have tons to do at home. We just stopped by to welcome you back. So nice to see you again, Callie. Do drop in the store if you need anything."

I was amused at their sudden hurry to leave. Perhaps my insinuation about the murder had touched a nerve.

They left. As the car rolled down the driveway, I wondered if they'd accomplished their mission and what they'd talk about on the drive back to town. Their probing hadn't been subtle, and I'd done my best to keep them in the dark—at least for now. I put both women on my mental list of people to watch.

I retrieved the remainder of my luggage from the car. I'd packed just enough to get by for the next few days. The rest of my clothes and toiletries didn't take long to put away. I had just reentered the kitchen when another car, a big black Cadillac, swept into the yard.

Once again, amused at all the attention so soon, I waited in the living room until the driver knocked at the back door. I opened up to a tall man in a business suit. His dark hair was liberally sprinkled with gray, and like my last visitors looked to be in his early to mid-fifties.

He smiled. "Little Callie, all grown up. It's so good to see you."

"Thank you, and you are…?"

He laughed. "I'm Bob Kendall. I was a good friend of your father's. May I come in?"

I stepped back and he entered, his gaze immediately scanning the room. The scent of an expensive cologne or aftershave wafted in with him. It smelled familiar, but I couldn't place it. I formed an instant dislike to the man, although I had no idea why.

"Needs updating, but in remarkable shape," he commented.

I didn't answer his remark, but offered him a glass of water.

"No thanks, I just thought I'd drop by and see if you need anything."

"I'm fine for the moment. Won't you have a seat?" I asked indicating the kitchen table.

He waved a hand. "No, thank you." His gaze shifted toward the café doors to the dining room. "Do you mind if I see how the rest of the house fared?"

"Why?" I didn't care if I sounded rude. My dislike intensified. I found his question pushy at best and his curiosity irritating.

Take it easy. No need to antagonize anybody yet.

"I'm sorry, Callie. I should have explained. Of course, you don't remember but I own Kendall Realty. I have a buyer over in Sheldon who's been after this property for years. Your aunt refused to consider selling. Said it was yours and Dennis's inheritance."

"My brother died two years ago, Mr. Kendall, and I have no interest in selling."

"He's willing to pay top dollar. Almost thirteen hundred acres with a house in good condition is a hot commodity right now." He mentioned a price that sounded like the national debt, yet was likely under the true value.

My irritation grew when he didn't so much as offer

condolences on Denny's death, but plowed on with his mission to get a listing.

"I'm still not interested."

"How long do you plan on staying?"

"Permanently."

His forehead furrowed. "Really? Why?"

"Why not?" Our exchange echoed mine with John Casey a few days ago.

"I'd think the memories would be unpleasant for starters."

"Not all memories are bad, Mr. Kendall."

"Callie, I'll be blunt. There's nothing here for you in Wellington. I'll give you a few days to think it over. At least give the offer some consideration."

"There's nothing to consider. Thank you for stopping by, Mr. Kendall."

He shrugged, fished in his pocket and withdrew a business card, laying it on the table. "Just in case you change your mind."

"I won't."

He left, paused by his car, and stared back at the house, then hesitated as if about to return and try to persuade me. Finally, he opened the car door, slid behind the wheel, and drove off, his tires kicking up a plume of dust all the way down the gravel road.

I was tempted to toss the card, but instead tucked it into a kitchen drawer. I had no recollection of Bob Kendall at all. If he were such a good friend of my father's, I'd have thought the name would ring a bell. His landing on my doorstep within a couple of hours of my arrival with an offer on the property was crass, and his obvious desire for me to leave piqued my curiosity.

He wants me gone. Why?

I put him on my mental watch list, too.

****

I shoved the list of groceries into my purse and gathered my keys when yet another car pulled into the drive.

Who now? I was getting tired of people intruding, even though I'd expected it.

This time, however, my visitor didn't come to the back door, but the front. I walked through the house and opened up.

A tall, good-looking man with light brown hair and a pleasant smile stood before me.

"Miss Bryant? Hi, my name is Josh Hendricks. I'm the owner, publisher, and chief reporter for the *Wellington News-Sentinel*. Would you be available for a little chat?"

A reporter? This *wasn't* something I'd expected—or wanted.

"I'm sorry, Mr. Hendricks, but I was just on my way out. Perhaps later. And what kind of a chat?"

"Call it a welcome home, if you like. I thought my readers might be interested in hearing why you've returned after all these years."

Curiosity got the best of me. I stepped back and invited him in. He entered and immediately cast his gaze around the foyer.

I just as quickly led him into the living room. He followed and sat on the sofa without asking. I chose Daddy's recliner.

"I can't see how I'm of interest to anybody."

He shrugged. "This is a small town. Naturally, people are curious."

"Tell me, would they have been nearly as curious if

my mother hadn't been murdered?"

His gray eyes narrowed slightly. "Perhaps not, but that's human nature."

"It's also a reporter's nature. I can tell you now I have no intention of discussing the murder or the trial with you or anybody else. If you want details, I suggest you consult your own newspaper files or those in Atwell. As the county seat, it has the only daily newspaper for miles a round, assuming it's still in business."

"It is, but I assure you I don't want lurid details of a crime committed a quarter of a century ago. I'm here for a human interest story about why a girl born in Wellington, and is then whisked off to the city, would return. That's all."

"I can tell you that in one sentence. I got tired of the hassles of city living. See? Simple and to the point." I glanced at my watch. "If you'll excuse me, Mr. Hendricks, I'm tired and need to run a few errands."

He rose, smiled, and said, "How about I take you to dinner? That way you don't have to cook on your first night back. Do you remember The Kozy Kafe? They still serve pretty good food."

Did dinner also include questions? Probably.

"I remember, but no thank you. As I said, it's been a long day. I'm tired. An early night is on my agenda." I paused. "By the way, how long have you lived in Wellington?"

"I bought the paper two years ago."

"And you came from a big a city, too, right?"

He gave me a funny look. "That's right. How did you know?"

"Nobody who ever lived in the country would

come to a farmer's front door."

He laughed, surprising me. It rumpled deep in his chest. It sounded comforting—the kind I wouldn't mind hearing again and again.

Shaking off this suddenly sentimental notion, I walked back toward the foyer. He followed, glanced at the stained floor, then opened the door and turned.

"The back door. You'd think after all this time, I'd remember that. Good afternoon, Miss Bryant. If you change your mind, drop by the paper. It's on Elm, just off Main."

He ambled down the steps to his car and waved as he drove away.

Interesting. A newcomer and a reporter to boot. He could have his uses. The fact he was good-looking was a bonus.

As I walked to my car, I thought things had gone well. In the last few hours, I'd had more than my share of visitors. I wondered how many more curiosity seekers would come knocking.

****

Not even Wellington, population three thousand-some-odd people, was immune to the passage of time. A small strip mall just east of town had sprung up during my absence. One end was anchored by a grocery store while an auto repair shop sat on the other. In between were a hardware store, a quick print place, a discount shoe store, an electronics establishment, and a photographer's studio.

I parked close to the grocery doors, walked in, and grabbed a cart. In the produce section, two women poking through the tomatoes stopped their conversation about someone named Myra and stared as I passed.

They put their heads together whispering as their eyes followed my progress. I ignored them.

Needing only the essentials, I spent a mere twenty minutes locating items before joining the checkout line. From behind, someone tapped me on the shoulder. I turned to find an elderly lady smiling.

"Excuse me, but aren't you Callie Bryant? Martha Bryant's granddaughter?"

"Yes, I am."

"I knew it. You look just like her. Your grandma and I were the best of friends. Shame she died so young. She was a lovely lady."

I didn't really remember my grandmother nor did I resemble her much. She'd passed away when I was five. After that, other events took over my life.

"Thank you very much, Mrs…"

"Comstock, dear. Eleanor Comstock. I taught at the local high school. My late husband and I had a farm south of town. When he died, I sold out and moved to a smaller place in town. So much more convenient."

As she paused, I became aware the others in line had grown quiet and listened while pretending to check the contents of their carts.

Mrs. Comstock cleared her throat. "I understand you're living on the farm now."

"Yes, that's right."

"So nice to see young folk returning to their roots. If you need anything, please call or just drop by. I live at 235 Maple Street. You're welcome anytime."

I decided the old woman was just being pleasant. There were no probing glances from her like I was getting from those around me. No direct questions about my motives, which I'm sure, buzzed through other minds.

"Thank you. And feel free to come by the farm."

The line had moved and I was next. I turned my attention to the checkout girl, a teenager who probably had never heard of either my parents or me.

I drove home thinking about my brief public appearance. Other than Mrs. Comstock, no one had approached me, although I could tell speculation ran rife and I'd be the object of more than one telephone conversation tonight. Ah, life in a small town. Some things never change. My mother had hated it, but then according to my aunt, she'd hated a lot of things in Iowa, including my father. But then Aunt Dee had admitted lying to the police. What else had she lied about?

Dinner was a simple affair—a baked chicken breast, broccoli in cheese sauce, home-fried potatoes, and a salad. After the clean up, I wandered into the living room.

Out of curiosity, I turned on the ancient TV. Nothing appeared except snow and interference. And then I remembered that all TV programming now was digital. Ah well, my flat screen LED would be here soon. I put getting cable or a satellite dish installed on my "to do" list. I'd also need Wi-Fi. I settled on the sofa with a glass of wine, my tablet, and read until a mammoth yawn told me it was time to call it a day.

I climbed the stairs to my room, turned down the bed, brushed my teeth, and slid between the covers. Moonlight streamed through the window and the curtains fluttered in the breeze. I yawned again and nestled my head into the pillow. My eyes closed with weariness.

I awoke to the distant moan of a train whistle.
Ah, midnight.

Chapter Two

I awoke from a dream feeling slightly disoriented. Sitting up, I wiped a line of sweat from my brow with the edge of the sheet, and waited for my racing heart to return to normal. It took a moment to remember where I was—my old bedroom in Wellington.

I'd had the dream before, one of those disjointed dreams with sights and sounds that didn't go together. Voices, a man and a woman, argued. Then the scene shifted and I viewed a room through bars. The latter I'd already deduced to be the spindles of the stair railings, but I never clearly saw what it was I viewed.

A quick glance at the clock on the nightstand showed five-thirty. I was wide-awake. Sleep wouldn't return until tonight. Tossing the covers aside, I rose, slid my feet into slippers, and grabbed my robe.

In the kitchen, I started a pot of coffee and slapped a package of bacon into a pan. I'd use the extra slices for sandwiches or on salads. I took a couple of eggs from the carton, and laid two slices of bread next to the toaster. It had been years since I'd had anything more than a bowl of cereal for breakfast. Maybe my country genes were coming back to life.

The old-fashioned AM radio sat where it always had on the counter next to the fridge. I turned it on. The dial was set to the local station. I didn't recall either Mom or Dad tuning into anything else. While the bacon sizzled, I listened to the latest commodity prices from the Chicago Board of Trade. All grain futures were up, corn especially, thanks to the increase in ethanol production.

I played the dream back in my mind as I sat at the kitchen table nursing a cup of coffee.

As usual, I couldn't place the identity of the arguing couple. Was it Mom and Dad? Probably. They'd often argued. But had they done so that night? I couldn't remember. What I did remember was telling the deputies I'd heard raised voices.

I closed my eyes and tried to visualize the foyer from the top step of the staircase as it had been then. The entryway was barely illuminated, yet I had the impression of shadows flitting about. They refused to materialize into concrete images.

For years, the dreams had tormented me. Were they glimpses into the past or merely figments of my imagination gleaned from bits and pieces of overheard conversations? I didn't remember much about Mother's funeral. I recalled how Daddy's sobs scared me. I'd never seen him cry before.

Shaking my head, I opened my eyes and rose. Maybe I'd remember later. I removed the bacon from the pan and added the eggs, then popped the bread into the toaster. As I ate, I planned my day.

The first order of business was to check on the outbuildings to see their state of repair. Since the acreage was leased to other local farmers, I assumed they also used the corncrib and barn.

Then, I'd head for town and drop in on John Casey. He'd been Daddy's defense lawyer and I needed answers. When I finished with him, the sheriff's office was next on my list. I hoped they'd kept the files on my mother's murder and would let me go through them. The bank would be third.

After that, I'd wander around town, introducing myself as I poked into shops and stores. Maybe I'd make a few inquiries to get reactions. People often blurted out the truth when confronted with a surprising direct question.

That appealed to me, even though it meant jumping in with both feet and no clear idea of what I thought I'd accomplish, but I was eager to get started. *No time like the present. Put off touring the outbuildings until later.*

As I sipped a second cup of coffee, I also decided to show up at the newspaper office. Josh Hendricks could be useful.

The fact he was good-looking had nothing to do with it.

****

I'll admit to not remembering much about Wellington, yet as I drove through town, some things clicked into place. The gazebo in the city park just north of town square still stood, gleaming arctic white against the light green of new leaves on the trees. Did they still hold concerts on warm summer nights?

I passed Connor's Ice Cream Parlor. Of course, concerts and ice cream cones. I could still taste the creamy mint chocolate chip as we'd sat on a blanket while waiting for the band to begin playing. Those concerts were Saturday night entertainment. We'd attended one the night of the murder.

And Lorna Bell's family's store, Mahon's Hardware, still occupied the same space. I wondered if the large home improvement stores had invaded

Northwest Iowa yet and if they had, could a family-run store survive in this day and age, especially with another hardware store in the strip mall. Did the Mahon's even still own it?

But as I'd noticed yesterday, time passes and things change. A cell phone tower sat on the western outskirts of town, and a cable company in Jasper had assured me they would be out this afternoon to make all the connections possible for TV and Internet access.

Welcome to the modern world, Wellington.

I parked on Main Street, walking the two blocks to John Casey's law office. I inhaled a deep breath before opening the door. A well-appointed waiting room was to my right. A receptionist, about my age, with an equally well-defined work area was to the left. She looked up and peered at me over her glasses as I approached.

"May I help you?"

"Yes, is Mr. Casey available? I know I don't have an appointment, but would like to speak with him if that's possible."

She looked at a book on her desk as if checking his schedule. I figured it was for show. How many clients could a lawyer in a town of three thousand have in one day?

"I think he can spare a few minutes. Your name?"

"Callie Bryant."

Her eyebrows rose and her spine straightened. "Callie? Oh my goodness, it is you. I'm Serena Smith—used to be Collier. We went to school together in the first grade."

Her surprise didn't ring true. By now, I assumed the entire town knew of my arrival, but I could be devious, too.

"Serena, of course, I remember you. How are you?" I lied. I didn't know her from Adam.

"I'm fine. Heard you were coming back to town."

Naturally, she'd heard. She was Casey's receptionist. She'd probably made the arrangements for the house to be cleaned.

"Yes, coming back to my roots. By the way, please send my thanks to the cleaning company. They did a wonderful job."

"Glad everything is all right." She lifted the phone and punched a button. "Mr. Casey, Callie Bryant is here to see you. Yes, of course." She hung up and smiled. "He'll be right out. Perhaps we can have lunch one day. I'd love to hear all about Chicago."

And how did *she* know I'd been in Chicago? After twenty-five years was it likely she'd remember where I'd gone? Casey must have had told her—or the gossipmongers.

"I'd like that. And you can fill me in on all the comings and goings in Wellington."

The door in the back wall opened and a smiling John Casey emerged. He strode forward, his hand outstretched. I accepted the offering.

I recognized him immediately. After Mother's death, he'd stopped by the farm several times to talk with Aunt Dee and Daddy. At the age of seven, I'd thought his sandy hair and blue eyes very attractive. And his smile was always in place. My gaze no longer stared at his belt buckle, but at his chin. I estimated his height as maybe five-ten. His sandy hair had grayed a bit around the temples, but his eyes and smile remained the same.

"Callie, welcome home. How nice of you to drop by. Please, come into my office where we can chat." He steered me toward the doorway. "Hold my calls, Serena."

He closed the door and led me to a plush leather chair in front of his ornate desk. "When did you get in? Was the house in good order?"

"Yesterday afternoon and the house is fine. I was a bit surprised to find the curtains and furniture in such good shape."

"Your aunt demanded regular cleaning by professionals. They'd come every few months to make sure all was well. Now, what can I do for you?"

I crossed my legs and smoothed my hand down the fabric of my navy blue slacks. "I'm wondering what you can tell me about my father's trial."

He sat back with raised eyebrows. "The trial? Good grief, Callie that was twenty-five years ago."

"But I'm sure you remember. You were Daddy's lawyer."

He waved a hand. "That isn't what I meant. Naturally, I remember. But your father died in prison. Why do you want to know at this late date?"

"Aunt Dee would never talk about it. Said it was water over the dam. She sheltered me from most of the nastiness. After she died, I searched all over the house for anything that related to Mom's murder and Daddy's trial, but came up dry."

"Callie, your parents had an argument. Your father lost control and stabbed her with a hunting knife." He hesitated. "Even you admitted they had fought that night."

I bit back a sharp reply. Ever since I was old

enough to understand the consequences of my statement, guilt had nagged at my soul. It wasn't until my aunt lay dying that I learned my comment alone was not responsible for Daddy's arrest.

Casey rolled on. "Plus his fingerprints were on the murder weapon. Your father denied everything of course, but the jury didn't buy it. Six stab wounds went against him. He was convicted of second degree murder."

"Mr. Casey…"

"John."

"John. That much I know. I was hoping to get a peek at your files, perhaps a transcript of the trial. It's no secret that I have memory gaps from that night. I want to fill in those gaps."

"I don't have the actual trial transcripts."

"Why not?" What kind of lawyer wouldn't keep records of his one and only murder trial?

He shifted in his chair and lowered his eyes. "It was a long time ago. The case was over and done with. I shredded a lot of old documents several years ago."

His body language suggested he was lying.

"That's it? What about the court? Would they keep the records?"

"No, not likely."

"So, there's nothing out there that can help me?"

He fiddled with a letter opener and stared at the blotter. "Callie, I don't think…"

"John, as you said, it was twenty-five years ago. My father is dead. What harm can it do for me to get a handle on what went down?"

He licked his lips. "A lot of old files are in storage over in Atwell. I'll see if I can find them." He glanced at his watch and came to his feet. "I'm sorry, Callie, but I have an appointment in a few minutes."

Not believing him for a moment, I also rose. He walked around the desk and escorted me into the waiting area. Serena hurriedly hung up the phone. My gut instinct said she'd been spreading the word of my meeting with John.

I turned. "Thank you for your time. I hope to hear from you soon. I guess time heals a lot. My memory has been slowly returning. Anything you can find might help."

"I'll do my best. The trial split this town. Some believed he did it, while others were just as adamant he hadn't. Don't go stirring up trouble. It might be smarter to let the old proverbial sleeping dogs lie."

I looked him straight in the eye and read worry on his face.

"It might, and then again, it might not. Goodbye, Serena. Let's do that lunch soon."

She made no attempt to mask her surprise at the conversation she'd just overheard. "Yes…yes, soon. Have a good day, Callie."

I swept out the door disappointed the transcripts might not exist. Murder wasn't a staple in Wellington. His practice would deal with wills, inheritances, and property disputes. Why did he seem so concerned? Was he afraid I'd uncover a botched defense?

I turned and marched down the sidewalk toward the police station.

****

"Ms. Bryant, I'm Officer Young. Chief Jackson is over at the courthouse in Atwell this morning. Is there anything I can help you with?"

The man standing before me smiled and extended his hand. I shook it and admired the crisp khaki uniform. I remembered the sheriff as rumpled and slightly unkempt.

"Nice to meet you. Jackson? I seem to remember a different name."

He motioned me to a chair in front of a desk. I sat as he perched a hip on the edge of it.

"Roy Wilson retired about fifteen years ago. Bill Jackson took over. Was appointed Chief of Police by the mayor about a year later."

Of course, the time thing again. Naturally, Roy Wilson wouldn't still be around.

"I noticed the cars outside marked Wellington Police. I don't remember Wellington having its own police force."

"The change came about the time Roy left. We have exactly three cruisers—one for the chief, one for me, and one extra for the weekend deputy. How can I help you?"

If he could get down to business, then so could I.

"Officer Young, I need to talk to the sher...I mean, the chief about a personal matter. Any idea when he might return?"

"Not offhand, but I know he made plans to have lunch here in Wellington."

I glanced at my watch. It was a few minutes after eleven.

"I see. Perhaps you could have him give me a..."

The front door opened and a tall, slender man with reddish-brown hair walked in. I immediately recognized him as the deputy from long ago who had questioned me after Mother's funeral.

Another one of those disjointed memories flashed through my mind. Me sitting on the sofa in the living room with Daddy standing off to the side, and Deputy Bill Jackson facing him.

"I just want to ask her a few questions, Eric. That's all."

"And I told you she was asleep. She doesn't know anything," Daddy said.

"Why don't you let me be the judge of that? She may have information we don't know about."

I remembered him asking me questions. When did I go to bed? Did I hear a car drive up? Did I hear my mother let someone in the house?

I'd answered no to everything. It wasn't until Aunt Dee got a hold of me later that I mentioned the argument. I'd never seen my father again after that.

Confused and frightened, I'd needed reassurance. I craved cuddles and to hear the words, "everything will be all right." But those words never came and my aunt was not a cuddling sort of person. Being unmarried, she had no clue how to deal with children. I was docile enough at that age to do as I was told. Denny, my half-brother, was another story. He resisted. Another long forgotten conversation popped into my head.

"I don't want to move to Chicago. I want to stay here," he argued.

"Dennis, if I could find a relative to take you in, I would, but since I can't, you will come with me. Even though you're not of my family, you are my responsibility," my aunt had replied.

Even I had heard the coldness in her tone and had seen the disdain on her face, although I didn't recognize it at the time. She didn't like or want my brother, but did so because it was her duty.

"I want to stay with Dad!"

"That won't be possible for a while," my aunt had replied.

"He's in jail, and I want to help him."

"Dennis, don't argue with me."

"Why can't we stay here? Why do we have to go to Chicago?"

"Because I said so."

My mind snapped back to the present when Officer Young slid off the desktop. "Chief, you're back early."

"Continuance until next week." He stared at me and smiled. "Let me guess, Callie Bryant. Heard you were back in town. What are you doing here?"

"If you mean the police station, I'm here to ask a favor."

His eyebrows rose. "Of course. How can I help?"

"I'd like to read the notes you and the sheriff at the time made on mother's murder and the investigation that sent my father to prison."

Deputy Young's eyes widened. The Chief's narrowed.

"I'm not sure that's possible, Callie," Bill replied.

"Why not? It's a closed case. Has been for a while."

"Because I'm not sure they even exist anymore." He shook his head. "No, Callie. I'm sorry. It's over, done with, time to move on. Justice was served."

Anger bubbled in my chest. All those years of wondering, of the nightmares, the shrinks, Aunt Dee's manipulation and deathbed confession, even Denny's death, and Bill Jackson had the gall to say justice had been served? Not by a long shot. I swallowed the anger before replying.

"I don't agree. In spite of my aunt's beliefs, I never thought Daddy did it."

"I know it must have been hard, but sometimes good people lose control and do bad things."

"Chief, I'm the only surviving relative and I want to see those files." I tucked a strand of hair behind my ear. "Look, I don't want to go on some lost crusade. I just want to fill in memory gaps. Lately, I've been remembering."

He drew in a breath as though startled. "Remembering? Remembering what?"

"That's what I'd like to know, too."

"A lot of stuff was boxed up and put into storage a few years ago. What could it hurt, Chief?" Deputy Young said.

"A lot of people might be upset at bringing it all up again. It's the only murder ever to occur in Wellington. Split this town apart. People took sides." His sharp words echoed those of John Casey. I wondered if they'd been talking about my imminent return to Iowa.

"No one needs to know except me. I just want to see if my nightmares are based in reality. And if you and Sheriff Wilson were wrong, don't you want to know?" I spoke softly.

The chief hesitated. "I'll see what I can do, Callie. Files that old are in storage over at Gleason's Self-Store in Atwell. The department has several bays. Old Roy Wilson never threw away a thing. If I'm not mistaken, your mother's file took up several boxes. Most of our more recent files are electronically stored, but with something that old… I'll call you if I find it."

I rose and extended my hand. "Thank you, Chief

Jackson. I appreciate your cooperation."

He shook my hand, but his expression showed he wasn't happy. I suspected his cooperation would be limited. I'd also told a little white lie. I had every intention of turning this into a crusade to prove Daddy's innocence.

****

Opening a checking account at the bank took all of fifteen minutes. Most of my banking was done online, but an account in Wellington made me feel more at home. I recognized no one and no one recognized me. Finished, I wandered up and down Main Street window shopping and occasionally entering a store to look closer at items. The sales clerks smiled, said hello, and then left me alone. For the most part, they were young and, like the checkout girl at the grocery, had probably never heard of Eric and Grace Bryant, much less their daughter.

I paused in front of Bell's Secondhand Store. Peering through the window, I spied Lorna at the counter talking on the phone. Maybe now was the time to ask a few questions of my own.

Lorna glanced up as I entered and froze a moment before saying to her caller, "I've got to hang up now. Customer just walked in. Talk to you later."

She hung up and smiled. "Callie, what a surprise. What brings you here?"

"Oh, I was just in town running some errands and thought I'd drop in. My furniture will be arriving from Chicago soon. Most of the stuff in the house now is dated, and I wondered if you'd be interested in it. Do you work on consignment or prefer outright sales?"

Lorna preened, patted her out-of-style hairdo, and

then moved from behind the counter. She wore a below the knee pleated skirt and a twinset. *Hello, early '60s.* Didn't the woman even look at the clothing stores in Wellington? But maybe she was just into vintage clothes, although why I had no clue. They did not flatter her.

"Oh, I do both. Which were you thinking?"

"I'm not sure, but I imagine an out and out sale would work best."

"And which pieces are you letting go?"

"I haven't done an inventory yet, so I'll have to get back to you."

As I spoke I wandered around the store stopping to look at the merchandise. It was in good shape and I could see how a new couple just starting out would gravitate toward Bell's.

"Certainly. Here let me give you my card. Just call when you're ready." She reached for a business card holder on the counter and extracted one.

I tucked it into my purse. "I'm so glad you and June stopped by yesterday. It was nice to meet a couple of my parents' friends. I know you said you grew up with Daddy, but did you know Mother well?"

"Oh, yes. She and I were great friends. Played bridge together for a while."

"I don't remember much about life here in Wellington. Being from Chicago, she must have felt a bit like a fish out of water."

"At first, I suppose." She sighed. "I can still remember when your daddy pulled up in that cherry red convertible of hers and calmly introduced her to Rich and me as his wife. Could have knocked me over with a feather, that's for sure. She was quite the beauty—long blonde hair and big blue eyes. It's no wonder your daddy was smitten. Guess he was lonely all by himself on the farm after his first wife, Sally, died. Can't remember why he was in Chicago."

"According to my aunt, he'd been up at a farm implement show, met mother's father, and the rest is history as they say."

"Which is why I just simply never believed your daddy could harm a fly. He was crazy about her. Oh, lots of women flirted with him—he did have a way about him, you know—but he loved Grace."

I stared her in the eye. "Yes, I understand more than one woman in town thought he was too good for mother—her being an outsider and all."

Lorna patted her hair again, and shifted her gaze around the room. "Yes, well, small towns can harbor small minds."

I wasn't sure I could elicit any more information from Lorna today. I needed to gain her trust first. And she struck me as the sort that once unleashed, would spew gossip like a fire hose.

"Well, thanks, Lorna. I'll see what I want to let go this weekend and be in touch."

"You do that, dear. Thank you so much for thinking of Bell's."

I said goodbye and left, deciding it was time to drop in on Josh Hendricks.

Chapter Three

I had no problem finding the office of the *News-Sentinel*. It was just around the corner from the Kozy Kafe, a staple in Wellington for close to seventy years—maybe more. The paper was housed in a narrow, older building with weathered bricks and a cornice depicting leaves of some sort. A stone inset over the entryway set the date at 1922.

I pushed the door open and entered the front office. The room was larger than I imagined, perhaps twenty by thirty feet. To my left sat a utility cart with a coffeemaker and the usual coffee additives. A water cooler was in the corner. File cabinets lined the walls down both sides of the room. To the right at the back of the room was a hallway.

The right hand side of the space boasted a modern computer set up manned by an earnest looking young woman busily typing at the keyboard. She looked up with a smile as I closed the door.

"Good morning. How may I help you?"

"Good morning. I was wondering if Mr. Hendricks was available."

"I'm sorry, he's out at the moment. Is there something I can do for you?"

"Would you just tell him Callie Bryant stopped by and have him give me a call?"

Her eyes widened, as did her smile. "Oh, yes, I

heard you'd come back to town. I'm Mindy Regis. Welcome home."

She stood and extended her hand. The woman was nine and a half months pregnant. She looked ready to pop at any moment.

"Please, sit down. When are you due?"

"Last weekend. This is my first and I can't wait for it to be over." She shook my hand and immediately resumed her seat. "I'm supposed to walk around, but to tell you the truth, my back is killing me. I feel like a beached whale."

I laughed. "I can imagine. I'd be home with my feet up."

She laughed with me. "Josh sent me home last week to do just that, but I was so bored out of my skull that I came back. I think he's terrified I'll go into labor here and he won't know what to do. For pity's sake, my husband's at home five minutes away and the hospital is a twenty minute drive." She rolled her eyes. "Men!"

I liked Mindy and her fresh-faced smile. In her mid-twenties, she exuded a glow only women about to give birth could. Plus, she didn't look at me like I'd just dropped into Wellington from some distant planet.

"Have you lived here long?"

"All my life. My parents owned a farm east of town. Daddy retired three years ago and my husband, Dave, and I took over running it. My maiden name was Norcross."

The name did more than ring a bell. My brother, Denny, had had a sleepover with Jimmy Norcross that fateful night. I estimated Mindy had been either a baby or not yet born.

"Oh, of course, our brothers were friends. Is he still

in the area?"

She shook her head. "No, 'fraid not. After high school, he went to Purdue and is now a vet up in Wisconsin."

The front door opened and Josh Hendricks walked in carrying a Styrofoam carton. His eyebrows rose at my presence.

"Miss Bryant, hello again." He set the carton on Mindy's desk. "Here you go. Meatloaf with mashed potatoes, gravy, and green beans. Elvira even tossed in a couple of biscuits for you."

She pulled the lid open and sniffed. "Oh God, that smells good. I'm starving. Maybe a good solid meal will convince this kid to make an appearance. Mind, I'll only be able to eat a few bites, but it'll last the rest of the day."

Mindy unwrapped the plastic utensils and dug in. I didn't blame her. It smelled good.

Josh turned to me. "Were you waiting for me?"

"Oh, I'm sorry, Josh," Mindy mumbled with her mouth full. "Yes, Ms. Bryant came in a few minutes ago."

"Come on back to my office."

He smiled, led the way to the door and closed it behind me.

"How can I help you?" he asked indicating the chair in front of his desk.

I sat and took a deep breath. Twenty-four hours hadn't changed his good looks. In a way, I'd hoped it had. Today he wore a pair of khaki slacks with a maroon polo. A navy sport coat topped it off. The casual elegance of the outfit told me he'd been exposed to a big city atmosphere most of his life. So what was he doing in rural Iowa? I wanted to find out.

Sucking in a deep breath, I replied, "First of all, I want to apologize for my rather rude behavior yesterday. My only excuse is that I was tired."

He waved a hand in dismissal. "Don't worry about it. I shouldn't have landed on your doorstep ten minutes after you arrived."

"You were the last of four visitors. Which brings me to a question—how did you know I was even home yet?"

"I didn't know for sure. I talked to Serena Smith, John Casey's receptionist, on Wednesday and she told me you were due back by Thursday afternoon. I took a chance and dropped by." He picked up a pencil and tapped it on the blotter. "Who else had the bad taste to show up before you had a chance to unpack?"

I had to laugh. He'd nailed it, himself included. "June Simpson and Lorna Bell practically followed me into the driveway."

"Good old June. You can always count on her to try and get the story first. Probably was waiting around the corner until you appeared. She should have been a reporter."

"Maybe you should hire her," I suggested.

Josh grinned. "No way. I deal in facts, not gossip. She'd drive me nuts in ten minutes and Mindy would shoot her by the end of the day. Who else gave you grief?"

"Bob Kendall. Started telling me all the updates the house should have before it goes on the market."

He ceased tapping the pencil. "You're selling?"

"No, and I don't care how many buyers he has lined up. This is my home and I intend to live in it."

The fact that Bob had so clumsily urged me to leave Wellington still struck a nerve.

Josh tossed the pencil onto the desk and straightened in his chair.

"Why are you here, Ms. Bryant?"

"In Wellington or your office?"

He smiled. "Both."

I stared into those penetrating gray eyes. My nerves jumped as if goaded with a cattle prod. For the first time, I noticed his wide mouth. When he smiled, the right corner lifted slightly higher than the left giving him a lopsided, but charming expression. He had a strong, firm jaw indicating a stubborn streak. His nose had a distinctive crook as though at some time it had been broken. His face oozed character.

I tore my gaze away, inhaled, and then released a deep breath.

"I came home for lots of reasons. My aunt was dead and city living is expensive. I was tired of the noise, the traffic, too many people, and the crime. I'm ready for a change of pace." I paused and allowed my gaze to once again make contact with his. "I'm in your office to say that if you still want to do that interview, I'm game."

His eyebrows rose. "Wonderful."

"I do have one condition—no mention of my mother's death or Daddy's trial. That's in the past. I'm interested in the future."

It was a stinking lie. I was very interested in the past.

"Very well, although not mentioning anything will sound kind of silly since the whole town knows what happened."

"Perhaps a simple referral to it as a tragedy will suffice. When would be a convenient time to do this?"

He shrugged. "How about now? Have you eaten lunch yet?"

I shook my head. "No, that was next on my agenda."

"Then why don't we go to the Kozy? You can have lunch while I ask questions."

I rose. "Sounds like a good idea. That meatloaf is tempting."

He laughed and also stood. "Then by all means, let's go before they run out."

The interior of the Kozy hadn't been redecorated since the joint opened. Blue vinyl seats in the booths and on the chairs looked worn and in several cases, cracked. Repairs had been made with duct tape. The Formica tabletops, however, gleamed. A long counter with stools graced the rear wall. A large window peeked back into the kitchen. I heaved a deep breath. Bacon, onions, and a myriad of other cooking smells tickled my nose. It smelled damn good. My stomach grumbled.

Josh led me toward a booth midway down the side wall. As we slid in, a waitress sporting a nametag with Elvira printed on it appeared with two menus.

"You must be hungry today, Josh," she said with a grin.

Josh smiled back. "Tell Bernie if he keeps cooking that good, I'll soon weigh five hundred pounds. Just iced tea for me. The lady needs lunch."

She laughed, and turned a curious gaze onto me. If she didn't know my identity, she certainly assumed.

"The meatloaf Mindy was eating smelled great. I'll

have that."

"It's the best. You get a choice of green beans or salad with it, and for an extra five dollars, a slice of the world's most delicious apple pie. Made fresh every day."

"Can't beat that with a stick," I said, laughing. "And I'll have the green beans along with iced tea."

She nodded and walked behind the counter to the order window.

I took the opportunity to gaze around the restaurant. It was nearly noon and most of the counter and the tables were occupied. The buzz of conversation had dropped when Josh and I entered. Now, amidst covert glances, it regained volume.

Already tired of the endless speculation, I shifted in my seat and stared at the tabletop. When our tea arrived, I glanced up to Josh's face.

He smiled. "It's a small town, Miss Bryant. People remember the past and can't help but stare."

Miss. I wanted to smile back at the old-fashioned title for an unmarried woman. No *Ms.* for Josh Hendricks. I didn't mind. I considered the more modern term cold. And I had the impression this man was not cold in any way.

"I suppose, and please, call me Callie. Like you said, it's a small town."

He pulled a small notebook from his coat pocket along with a pen, opened it, and then paused.

"Tell me about your life in Chicago. Was it hard to adjust to the big city?"

The question surprised me. "I remember being lost and lonely at first. My Aunt Dorothea lived in the Conrad mansion with her father for years. He died not long after I was born, so I never knew him."

Josh stopped writing and stared. "Conrad—as in Conrad tractors and Conrad Coliseum, the downtown sports arena?"

"Very distant relatives of different branches of the family. I'm not sure how we ended up with the house."

"Still, you grew up, if you'll pardon the cliché, in the lap of luxury?"

"Yes. The house was enormous and stuffed with antiques. As a child I remember thinking it was dark and gloomy, which is why I moved out soon after college." It also explained why I loathed antiques. Give me clean, modern lines any day.

"So, you were unhappy?"

I shook my head and lied only a little bit. "No, not really. Only at first. It was so different from farm life. Do you know I never learned how to ride a bike? My aunt was afraid I'd not only get hurt, but kidnapped as well." His eyebrows rose. I rushed on. "Don't get me wrong. I never wanted for anything. And Aunt Dee could be stern, but never without cause."

"How did she react to your moving out?"

"She wasn't happy, but accepted it, especially when I got a place only five minutes away. That way I could maintain being on my own while she kept the illusion of keeping tabs on me."

"She was controlling?"

"Very much so when I was little. Not so much after I went to college. She and I often butted heads about rules and regulations when I was a teenager."

"Where did you go to college?"

"Northwestern. I lived at home, but did manage a social life, made new friends. Aunt Dee wasn't thrilled, but learned to live with it."

I didn't add that my social—not to mention my sex—lives were very active. That information didn't go with the image I wanted to project in Wellington.

My lunch arrived. The aroma was as enticing as it had been in Josh's office. I unwrapped the utensils from the paper napkin. I knew I wouldn't need the knife. I popped a morsel of gravy covered meatloaf into my mouth and sighed.

"Good, huh?" he said with a smile.

"Wonderful."

"You said your aunt recently passed away?"

"A couple of months ago."

"So, why leave a mansion in Chicago that's been in your family for generations to return to a farm that only knew tragedy?"

His question made sense, but I skirted around the truth. He didn't need to know the whole story—not yet.

"The house in Chicago is old—really old. Built in 1900 or something close by my great-great-whatever grandfather. It was renovated by various ancestors throughout the years. The taxes are horrendous, almost as bad as the cost of maintenance, and to update everything yet again would take more time and money than I'm willing to spend."

That much was true. The stately old mansion sitting behind a six-foot high stone wall on an acre of ground near Lake Michigan had been slowly crumbling around our heads for years. Rejuvenating the place would have come close to wiping out the rest of my inheritance. And to be honest, I'd never felt like it was home. Plus, Aunt Dee had been heavily invested in the stock market. Her broker, an old codger and family friend, had long ago lost his touch. The latest recession was a powerful gut punch to the family finances.

"But why here?" Josh asked.

"Why not? The farm was the one thing put aside by my father for my brother and me. It would always be here if either of us needed it. I needed it."

"What about your brother?"

"Denny died two years ago in Afghanistan."

He stopped writing in his notebook to lift his head and stare.

"I'm sorry, Callie. Were the two of you close?"

"Yes. Very."

"You must miss him a lot."

"I do."

I took a sip of my iced tea to ease the rising lump in my throat, and then resumed eating. Miss Denny? God yes, I missed him. My resentment toward my aunt after she sent him to boarding school had never gone away. He'd been protective of me. Now, I could see the truth was he'd never adjusted to Mother's murder or Daddy's incarceration. And Aunt Dee hadn't helped matters by insisting her brother-in-law was guilty of the crime.

The waitress appeared whisking away my now empty plate. A moment later she returned with a huge slab of apple pie, refilled the tea glasses, and left the check on the table.

I stared at the pie wondering where I'd put it in my already full stomach.

Josh grinned. "Forget this is a farm community? The people expect a lot for their money at the café."

"Apparently so."

He tapped his pen on the notebook. "So, now

you're back in Wellington and doing what? Any plans?"

I eased a bite of pie into my mouth. Oh my God—delicious, sweet and tart at the same time.

"I want to get acclimatized first before I make any decisions."

"And then what?" he persisted.

"I was an English major and took enough creative writing classes in college to know I liked writing. Over the years I've sold a few articles to magazines and such, even had a short story published, but the lure of a novel is appealing. I don't know. I'll play it by ear."

"A novel? What kind of novel?"

He didn't say it, but I could almost hear the words, murder mystery, hanging in the air.

I leaned forward and lowered my voice. "I'm a sucker for romance. Sneaked my first Harlequin when I was twelve. If Aunt Dee had known, she'd have died on the spot."

Josh laughed. "Let me guess—a flashlight under the covers?"

"You got it!" I pushed the unfinished pie away. "This is the best apple pie I've ever tasted, but I've hit the wall."

He picked up my unused spoon and finished it off. "Can't resist Miss Emma's apple pie. Or anything Miss Emma makes for that matter."

"Miss Emma?"

"Emma Grandview, the owner of the Kozy Kafe. Does all the baking herself."

The Grandview name rang a bell, but I couldn't place it at the moment. Maybe later.

Josh closed his notebook returning it and the pen to

his pocket.

"I guess that will do for now." He smiled, reached across the table to take my hand, and squeeze it. "But I wouldn't mind getting to know you better, Callie. How about dinner tomorrow night? There's a nice Italian restaurant in Atwell."

His hand not only warmed mine, but the heat spread to the rest of my body, too. I should have refused, but instead found myself agreeing. "I'd like that, Josh."

To my disappointment, he released my hand and picked up the check. "Guess I'd better get back to work." He slid from the booth and helped me to my feet. "I think I have enough information for a short column."

"When will it come out?"

"Next week. The paper's published on Thursdays. I'll save a copy at the office for you."

"Put me down as a subscriber."

Josh tossed some money onto the table for a tip, paid the bill, and escorted me outside.

"Thank you for lunch," I said. "It was delicious. I'm not sure I'll be able to eat dinner."

His gaze swept down my figure making my nerves jump and sending a rush of heat to my fingers and toes.

"I like what I see. How about I pick you up tomorrow night at six?"

I nodded. "Six sounds fine."

He turned and walked toward the corner. I inhaled a deep breath and strolled to my car. Tomorrow night couldn't come fast enough.

On my way home, I stopped once again at the store to stock up on groceries for the rest of the week.

I had just finished putting the last can in the pantry when a Mercedes pulling into the driveway caught my attention. A woman wearing a business suit emerged and walked gingerly across the gravel in high heels. *A Mercedes, high heels, and a business suit? How un-Wellington.*

The woman made her way to the back door. I shut the pantry door and answered her knock.

"Hello, Callie, I'm Ruth Kendall, Bob's wife. I understand he dropped by the other day. I thought I'd do the same and welcome you home again."

"Thank you. Please, come in."

Ruth Kendall. Now *this* was a surprise.

She entered and flashed me a smile. "Hope I'm not interrupting you. I was in Atwell at a Humane Society luncheon and thought I'd drop by on my way home."

"Not at all. Please come into the living room."

I led her out of the kitchen, through the dining area, and into the living room.

"My goodness, this looks just like it did twenty-five years ago," she commented taking a seat on the sofa. I chose Daddy's chair, not sure if she was being critical or not.

"My stuff doesn't arrive until Monday. Bell's will get most of this."

"Yes, I suppose Lorna was on your doorstep before you could unlock the door." Her crisp tone suggested she didn't care much for Lorna.

I laughed to cover my suspicion. "Just about. She and June Simpson dropped by."

Her gaze lowered. "Ah yes, June. She's probably hoping you'll hold an enormous yard sale."

I got the impression she didn't like June either.

"I don't have the time or patience for something like that." I didn't mention *her* husband had wanted more than a garage sale.

She laughed. "Neither do I. So tell me, why have you come back to Wellington?"

I found her to be almost as irritating as her husband. In less than five minutes, she'd eyeballed the furniture, politely declared it out of style, and dissed two of her acquaintances. Now, she asked the same question everyone else had. I bit my tongue to keep from telling her to take a hike. I needed to keep things in perspective. My burning desire to ferret out the truth might turn people off. She could prove useful in the future, so I gave her the now stock answer of city life versus a quieter venue.

"I suppose I can see that, but I'd think the memories here would be overwhelming."

Funny she should echo her husband's comments. Did he send her as some sort of emissary to change my mind about selling the farm? Better set this straight immediately.

"As I told your husband the other day, not all memories are bad, Mrs. Kendall."

Her eyebrows rose. "Mrs. Kendall? Oh, don't be formal, dear. I'm Ruth. And I apologize for Bob. Sometimes he's a little over-enthusiastic about real estate and comes off sounding pushy. That's just the way he is. I'm glad you don't plan to sell. Your mother and I were great friends, you know. Her death devastated me. We both came to Wellington from large cities as brides—she from Chicago and me from Cleveland. The locals had a hard time accepting us at first, but eventually we won them over."

"From what I heard, Mother never quite felt comfortable in a small town."

Ruth lowered her gaze again and fiddled with the large wedding set on her finger. "That's true, but she loved your father, more's the pity."

My senses soared to red alert. "Why do you say that?"

She bit her lip and smoothed an imagined wrinkle in her skirt as though realizing she'd said too much.

"Oh, dear," she murmured.

"Oh, dear what, Ruth?"

She locked her gaze on my face. "Honey, your father was having an affair, and when Gracie confronted him, he killed her."

Chapter Four

I stared, too stunned to respond. How dare she? How dare this…this person come into my home and tell me my father was having an affair? I didn't believe it. Not for a minute.

Ruth sighed. "Oh dear, I shouldn't have told you. You obviously had no idea. I'm so sorry, Callie. I thought your aunt would have spilled the beans by now."

I cleared my throat. "Aunt Dee? How would she know something like that?"

The words came out in a raspy tone. I have no idea how I managed to keep my voice calm when the urge to rip her tongue out was overwhelming.

My babbling guest wrung her hands, an embarrassed expression on her face.

"She…she spoke to me at the funeral. Asked if it was true Eric was being unfaithful to her sister. I told her I didn't know. That was a lie. The rumors had been flying around the garden club and various bridge games for months. When I asked her where she heard this, she said Gracie had called her the week before all upset and confessed her husband was fooling around."

"And exactly whom was he supposed to be sleeping with?"

"I have no idea. Nobody did. And after the murder, nobody came forward to admit to it."

"Yeah, I can see why."

Had the jurors at Daddy's trial heard the rumors? If so, then that could have thrown doubt into their minds about Daddy's guilt, especially if the other woman was married. A jealous girlfriend would have had a hell of a motive. On the other hand, it could also be construed as evidence he'd killed her. Had he asked for a divorce and been denied?

Ruth, the embarrassment still on her face, checked her watch. "Callie, I'm so sorry. I didn't mean to upset you. I...I just thought you knew."

"This is the first I've heard of it and there's no need to apologize. This is Wellington. I'd have heard sooner or later."

She rose. "I'd better be going."

I also stood and swallowed to keep my temper in check. "But you just got here."

"I...I just dropped in to say hello. Bob and I are having some guests over tonight. How about lunch sometime next week? You pick the day and time. I'll pick the place. Is that okay?"

"Yes, yes, fine," I answered in a taut, distracted tone.

I followed Ruth back through the kitchen. She paused to glance around the room. "It hasn't changed a bit. Everything's in the same place as it was years ago. Very vintage. Even the stove is a relic from the fifties. You know, Callie, if you do decide to sell, I'd remodel it in a retro style using that stove as a start. Goodbye, dear. We'll be in touch."

I plunked my fanny down at the table as she drove away. Daddy having an affair? Why hadn't Aunt Dee said anything during her deathbed revelations? Or any other time for that matter? Given how much she hated my father, I'd have thought that snippet of information would be her final triumph in convincing me to hate him, too. Perhaps, she hadn't wanted me to know at that age what constituted an affair. *And after Daddy died, why bother to say anything?*

And who the hell was the other woman—assuming she even existed? The rumor mill in small towns often ran like a swiftly flowing stream, tumbling and churning out information before moving on. I needed a pipeline into that stream. Lorna Bell came to mind. I'd drop by the shop and strike up another conversation, suggest lunch—my treat since Lorna didn't strike me as a picking-up-the-tab kind of person, then pump her for information. Carefully, of course. For all I knew, Lorna could have been the other woman—if the rumors were true.

Of course they aren't true!

The cable company arriving took my mind off the problem. In less than two hours I had both television and Internet access. Although I'd have to wait for my furniture to arrive before enjoying my favorite TV shows on a screen larger than twenty-seven inches, I could catch up on my Facebook page and e-mails.

Dinner was of the microwaved variety tonight. It took me a few minutes to decipher how to use the outdated appliance in this kitchen. No push buttons to help the process along. Afterward, I watched some TV and did my best to push Ruth's unsettling news to the back of my mind. I needed more than just Lorna's input into the situation, too. Out of a population of three thousand there had to be more than one or two candidates for the position of "other woman."

Later that night, as I lay in bed on the cusp of sleep, the train whistle echoed in the distance.

****

I awoke the next morning energized. Ah, Saturday mornings. I remembered them and assumed Saturdays were still big with farmers and their families as the designated go-to-town day. My presence in Wellington again this morning would have tongues wagging for the rest of the week. So, I avoided gossip by making a list of all the old furniture I could sell to Bell's. In defiance of the past, I began in the foyer.

The grandfather clock would remain. I tried moving the weights to see if it worked, but they refused to budge. I made a note to call a repairman.

An antique table sat along the wall below the stairs, the marble top bare of ornamentation. In my mind's eye, I saw a vase with roses in it. A memory flashed—the sound of a scuffle and a crash. Had there been a fight that fateful night? Was the crash the vase falling and breaking? I shook my head. Perhaps I remembered Denny and his friends horsing around.

The living room was next. I marked it all for Bell's. My furniture would fit nicely. I remembered Sunday dinners in the dining room and couldn't bring myself to part with anything. In the kitchen, I liked the old farmhouse table my parents and grandparents had used. My kitchen table was more modern. I caved in to nostalgia and added the newer set to the list for Bell's.

The bedrooms didn't take long. The master held nothing I wanted to keep. I'd replace it with my bedroom furniture. I by-passed Denny's room and instead concentrated on the small room across the hall. I put all of the furniture down as gone.

My room remained intact. The two east facing windows let the light pour in and in spite of everything, I liked being reminded of my childhood.

The last two bedrooms and the bathroom ran along the back of the house. All items made the list.

I saved Daddy's office on the main floor for last. The back steps emptied into the hallway next to it. I entered and swallowed hard. Memories flooded my mind. Daddy would often hold me on his lap while doing the books. The huge roll top desk and swivel chair had been there in my great-grandparents' time. I opened the top. It was stuffed with papers secured into neat bundles. Same with the drawers. I imagined the cops had been through it searching for evidence. At least somebody had made an effort to tidy the mess later. I picked up an envelope marked "Feed Receipts." My eyes filled with tears as I recognized Daddy's writing.

I replaced it, then turned and walked away. This furniture stayed. I'd deal with the paperwork later.

With that task finished, I decided a trip into town might not be such a bad idea after all. Perhaps now was a good time to re-visit Bell's. And I could make an appointment at the local beauty salon for a trim. Small town beauty salons bred gossip like fleas in summer. Just because it's gossip, didn't mean at least some of it wasn't true.

The town was crowded and I had to search for a parking spot before finding one on a side street not far from the newspaper office. I was tempted to drop in on Josh, but then dismissed the thought. Josh Hendricks and the word distraction seemed to be synonymous. And I refused to be distracted. Besides, I'd see him tonight.

I had to wait at Bell's for Lorna to finish with a customer. As that person left, she turned her hesitant smile on me. I didn't think she was glad to see me.

"Back again, Callie? What can I do for you?"

"Here's the furniture I'd like to sell," I replied, handing her the list.

Lorna read the items. Her smile widened. "Callie, this is wonderful. I'm sure we'll both see a profit."

After assuring her the items were in good shape, we spent the next several minutes negotiating a price for the whole lot.

"Excellent. When can you pick up everything?" I asked. "My things are due to arrive on Monday."

"How about I send a man out with a truck early Monday morning? That way you won't be without furniture to sit on Sunday night," she said with a laugh.

I laughed along. "Sounds like a plan to me." I leaned in closer to her. "I can't tell you how glad I am to find a place like Bell's. Customers can come in, look at the merchandise, and make a selection with no fuss. And they get to deal with someone they know. I find all those online places, well, uncomfortable. Know what I mean?"

She sucked in a sharp breath. "I do indeed. As a seller you have to let strangers into your home. And as a buyer, well, you just can't always trust people to tell the truth about what they sell, can you?"

"My thoughts exactly!" I heaved a sigh. "I'm so glad to be back in small town with people who have values. I just wish Mom and Dad were here, too. I don't remember much about them." I checked my watch. "It's almost noon. Perhaps we can have lunch—just to talk about old times?"

She hesitated before answering. "Now? Well, I don't know... Yes, that might be nice."

"Great. Is the Kozy all right with you or would you like to go someplace else?"

"The Kozy is fine. I rarely eat anywhere else."

Lorna locked up, and then we walked the two blocks to the café. The waitress showed up at about the same time we sat down. The place was filling up fast.

After ordering, I got the ball rolling.

"It's funny, but one of the things I do remember about Wellington is the Kozy. Seems like Mother or Daddy brought me here often."

"It's the most popular place in town. Breakfast and dinner aren't such a big deal, but lunch is."

She hugged her cardigan closer around her chest and stared at the placemat.

"You said you grew up with Daddy?"

"Oh my, yes. We were classmates all through grade and high school. He was so good looking. I had such a crush on him."

I laughed. "Daddy was very handsome. Did you ever date?"

"No, but he and June did."

"June Simpson?"

"June Cranston then. Oh, they were quite the item all through high school. She was a cheerleader and he played just about every sport there was: football, basketball, baseball. I think he even ran track. But he and June busted up the summer of their senior year."

"What happened?"

"Not what, but who. Sally Renfrow moved to town. Her daddy became the new town doctor when old Doc

Carter retired."

"Sally? Denny's mother?"

"Yes, indeed. Your poor father fell like a ton of bricks for her. She was a looker, that's for sure *and* knew what she wanted. Took one look at Eric Bryant and went right after him. Happened so fast June didn't know what hit her. One minute she was going steady and the next she wasn't."

At last, some useful information. June Simpson and Daddy? I pressed for more.

"Bet she was mad."

"Honey, she cried and cursed Sally Renfrow for weeks. And when they ran off and got married a year later, June threw an absolute fit." Lorna leaned forward and lowered her voice. "Don't tell anybody, but when Sally was killed in that car wreck, June actually laughed and said something like, 'I'll give him a few months grieving, and then reel him in again.'" She sat back. "Didn't work out the way she hoped. Eric had his hands full with a two-year-old son and to be honest, nobody compared to Sally. Not even his old flame."

Her satisfied expression suggested she enjoyed that June no longer measured up. I probed further.

"Until my mother came along."

"By that time, June felt she was making headway with your daddy and was all set to pounce when, lo and behold, he went to Chicago and came back with your mother. June was livid, and I mean livid. She was so mad, she up and married Roger Simpson two months later."

The satisfied smirk deepened, suggesting maybe Lorna and June weren't the BFFs Josh thought. Lorna had a crush on Daddy, but June dated him and had expected to make it a permanent arrangement. Mother was another brick on the load of disappointment.

"Tell me a little about my mother. I don't remember too much." I let a wistful note creep into my voice.

"She was beautiful, of course. Your daddy knew how to pick the pretty ones."

"But she never really fit in here, did she?"

Lorna sighed. "No. She and Ruth Kendall became good friends. Both were outsiders and both were used to living a life of luxury. I don't think Grace ever adjusted to the farm or Wellington."

"What a shame. Too bad she didn't have many friends."

"Oh, Rich and I saw them frequently. I liked her. She was a perfect hostess at barbeques and such."

"What about the Simpsons? Did they socialize with Mom and Dad?"

Lorna shifted her gaze to look around the room and bit her lip. "I probably shouldn't tell you, but June pretended to like your mother just so she could garner invites and see your dad. She never got over him. Never."

"Did Mother know?" This was a new wrinkle I hadn't expected.

"I think so. A woman can always tell when another woman is after her man. And I'll say this, your mother tried to be friendly with June, she really did. And she doted on you. You were her little princess."

During this conversation our food arrived—a club sandwich for me and the venerable meatloaf for Lorna. We were just about finished when an older woman approached the table.

"So, what kind of pie are you ladies having today?"

"Uh, I'm not sure…" I began.

"Of course you're having some of my pie. I've got cherry and apple today along with lemon meringue. Which will it be?"

Lorna actually giggled. "Callie, this is Emma Grandview. She owns the Kozy and makes all the baked goods."

I remembered the woman now. She'd often stopped by to talk to Mom and Dad whenever we'd come in. "Hello, seems I remember you from the old days."

She nodded. "I was here, that's for sure."

"Miss Emma, don't you have any carrot cake for my sweet tooth?" Lorna asked.

"I got it, but my pies are better." She smiled at me with faded blue eyes. "Welcome home, Callie. Heard you'd been in with Josh yesterday. How do you like country living again?"

"I like it just fine and will have the cherry pie."

Emma laughed. "Good for you. Come back sometime soon and we'll have a talk."

Lorna ordered the carrot cake. When Miss Emma had left, my companion eyed me. I had the feeling she was sorry she'd told me so much.

"I'm so glad we had this chat, Lorna. It's sad not knowing one of your parents. In my case, both of them, what with Daddy being arrested and sent to prison. I think I would have liked growing up in Wellington."

She smiled, but her eyes were wary. "I'm glad I could help."

An idea so radical it would send a normal person into cardiac arrest popped into my head. If I stopped to think it over, I'd chicken out.

"Oh, I just had a wonderful idea, Lorna. Suppose I throw a party?"

She stared with a blank expression. "A party?"

"Yes! I want to fit in again. After all, this is my hometown and I'm going to live here. A little get-together to say hello to everyone—nothing elaborate. Just some cocktails and a few hors d'oeuvres. Let's see, my furniture won't arrive until Monday, and I'm not certain how fast I can get this together, but I'm thinking Tuesday night—or maybe Wednesday. Yes, Wednesday. What do you think? I know its short notice, but this is Wellington and I'm sure most people will attend. You'll come, won't you?" I leaned forward and let the eagerness creep into my voice as though her presence was essential to the success of the gathering.

For a moment, she looked totally flabbergasted at the idea, but then smiled as though happy to be included. "Of course, I'll come."

"Wonderful. By the way, my hair needs a trim. Is there a beauty shop in town?"

"Of course, the Elite Beauty Salon is a couple of blocks down Juniper Street just off Main. Clovis Fisher is the owner. Do you remember her?"

"Can't say that I do."

"Oh, she was a great friend of your mother's, too. Had her hair done by Clovis every Saturday morning."

"Well, I'll have to hurry right on over. I'll call with more information about the party later."

The party was likely a terrible idea and might cause people to doubt my motive for returning to Wellington, but as much as I wanted to learn more about my parents, I had also told the truth about fitting in again.

This was my home and I wanted friends. I wanted to belong. Chicago was never home, it was just where I'd lived.

Our desserts arrived and lived up to their reputations—or at least to Miss Emma's. I paid the bill and strolled down the street with Lorna, saying goodbye as she unlocked the shop door. She waved from the threshold and entered while I continued on toward the beauty shop.

With just a few questions, Lorna had done what I expected—gushed information. And what interesting information.

I had no trouble finding the Elite. The building, complete with a hideous pink and white striped awning over the door and gold curly-cued writing on the window, stuck out like a wart on a model's face. I entered and strolled up to the counter. Behind it were glass shelves laden with shampoo, conditioner, and various other beauty enhancing items.

Three hairdryers, each separated by a small table complete with the latest gossip magazines and tabloids graced the wall to the right beyond a partition. Two shampoo bowls were on the back wall. To the left, three corresponding work stations stood, all occupied.

Conversation ceased when I walked in. Everyone stared. Finally, a woman with a bouffant hairdo stepped forward. I had no doubt found my mother's beautician. I put her age as somewhere between sixty and death.

"Good morning, may I help you?"

"Yes, I was just wondering if I could get a trim?" I let my gaze wander to the customers in chairs and under dryers. "It looks like you're busy, but I don't mind waiting."

The woman smiled and held out her hand. "You're Callie Bryant, aren't you? I'm Clovis Fisher. I don't suppose you remember me, but your mother was a client."

"Well, fancy that," I said shaking her hand. "I remember my mother's hair as always looking so pretty."

Clovis patted her out-of-style hair and harsh dye job.

"Why thank you, honey, that's sweet, and of course I can take you. I'll do you myself. Won't be a long wait. Maybe twenty minutes. Have a seat and I'll be right with you."

She gestured toward the waiting area opposite the glass counter. I hoped Clovis did a better job of cutting hair than she did of dying and styling it. The poor woman obviously hadn't kept up with industry changes in the last thirty years.

I sat in a gilded chair and picked up a magazine from a coffee table as she returned to her client. The conversation resumed with a discussion about an upcoming election. The clients often glanced at me through the mirrors as they spoke.

I pretended to read while giving the salon an evaluation. The décor was a cutesy-pooh nightmare of pink and white with velvet pillows and faux-gilded furniture. Interior decorating obviously wasn't high on the owner's list either.

Clovis walked her customer out to the waiting room. The woman's hair was poufy and glued in place with a ton of hair spray.

"Thanks a lot, Clovis. See you next week, same time, same place." The client paid, cast a casual look at me, nodded, and left.

Clovis turned her attention toward me, a predatory gleam in her eyes. "Your turn, honey. Do you need a shampoo and set, too?"

"Why not? But no set, just a blow dry will do."

I rose and followed her back to the shampoo bowls. After a brief lather, rinse, lather, rinse, conditioner, rinse cycle, she wrapped my head in a towel and led me to a pink vinyl chair in front of her station. A gold polyester cape was thrown around me.

"My goodness, this is certainly a very plain style. Are you sure you don't want me to use some rollers? Would give you more volume, you know, some pouf."

"No thanks. I like to keep it simple."

She picked up a comb and sighed. "Well, if you say so. Have you ever considered a perm?"

The image of a poodle flashed through my mind. "Uh, no. Curls and I just don't go together."

She sighed again, no doubt disappointed at being unable to make a sale. Manipulating the comb, she parted my hair and smoothed it, then lowered her arms and smiled.

"I knew it. I just knew you were a natural blonde. Same as your mother. The color is almost the same, too." Still in full selling mode, her smile widened. "Would you like me to add some highlights? Highlights give you more depth."

"Maybe later. But for now just a trim will do."

Clovis brightened at the thought of me returning and reached for a pair of scissors. "Whatever you say, sweetie."

I held my breath hoping she knew what she was doing, and then let it out when she did. I'd had this hairstyle for a couple of years courtesy of Christof, one of the pricier Chicago stylists. At least, Clovis wouldn't butcher an expensive hair cut.

A steady stream of chatter came with the cut. She asked questions non-stop, most of which I answered. The silence from the other two customers and operators told me they were taking in everything I said.

Half an hour later, she whipped off the cape and declared me finished. All in all, it wasn't bad. The ends curled under just enough. I followed her out to the waiting area where two more clients sat, eyeing me with curious expressions. I ignored them.

"Okay, honey, that'll be twenty-five dollars. Would you like to make another appointment?"

Twenty-five bucks? Was she kidding? I'd save a bundle at the Elite Beauty Salon as compared with Christof's, and then remembered Wellington was not Chicago. Twenty-five dollars here was likely viewed as top-end.

"Not right now. I'm thinking of letting it grow out a bit." I handed her three tens. "Keep the change, Clovis. You did a nice job."

"Why thank you, honey. You just give me a call anytime, you hear?"

I nodded and left. I'd be back in a few weeks. Perhaps by then, I could ask a few questions regarding my mother.

It was after two before I arrived home. Josh wasn't due to pick me up until six. It wouldn't take four hours to shower and change clothes. I decided to kill time on the Internet when inspiration hit me. Why not Google a few people? I set my computer on the kitchen table and fired it up.

John Casey was my first choice. I pulled up his website. As I suspected, he dealt with wills, trusts, and the needs of small town America. No mention was made anywhere of his one and only criminal case.

Very little was available on Richard and Lorna Bell. I didn't see Lorna as a big fan of computers. She likely kept all records in a file drawer in the back room of the shop. I pictured her sitting at a desk with a ledger in front of her doing the books.

The same held true for June Simpson. Other than organizing a recent quilt show in Atwell, she kept a low profile.

Bob Kendall's name yielded more. His website was up to date and I suspected he paid someone to keep it that way. From his bio, both personal and professional, I gleaned that he sat on the city council and had been appointed vice-mayor three years ago.

I Googled Ruth next. She sat on the city beautification committee. She was also active in various clubs around the town and in the county serving as president of the Wellington Garden Club and as vice-president of the Atwell County Humane Society.

I saved Josh Hendricks for last. He was born and raised in the Minneapolis area, attended the University of Minnesota, and graduated with a degree in journalism. His work history profiled stints at newspapers in St. Paul, Des Moines, and numerous other cities, including St. Louis. He left his last job after only six months. Four years later, he bought the *Wellington News-Sentinel*.

Why only six months? All his other employment stretched for several years. Didn't St. Louis agree with him? And what had he done in those four years between

St. Louis and Wellington? The military? Lounging on a beach in some exotic locale? I liked a man with a hint of mystery surrounding him. And I was beginning to suspect Josh Hendricks might be very likeable.

Chapter Five

"May I compliment you on how nice you look?" Josh asked as we drove down the two-lane highway to Atwell.

I laughed as the breeze from the open window ruffled my hair. I hadn't consciously considered the time of year when I'd selected my clothing.

"Thank you. With most of my clothes on a semi somewhere between Wellington and Chicago, I made do with what I had."

"You look like spring."

"Now, that was spoken like a romantic."

He grinned. "I'm just an old softie."

He had a point about spring. I'd chosen a lime green skirt with a white blouse. A pair of bronze-colored flats graced my feet.

I cast a glance at him. His navy blue slacks and light blue polo shirt fit him like a male model. I could easily see him posing in a catalogue. The black loafers shined to perfection added elegance. Yes, his likeability rating had climbed.

"Where is it we're going again?" I asked.

"Morelli's. It's an Italian restaurant. Been in Atwell for years. Didn't you ever go as a kid?"

"No, at least not that I remember. My parents didn't take my brother and me out to eat much, and when they did, it was to the café in town."

"In that case, you're in for a treat." He glanced over at me. "Have you been keeping busy since we last talked?"

"Busy enough. I took an inventory of furniture I didn't want and arranged for Lorna Bell to pick it up on Monday. Then I went to the Elite Beauty Shop, met up with Clovis Fisher, and got a haircut."

Josh laughed. "Ah, good old Clovis. I'll bet she talked your ears off."

"Pretty much." I paused and decided to see how much he knew concerning the town. "I had another visitor yesterday—Ruth Kendall."

"Ruth? What on earth did she want?"

"Just to say hello and welcome me back. At first I thought she might have come at her husband's request to push for a sale of the farm."

"Not Ruth. She doesn't give a damn about the real estate business. She was probably checking you out as competition."

"Competition?"

"She's got her finger in every social pie in the county. Head of this, chairman of that. She wouldn't take lightly to giving up any of it to a newcomer."

"She has nothing to fear from me. I'm from the city, so gardens and I aren't on the same page. I play bridge, but to be truthful, never cared for it. I'm not much of a social butterfly."

"Too bad. Wellington revolves around its clubs and social events, including politics."

"I'm not political either."

"Believe it or not, small towns can be hotbeds of politics. The Wellington Republican Club meets once a month at the American Legion Hall. Same for the

Wellington Democratic Club."

"Not at the same time, I hope."

He chuckled. "No. Every third Wednesday for the Republicans and every fourth Tuesday for the Dems. Even the Libertarians get into the act. They meet at Horace Fielding's house whenever they can find five members who aren't busy elsewhere. I attend all as the one and only media source."

We entered the Atwell city limits, population 9,996 according to the sign. I'm sure I must have been in the town at some point in time, but had no recollection. Josh maneuvered the car into a parallel parking space, got out, dropped a couple of coins into the parking meter, and then opened my door.

"Morelli's is just down the street," he said.

Just down the street turned out to be on the square opposite the courthouse. It was Saturday night and the town was crowded. Most shops were open in the hope of snagging a casual window gazer as they strolled past. Not familiar with small towns, I found the cheerful greetings called out from doorways charming.

The fabulous scents of garlic and oregano led me to Morelli's. Josh pulled the ornate front door open and we walked in to a little bit of Italy. Several murals depicting Italy and all things Italian brightened the dark wood on the floors and walls. Large chandeliers hung throughout the room. Wine racks filled with bottles were placed along the walls in a random fashion. I found the décor dated and on the depressing side.

A hostess showed us to the last table for two along the wall. The snowy white tablecloth impressed me, along with a perfect place setting. My aunt, the snob that she was, would have approved.

"Josh, this is lovely," I said as I placed my napkin on my lap.

"I knew you'd like it. As you can see, people come from all over to eat here."

He spoke the truth. Most of the tables were full. The well-dressed patrons chatted, ate, and sipped from wine glasses. Dinner at Morelli's was obviously a big occasion and an excuse to dress up.

Our waiter appeared. Josh ordered Chianti while I went with my favorite Italian white wine, Pinot Grigio. As soon as we were alone, I opened the menu. The selections made me want to order everything, but I settled on Chicken Parmesan. Josh decided on Veal Sinatra. We placed our orders when the server brought our drinks.

Alone again, I asked questions even though I already knew the answers.

"So, tell me about Josh Hendricks. How did you get to be the owner of a small town weekly in the middle of Iowa?"

He smiled and sipped his wine. "Journalism was in my blood, I guess. My father was an opinionated soul. It came naturally from his father. They both wrote numerous letters to the editor of the local paper."

"And where was that?"

"Bennettsville, Minnesota, a suburb just outside Minneapolis. My father was an attorney and my grandfather owned the local bank. Neither the law nor banking appealed to me, but I romanticized the life of a reporter. All those far away places, covering war and social upheaval. At the time, journalism just seemed like the best road to take."

"At the time? You sound rather lukewarm on the

subject," I commented.

"A few years ago, I was, but the enthusiasm came back. At any rate, after college I landed a job on the *Twin Cities Chronicle*. I had delusions of my own byline and winning awards for my scintillating writing." He laughed. "What I wrote were obituaries and updating the calendar of events in the area."

"Calendar of events?"

"'The Ladies Garden Society will hold their monthly meeting at ten o'clock this coming Thursday at the Bennettsville Public Library.' 'The Universal Club of Minneapolis will be electing its Board members next Tuesday at seven o'clock in the evening. All members are urged to attend.'"

"Oh, good grief. Sounds boring as hell."

"It was. The Chronicle was a small paper struggling to survive against the established Minneapolis and St. Paul newspapers. I stuck around for a year, and then beat it."

The salad course arrived and as we ate, Josh filled me in on his journalistic wanderings. The story followed what I'd Googled earlier. Still, I sensed there was something he wasn't telling me, but then, I wasn't telling him everything either.

"And you've been in Wellington how long?"

"Two years now. I like the slow pace and the people. It's a perfect refuge to gather thoughts and relax."

"Refuge? You make it sound like a hideout."

I'd meant the words in a facetious manner, but he looked at me sharply, his brows drawn together. Then the semi-scowl faded and he smiled.

"Not a hideout, just a nice town with nice people."

Except when one of the nice people turns out to be a killer. I kept my opinion to myself for the moment.

Our meal arrived cutting off the conversation. The Chicken Parm was golden brown, the mozzarella cheese melted just enough to bubble, and the tantalizing aroma made my stomach growl. Josh's Veal Sinatra looked just as appetizing. We both opted for Parmesan cheese on our food and ordered another glass of wine.

I popped a bite of my chicken into my mouth and almost swooned. The hint of garlic and oregano along with the strong flavor of the Parmesan was delicious.

We ate silently for several minutes. After the wine was served, I threw the small talk back into his court.

"So, tell me about Wellington."

"What do you want to know?"

"What does one do for fun? Is there a movie theatre? A bowling alley? Any restaurants besides the Kozy Kafe?"

"Atwell boasts the only four-plex in the county, but the old Doc Jones Theatre in Wellington is still in business on weekends. It tends to show second runs and only costs two dollars."

"Quite the bargain."

"Yes, it is. The Kendalls own it."

"Why Doc Jones?"

"From what I was told, he was the original owner and town dentist."

"I see. Anything else in town?"

"No bowling alley. Once again Atwell claims that distinction, but Wellington does have a miniature golf course just south of town. The Kendalls own that, too. And if you want to upgrade from the Kozy Kafe cuisine, there's a cafeteria on West Green Street or the

Chinese Palace on South Main. And if the urge for pizza strikes, you can always stop by Paisano's Pizza on East State. And don't forget the usual fast food joints. Most of those are near the strip mall and grocery store."

"Do the Kendalls own all that, too?"

He chuckled. "No, but Bob probably sold the land or buildings. He never misses an opportunity."

"I'm surprised he's not mayor, justice of the peace, chief of police, *and* fire chief."

"Not yet, although the rumor mill is suggesting he's thinking about the mayor's office come next year."

"Thanks for the warning." I sipped from my glass. "I'll have to get used to small town vibes. I bet Wellington has a grapevine that never ends."

"Ah, gossip. Take my word for it, it's alive and well."

"And who is the gossip guru? Ruth Kendall?"

"Ruth likes to show she's above that, but June Simpson has her finger on every pulse in town—including the Garden Club, three bridge clubs, The Presbyterian Women's Auxiliary, and heaven only knows what else. Lorna comes in a close second. And all information whether factual or not, is disseminated at Clovis Fisher's. What the other mavens don't know, Clovis does."

"You seem to be well-versed in the pipeline. So what's the latest gossip?" I tried to keep my tone light.

Josh leaned forward slightly. "I have it on good authority that Callie Bryant is back in town, and I for one, am glad."

I laughed. "I can remember my aunt saying something about how small town gossip had upset my mother. I guess being a newcomer she must have been the object of discussion on more than one occasion."

"Before my time."

He sipped his wine and avoided eye contact while eating his last bites of food. He was being evasive. He'd probably heard plenty and either didn't pass along rumors, or wanted to spare my feelings. I admired that, but it didn't help much. I needed information, even of the speculative kind.

The waiter cleared our dishes. We refused dessert, but accepted coffee. I added cream and stirred watching the mixture turn a rich mocha color.

"So tomorrow's Sunday. Will you be attending church?" he asked.

"I suppose that's a must. In Chicago, my aunt and I attended the First Presbyterian off and on, but never regularly."

"In a small town, it's high on the list. Wellington boasts a Methodist church and a Presbyterian. There's even a small Unitarian church on the east side. Catholics have to drive into Atwell. And if you're Jewish, you're just out of luck."

I chuckled. "Guess I go Presbyterian if I go at all."

"Won't get off easy. Ruth and Bob Kendall are Presbyterians as are Lorna and the Simpsons, and just to warn you, Clovis is a firm Unitarian."

"Can't escape any of the gossipmongers, can I?"

He grinned. "Nope."

The waiter brought our bill. Josh settled up and we left the restaurant.

"Care to take a stroll?" he asked.

"Love to."

We walked down the crowded sidewalk stopping

every now and then to peer into store windows. I had fun. I could easily see myself wearing those styles.

The drive home was filled with chit-chat about the weather and the crops just planted. We pulled into the drive a little after nine-thirty.

"Would you like to come in for another cup of coffee? I'd offer a nightcap, but don't have anything other than wine."

Josh smiled. "A glass of iced tea sounds good."

"That, I have." Iced tea was a mainstay of country living.

He escorted me to the porch where I unlocked the back door.

"You locked the door?" Amusement seeped through his words.

"Sorry, I'm still in Chicago mode." I pushed the door open and entered the kitchen. I'd left several lights on in the house so I wouldn't be greeted with darkness. I hated the dark. "I guess there's not much crime here in Wellington."

"Not a whole lot. The occasional shoplifter is about as crime-ridden as it gets. Every once in a while a call comes in about vandalism, mostly around Halloween."

Don't forget the occasional murder.

I poured us each a glass of tea. Josh accepted his and sat at the kitchen table where I joined him.

"My mother's death must have sent shock waves through the town," I commented. Surely, he knew something about the reactions.

He drank as if collecting his thoughts. "From what I've heard and read, it was more like a tidal wave. A beautiful young wife and mother found by her husband with a knife in her back in the foyer of their home.

Gave the whole county a jolt."

Time to take the direct approach. "Exactly what have you heard?"

He shrugged. "Not much. Your father was accused of the crime, found guilty, and sent to prison where he died five years later. By the time I got here, it was old news. Why are you asking?"

I drank deeply to erase the dryness in my throat. "My memory gaps are beginning to close, but I need to know what's fact and what's fiction. You try going through life with a chunk of your memory gone."

"What do you mean by your memory gaps are closing?"

"I started having nightmares after we moved to Chicago. They came and went over the years. Lately, I've dreamed about the farm, Mom, Dad, the confusion after the murder. I want to find out what they all mean, if anything."

"Why is it I have the feeling you're not telling me everything? Why did you come home, Callie?"

"I'm hoping familiar surroundings from twenty-five years ago will put the pieces into place."

Josh finished his tea and set the glass on the table.

"Can I get you a refill?"

He shook his head. "What pieces? You were in the house that night, weren't you? Did you see something you shouldn't have?"

I raised my hand, and then let it fall back to the table. "I really don't know. I remember waking up to lots of commotion downstairs and calling for Daddy. He came up, tucked me in, and kissed me. I don't remember him saying anything other than to go back to sleep. When he kissed me goodnight, his cheeks were wet like he'd been crying. The aftermath is a jumble of memories and people. I need to get it all straight in my head."

"Why, Callie?"

I took a deep breath. He was the only person in town I trusted to know the truth.

"Because I don't believe my father killed my mother. He was innocent, and I intend to prove it."

Chapter Six

Josh stared, then rose abruptly and walked to the sink where he paused to gaze out the window before turning back. Leaning against the counter, he crossed his arms over his chest and frowned.

"What makes you think your father is innocent when the cops, a jury of his peers, and half the town believe otherwise?"

I folded my hands on the table, but looked at him with a steady eye. "You didn't know Daddy. He was the kindest, gentlest man I've ever known. I can remember him holding me on his lap in that big recliner while we watched TV. I remember his hugs and his laughter. He would never do anything as heinous as murder, especially to Mother. He loved her."

"Callie, you were a child who remembers a parent you loved. Plus, you also admit to having memory gaps," he reminded me in a soft tone.

"About that night and the immediate aftermath. Aunt Dee whisked Denny and me out of town a couple of days after the funeral. I think that's when Daddy was arrested. I never knew about the trial until it was over."

"Why are you telling me this?"

"Because in my eyes, everyone else in town is a suspect. They were here twenty-five years ago. You weren't. I need help doing this. Both John Casey and Bill Jackson were less than cooperative when I talked to them yesterday."

Josh uncrossed his arms and joined me again at the table. "John Casey? How does he fit into this?"

"He was Daddy's lawyer."

His forehead furrowed. "You mean for the trial? He does wills and trusts not criminal law. Why didn't your father get a criminal attorney from Atwell—someone with experience in that field?"

"I don't know. Daddy and John grew up together."

His frown deepened. "And you say you've already talked to him? He knows your plans?"

I fidgeted in my seat, then rose and grabbed a couple of wine glasses from the shelf. Opening the refrigerator door, I pulled out a half bottle of wine and poured.

"Not quite," I replied, setting the glass in front of him and resuming my seat. "I told him I wanted to see the trial transcripts to fill in memory gaps, but he says they don't exist. Same with Chief Jackson and any notes on the investigation. Both were reluctant, but said they'd 'see what they could do.'"

He sipped from the glass and stared over my shoulder at the kitchen door. "An ongoing investigation is the only reason for records to be kept under wraps."

"John Casey says he doesn't have much of anything—that he destroyed old files years ago."

"The transcripts would have been sent to the appellate court for the appeal. You may want to check there."

"I don't even know where that is."

"My guess would be Des Moines."

I drank half my wine in one gulp. "I'm not sure what to do next. I need help. You're a reporter. Tell a reporter no or stonewall him and you're asking for trouble."

"Callie, has it occurred to you that John or Bill, or both, suspect your real motives? Solving a twenty-five year old murder that was legally resolved through the court system might make them nervous. Make it seem like they didn't do their jobs."

"They didn't." I laid my hand on his arm. "Please, Josh, I need someone on my side. Someone who knows how to get information from official sources. I can deal with people like the Kendalls and Lorna Bell, but..."

I let the sentence hang and held my breath.

"Exactly what do you remember from that night?"

"I'm not sure."

"All right, let's try it this way. What kind of dreams are you having?"

I finished my wine and got up to pour another glass before resuming my seat.

"Disjointed is probably the best description. I hear voices—a man and a woman arguing."

"Your mom and dad? Did they argue?"

I nodded. "Frequently."

"So you heard them fighting the night of the murder?"

"I can't identify the dream voices or if when I heard them was the night of the murder."

"What else?" he persisted.

"I...I think I hear someone running and a cry along with a crash of some sort. Later sobbing. And then there are the flashing lights."

"Lights?"

"Like a strobe—white, and then red, then white again." I rubbed my forehead. "It's all so confusing.

Occasionally, I see the foyer from above like I'm floating near the ceiling or I'm at the top of the stairs."

Josh wrapped my cold fingers in his hand. "What do you see?"

"Nothing. Just shadows. I'm not sure what is real and what isn't."

"I assume you had a shrink to help you deal with the trauma."

I sighed. "Aunt Dee hired the best in Chicago. His name is Halloran, and before you ask, no, he doesn't agree with what I'm doing."

"I don't blame him. Did he ever hypnotize you to get the answers?"

"He tried on several occasions, but it didn't work. I must have a very strong mind."

Josh didn't smile at my feeble attempt at humor. "I've heard it said that a traumatic experience can bring on amnesia."

"Dr. Halloran brought that up several times, but never voiced if he thought I'd seen anything that night."

"What was your reaction when you found out your father had been convicted of second degree murder?"

"I was only seven and not even sure what second degree murder and life in prison was all about. All I knew was that Daddy wouldn't be coming to live with us in Chicago."

"What about your brother and your aunt? Did they agree with the verdict?"

"Aunt Dee was passionate that he was guilty. Denny was just as passionate he wasn't."

"Must have made for interesting talk around the dining table," he said.

"Denny and Aunt Dee were oil and water. He was

twelve, almost thirteen, and resented being ripped away from his home."

Josh nodded. "I remember. Puberty was around the corner waiting to pounce. Not a thing I'd like to repeat."

"Aunt Dee didn't know how to handle him, so as soon as it was possible, she shipped him off to a very expensive military school in Indiana." I sipped more wine. "You do know that Denny was my half-brother, don't you?"

"Didn't even know you had a brother until the other day."

"His mother died in a car wreck when he was just a toddler." I paused to drag in a shaky breath. "So, will you help me?"

He stared into my eyes. "I think you should forget about this crusade. It's only going to bring trouble. Sell the farm and go back to Chicago."

His words took me by surprise. I was so sure he'd see things my way. Disappointment gnawed in my chest.

"Josh, I can't give up now. I just can't! Someone didn't just kill my mother, they murdered my entire family. As a result of Mother's death, my father was sent to prison where he eventually died. And with Daddy in prison, my brother was forced to go to Chicago and eventually, military school. As a kid, all he'd ever wanted to do was be a farmer, but with a military background, chose the Army as a career. And that choice got him killed, too. I'm the last Bryant left standing, and I'll be damned if I give up!"

Josh's face softened. "I'm so sorry, Callie. I never thought of it like that. I suppose if I was in your shoes,

I'd be doing the same thing." He finished his wine. "I'll help you get access to the transcripts and police reports if they still exist, but I think you're fighting an uphill battle."

"It's one I expect to win."

"Have you considered the consequences if you do? If you find out he was innocent that means somebody in this town isn't."

Determination lifted my chin. "I know. I'm already talking to people and judging their reactions."

His hand covered mine making my heart beat faster. "Be careful how you tread on that one, Callie. If you're right, then a killer has spent the past twenty-five years thinking he's safe. Your questions, even innocent ones, could spook him. Don't make yourself a target. Don't put yourself in danger."

He was right, I could be putting myself in the crosshairs of a killer. Warmth surged through my body, not only from his touch, but for the concern in his voice. "I won't—although I *am* planning something special."

"Special? How special?"

"I'm going to have a cocktail party Wednesday night."

"A party?" Josh exclaimed.

"Why not? It'll bring all the suspects together and with enough liquor flowing, maybe someone will let something slip. It happens all the time in mystery novels. Agatha Christie would have Hercule Poirot or Miss Marple gather everyone in one spot before revealing the killer."

"For God's sake, this isn't a novel. It's real. And you aren't Hercule Whoever or Miss Whosiewhatsis.

This is a bad idea, Callie. Forget it."

"No, I won't forget it. Don't you understand? I have to know who killed my mother. And it wasn't Daddy. Besides, this is my home now. I want to fit in."

"So you throw a party designed to pump your guests for information? That won't endear you to them."

"How else can I learn anything?"

He spared me a quick glance. "And just who do you plan on inviting to this ill-advised party?"

I let his irritating sarcasm pass. "Well, Lorna for one. I had lunch with her today and she had plenty to say about June Simpson and Daddy." I gave him the lowdown on what she'd said.

"I never knew June was sweet on your dad, which might explain Lorna."

"How?"

"Did you ever see that old sitcom, *Cheers*, and the Norm character that practically lives at the bar to avoid spending time with his wife, Vera?"

"I catch it every once in a while on one of the oldies TV channels. Why?"

"The ongoing joke down at Sweet Daddy's Bar was that the characters were based on Rich and Lorna."

"You're kidding. Rich and Lorna didn't get along?"

"Can't say one way or the other, but he died a few weeks after I moved here. His was my first Wellington obituary. And from what I observed, Lorna wasn't all that broken up about it."

"How do you know so much about Lorna and Rich?"

"When I first moved here, I spent a lot of time at

Sweet Daddy's talking up the clientele. I wanted to know more about the town from the people who lived here."

I shifted in my seat and took a deep breath. "I guess that's how you found out about Mother."

"It was the first topic of conversation. I did some research, but since it happened so long ago and the family was no longer in the area, didn't pay it much mind."

"Until I came along."

He nodded. "Until you showed up."

"Gossip is alive and well and isn't gender specific," I said in a dry tone.

"I wouldn't call it gossip," he protested.

"Of course, it is. Just a different venue. Women use the beauty shop as headquarters while men use the bar."

"I never thought of it quite like that before. So, who else is on the invite list?"

"June Simpson and her husband, Bob and Ruth Kendall, John Casey and his wife, you, a few neighbors, and I think Clovis, too."

"Clovis Fisher? Whatever for?"

"She did Mother's hair, and like I said, a beauty shop is always a hotbed of gossip. I'll bet Clovis is just like Lorna, a fountain of unsubstantiated information, some of which might even be correct." I paused. Sifting through all the innuendos and such would take time, but I was willing to do it. "I wonder how happy June Simpson is in her wedded life?"

"Can't tell you that either, but I do know inviting Ruth Kendall and June Simpson to the same party is not for the faint of heart."

"They don't like each other?"

"Not one bit. When Ruth moved here, she pushed June right out of the queen bee social position. They're civil to each other, but that's about all."

"So, I may feel frost?"

"Polite frost, of course."

"How did an outsider like Ruth, push June aside in the social whirl?"

"Not real sure, but both women can be aggressive. Maybe some of the other women in the groups were tired of June calling the shots. A newcomer equals new ideas or something."

"Let me get this straight. Lorna and June pretend to be friends, but aren't really, while June and Ruth don't even pretend?"

"And John Casey's wife refuses to let Clovis touch her hair. Something about a botched haircut years ago."

"Maybe no one will show up at this party."

"Sure they will. Bob to pressure you into selling the farm. Ruth to lord it over June. June and her husband, Roger, to remind Ruth that even after over thirty years, she's still not from Wellington, and Clovis just because Clovis likes a good time. Lorna will come to needle everyone."

"And John Casey?"

"Community relations. He'll be running for county judge next year when current judge, Brad Shubert, retires. He wants my endorsement along with that of City Councilman, Bob Kendall who in turn expects an endorsement from John Casey when *he* runs for mayor."

"Holy crap! This is almost as convoluted as Chicago politics. What a bunch of hypocrites, which also makes them a bunch of liars as well."

Josh laughed. "And here you thought you were moving back to the simple way of life."

I shook my head. No wonder Mother had hated Wellington. Not only had she been an outsider, but also the center of gossip. I needed to get Ruth one on one soon. Another lunch loomed on my horizon, only I had the gut feeling this one wouldn't be at the Kozy.

I wondered how frustrated June Simpson was to have first lost Daddy to a couple of blondes, and then to have lost her social standing to Ruth Kendall. *And Mother was Ruth's best friend. Interesting development.*

He glanced at his watch. "I'd better be heading home. I'll make some calls on Monday morning. Maybe later we can head over to Atwell and read those newspaper files. I doubt there's anything online about this. Too many years have passed."

"I've already Googled and found nothing. And I can't do Monday. Bell's is picking up and the moving van from Chicago is due."

"Tuesday, then."

He rose and I accompanied him to the back door.

"Good night, Callie. Hope your dreams tonight are peaceful."

"Me, too. And thank you for dinner. I had a wonderful time."

He hesitated, and then leaned down to lightly brush his lips over mine. "So did I. You going to church tomorrow?"

"Wouldn't miss it. The Presbyterians need something to talk about other than the sermon."

Josh grinned. "I'll see you there."

He kissed me again and as he left, I placed my fingers over my tingling lips. My stomach fluttered and suddenly the kitchen was much warmer than earlier.

Don't let physical attraction get in the way of finding the truth.

Yeah, right. Easier said than done—on both counts. I'd discovered an earthier side of life my freshman year in college along with the ability to enjoy it. I'd also learned how to hide it from Aunt Dee.

I poured the last of the wine into my glass and took it into the living room. Instead of sitting, I paced.

I hadn't meant to tell him so much, but was glad I did. I had more to disclose, but decided to keep those secrets a while longer. Secrets like Denny's last visit before he left for Afghanistan, Aunt Dee's deathbed confessions, and Ruth Kendall's information about Daddy's so-called affair. I wanted to investigate the latter.

I finally went to bed. The light breeze fluttered the curtains bringing with it that country smell of clean, fresh air. I hadn't realized how much I'd missed it.

As I drifted off to sleep, a train whistle in the distance sent a comforting note to my tired brain.

****

I sat in my car in the First Presbyterian Church parking lot fingering my purse before opening it and extracting an envelope. Torn by indecision, I bit my lip. In all the hubbub of yesterday, I'd forgotten to check the mailbox, so I stopped this morning on my way into town. It contained the usual assortment of junk, forwarded mail that didn't matter, and the envelope I now held. No stamp, no postmark, and no return address. Just the envelope. Curious, I'd opened it and read the single sheet of paper inside.

Go back to Chicago. There's nothing for you here.

Stop asking questions and stirring up trouble. Your mother stirred up trouble, too. Look where it got her. Go home!

The note was printed in big block letters. There was no signature.

The contents scared me on several levels. First, my questions regarding details of Mother's death and Daddy's incarceration had been fairly benign—just a daughter seeking answers to a tragedy she didn't quite remember. They had also been limited to John Casey and Bill Jackson.

Second, I had only referred to my parents in a nostalgic way when speaking with people like June, Ruth, and Lorna. The only person who had suggested I leave town had been Bob Kendall.

And last, I remembered Josh's warning from the night before about seeking to prove Daddy's innocence. If he didn't kill my mother, then someone else did. This note indicated I might have struck a nerve.

Should I show it to Josh? Take it to the police? Let it be known publicly, I didn't like the implication or being threatened?

Anonymous letters are the work of cowards. If it's true Daddy was having an affair, then this could be the other woman hoping to cover her ass.

I shoved the envelope back into my purse and exited the car. I was undecided whether or not to tell Josh. I'd have to think on it.

Josh met me on the steps outside the church with a smile. "Ready to run the gauntlet?"

Already people stared as they hurried inside. Had one of these church-going, upright citizens written the note? "Ready as I'll ever be."

The usher smiled and handed us a program. We slid into a pew near the back, nodding to those who looked us in the eye. Like a wave, parishioners stared over their shoulders before focusing their gazes back to the front. Heads got together to whisper.

"Miss Ballou, you have arrived," Josh said in a low tone, misquoting from an old movie, *Cat Ballou*.

The Presbyterian Church hadn't changed since it had been built in 1945. The dark brown wooden pews gleamed with care. The long center aisle was wide enough to allow a bride wearing a ball gown to pass without fuss. Brass candlesticks on the raised altar shone bright. Yellow and white flowers stood on either side of the steps. The mid-morning sun streamed through the stained glass windows with a multi-hued brilliance. I wondered if the Sunday school rooms and the reception hall downstairs had also stayed the same.

Organ music swelled from the balcony behind us as the congregation rose to praise the Lord. The choir marched down the aisle where they took seats on the right hand side of the altar area.

My throat tightened as I sang. Tears welled and I blinked them away. It had been a long time since I'd been in church. Mom and Dad had attended every Sunday. I remembered the fun of Sunday school and how proudly I'd shown them my awards and certificates. Aunt Dee had been more of a special occasion churchgoer, like on Christmas and Easter. Denny had turned into an out and out agnostic.

During announcements, I allowed my gaze to wander from pew to pew. Up front, I spotted Lorna Bell. A few rows in back of her June Simpson sat with a man I assumed was her husband. Across the aisle,

Mrs. Comstock from the grocery store nodded and smiled at me. I nodded back. I didn't see the Kendalls anywhere.

The sermon dealt with the prodigal son, which given my circumstances seemed appropriate. After the benediction, the minister announced that coffee and cookies would be available in the reception room.

As we filed out of the church, the minister shook my hand and smiled. Tall and distinguished, he didn't look a day over forty.

"Welcome home, Miss Bryant. I hope we'll be seeing you again soon."

"I'm sure you will. Very nice sermon."

"Thank you." He turned his attention to the man by my side. "Nice to see you, too, Josh. It's been a while."

"Yes it has." He glanced at me. "I think that may change soon."

We moved on down the steps to the sidewalk.

"So, do you want coffee and cookies?" Josh asked.

"I suppose one cup of coffee and one cookie won't kill me."

We walked down the sidewalk to the side entrance of the church and made our way to the large room. A sizable crowd had assembled. The babble ceased when we entered, and then resumed. Sooner or later, the people of Wellington would get used to me coming and going.

I chatted with Mrs. Comstock and mentioned the party on Wednesday night. She smiled and accepted. I couldn't avoid June Simpson who introduced me to her husband along with several other people. I took the opportunity to invite the Simpsons to the party. Her husband beamed and accepted immediately. June nodded her acquiescence, but with a strained smile. Lorna said a quick hello reminding me a truck would be at the house for the furniture pick up around nine. Before she rushed off to speak to another woman I managed to give her the details of the party, too. Frankly, I couldn't see any of them sending me an anonymous letter. Half an hour later, Josh and I were back on the sidewalk. I asked him about Bob and Ruth.

"I think they're more of the if-I-get-up-in-time attendees. Would you like to indulge in a Sunday meal at Wannamaker's Cafeteria?"

"Where?"

"That's where everyone meets to discuss the various sermons delivered by each denomination."

I shook my head. "No thanks. If Lorna is sending the truck at nine tomorrow, I have to go through drawers and such to make sure everything is empty. My stuff should arrive later."

"I'd offer to help, but have to interview someone in Center City this afternoon. However, I can help you set up things that arrive tomorrow. Would you like me to bring dinner?"

I decided to hold on telling Josh about the note. "That sounds wonderful. Why don't you come around five?"

He nodded, smiled, and much to my disappointment, headed for his car.

"Did you expect him to kiss you in front of God and the entire Presbyterian congregation?" I muttered to myself.

Back home, I changed into jeans and a t-shirt, then padded barefoot downstairs where I made a brunch of French toast, bacon, and fruit. I had to chuckle. Aunt

Dee would have a cow at my attire. To her, jeans, t-shirts, and bare feet symbolized someone who didn't care about themselves or how they appeared to others. To me, my clothes spelled comfortable. My roots were re-establishing themselves. It felt good.

After eating, I did a search through the drawers of the furniture in the living room going to Bell's. As expected, they were empty. I supposed Aunt Dee had seen to the clean-out when closing the house or had had someone do it for her.

I wondered why the desk in Daddy's office had been left almost intact, and then shrugged. Maybe it had been ignored for tax purposes. After all, someone had to have done that final year of taxes, not to mention the filings for the past twenty-five years. Had my aunt employed an accountant to oversee the job? Had he or she been in Chicago or local? I had no idea and made a mental note to ask John Casey the next time I saw him. I did not need problems with the IRS.

Next, I turned my attention to Mom and Dad's bedroom. Long and narrow, it ran the entire width along the front of the house. At some point in time, a smaller bedroom had been converted into a large closet and a master bath. Mother had called this room her retreat from reality and I'd known from an early age that if the door was closed, not to intrude. Of course, I'd also often heard angry words coming from behind that closed door.

Today, the room had a sterile look to it. Gone were the little personal touches like the Hummel figurines my mother had adored. I had no clue where they were now. I hadn't even attempted to go into the attic or the basement yet.

I checked the dresser and nightstand drawers. They were empty. The closet gaped naked, too. The curio cabinet, home to the Hummels, sat forlorn in a corner. An antique bookcase, its glass encased doors closed, graced the opposite corner. With the exception of the bookcase and cabinet, the rest would go to Lorna. I exited the room leaving the door wide open.

I paused in the doorway of Denny's room before finally stepping inside. Twin beds flanked the east-facing window. In my mind's eye, I pictured the matching bedspreads and the braided rug between the beds. Little league trophies had graced the shelves along the wall. The shelves were bare now. A dresser and a chest of drawers nestled against the wall near the door, the hairbrushes and other boy paraphernalia long gone.

My gaze swept toward the nightstand between the beds. Denny had claimed the one furthest from the door as his. I remembered him reading the latest comic book in bed when I'd come in to wish him goodnight.

My throat tightened at the memory and I blinked tears from my eyes. God, how I missed him. I wished he were here now to help me. His military training gave him an air of authority I didn't possess. Captain Dennis Allen Bryant would not be given the runaround by lawyers or police chiefs.

Unbidden, other memories also intruded. Aunt Dee, cold and controlling, had her way. We moved to Chicago. That's when the nightmares began. Just a few at first—Mother and Daddy arguing, the sobs, the shouts. I got little sympathy from my aunt.

"Calista, you must put these silly things out of your mind. I will not coddle a weakling."

Then she and Denny reached the boiling point and he was shipped off to military school. With my last thread to the life I'd always known now cut, my dreams became more terrifying, more vivid, and more frequent. Eventually, my aunt had brought in a psychiatrist.

"You're just like your mother. She was weak, too. I will not tolerate weakness. You need to be strong, Calista. I'm sure this doctor can help straighten you out."

Only he didn't. Now, for the first time in years, I no longer depended on him or anyone else—just me. And now Josh, of course.

I closed my eyes and bit my lip. I'd kept my deepest fear hidden—even from Dr. Halloran, tucked away in the furthest corners of my mind and heart.

I feared that for a quarter of a century, I'd been fantasizing, that the dreams and nightmares were not based in reality.

I feared I was crazy.

Don't think about that. Focus on what's important. I don't have time for fears. I have a job to do.

Inhaling a deep breath, I reopened my eyes. The room was no longer my brother's. It was cold and lifeless. I turned and left, this time closing the door behind me. I couldn't bring myself to sell Denny's things yet.

I had just entered the kitchen when my landline rang.

"Hello?" Silence greeted me. On the other end, I heard heavy breathing. My throat tightened. "Hello, is anybody there?"

"Church won't help you anymore than it helped her. Go home," a voice whispered before disconnecting.

I hung up slowly, my heart pounding. It's hard to tell gender from a whisper. I now regretted not telling Josh about the note and wished I'd suggested dinner here tonight. I was nervous, but not particularly frightened—at least not enough to call the cops. Besides, what could they do? So far, I hadn't been directly threatened.

The walk-through depressed me, and now this phone call, on top of the note, left me anxious. Dusk was settling. I needed to get out of the house, to be surrounded by people. Perhaps a meal at the Kozy Kafe would help. Maybe a movie at the local theater was just the answer.

Without stopping to think, I grabbed my car keys and drove into town. The Kozy was only a couple of blocks from the movie theater. A quick dinner of pot roast with all the trimmings satisfied my hunger. The two-dollar movie, a romantic comedy I'd seen several years ago, kept most of my attention focused.

Back home, I checked the mailbox. It was empty. Restless energy had me pacing much as it had last night. I replayed the part of Josh's and my conversation about not making myself a target in my head.

Were my questions and curiosity like poking a cornered animal with a stick? Was Josh right? Could the person who killed my mother turn on me?

Of course they could—probably would, too. But were the writer and the caller the same person? Or the killer?

For the first time since moving back, I locked the doors before going to bed. I needed to be careful. I had no desire to become a victim, too. Someone in this town was a cold-blooded killer. I intended to find out whom.

Chapter Seven

I awoke at six-thirty from another dream, only this one didn't involve strange voices or visions. This one centered on Josh Hendricks. Perhaps it was a combination of the romantic movie I'd seen last night and the kiss he'd bestowed on me Saturday evening, but my dream bordered on the erotic. That earthier side was coming through.

The cawing emanating from the tree outside my bedroom window gave me a clue as to what had interrupted my very pleasant imaginings.

"Damned crows," I muttered.

The first red streaks of dawn were touching the horizon. I threw back the covers and got up. No more dreaming for me. It was time to face the day. In spite of my worries about the note, the phone call, and who had killed my mother, I'd slept like the old proverbial log. Not even the midnight train interrupted my slumber.

Breakfast consisted of a bowl of cereal, orange juice, and coffee. With a couple of hours to kill before the truck from Bell's arrived, I decided to inspect the out buildings and see if any repairs were needed. Farmers had priorities when it came to structures.

Barns housed livestock and hay. Machinery sheds sheltered tractors and other expensive pieces of equipment. Corncribs held field corn until it was needed as feed for the animals or sale. Those buildings were more important to the farmer than his house and often had better maintenance.

I rarely indulged in nostalgia. Yet now it rolled over me in waves. For reasons, I couldn't explain, I needed to let it in. Perhaps if I dwelt on the good memories, my mind would relax and allow me to remember the bad.

The buildings were in good shape. The corn crib was almost empty. I jumped as a mouse shot out from between the slats and scurried through the door. At least it wasn't a rat. I hated rats. A cat might be a good investment.

Just behind the barn, a small house nestled near a wooded area. It was the original farmhouse, built when the place was homesteaded in the 1880s. I'd used it as a playhouse during the summer months.

The covered front porch sagged as I mounted the steps. I entered and let the memories flood over me. Gina Howell and I, along with our imaginary friends, had played pioneer on many a day. Gina had lived on the farm down and across the road from us. The same age, we'd become inseparable as kids. I wondered where she was now and what she was doing.

I walked slowly back to the main house. So many memories crammed into my mind demanding to be set free. I'd need to revisit them all—the good with the bad—if I was going to live here for the rest of my life. I still stood on the back steps when the truck from Bell's pulled into the drive.

I pushed the childhood fantasies away. It was time to deal with the present.

****

The old furniture had barely been loaded when the

moving van with my things arrived.

"Upstairs, to the right, bedroom in the front of the house…Kitchen…Living room…"

I'd directed, they'd lifted, and by two o'clock had left. Even the TV had been hooked up properly.

Now, three hours and several placement arrangements later, I stood in the dining room archway, hands on my hips, and surveyed the new living room. My apartment in Chicago had been blessed with large rooms, so I had filled it with furniture to match.

The long portion of my sectional rested against the inner wall, the shorter section curving around with its back to the dining room. Two large chairs were opposite, making for a nice framing effect. The glass top of the coffee table displayed the rug beneath it. A couple of end tables with lamps, and another between the chairs gave good light.

In a last second decision, I kept Daddy's recliner. Too many happy memories were associated with the plush leather. It now nestled in the corner.

My sixty-inch LED TV was mounted on the wall opposite the sectional. A sleek entertainment center holding the rest of the equipment needed for good viewing ran under it. I hadn't as yet combined my Internet and TV services. Too old-fashioned, I guess. I grabbed the remote and pressed the buttons. A picture immediately leaped onto the screen. *Ah, civilization finally arrives.*

I ran upstairs to the front bedroom and rummaged in a box marked linens until finding a set of sheets. This would now be my room. I liked the idea of a master bath and the big closet to hold all those shoes I clung to, but would probably never wear in the country. The only reason I hadn't claimed it before was the furniture. I just couldn't bring myself to sleep in Mom and Dad's bed. My king-sized platform went between the two front facing windows with room to spare. The rest of the furniture fit perfectly.

As I moved my things from my old room, I turned and paused in the doorway. It had been a nice bedroom, but I wasn't a kid anymore. Once again, time to move on.

I tweaked the comforter one last time and headed for the back staircase even though the front one was closer. I knew why—the foyer still set my teeth on edge. I wondered if I'd ever get past my fears.

I took a few minutes to call John Casey about the party on Wednesday.

"A party?" His tone held a hint of reserve.

"Yes. I want to reintroduce myself to Wellington, so I thought a little get-together might be nice. I do hope you can come."

"I'll have to clear it with Jessica and get back to you."

As I hung up, a loud banging on the back door had me scurrying to answer.

Through the panes of glass, I spied Josh both hands full of bags and using his foot to knock. I quickly opened up.

"Thank goodness! I wasn't sure how much longer I could have held this stuff," he exclaimed setting the bags on the counter.

"What is it?"

"Dinner."

"Dinner? Good grief, how much do you plan on eating?"

He laughed. "I'm starving and since I wasn't sure what you liked, I ordered just about everything on the menu."

"What menu?" I peeked in one of the bags. The delicious aroma of General Tso's chicken hit my nose. "Oh, Chinese."

His face fell. "You like Chinese, don't you?"

I started to unpack the goodies. "I love Chinese, and have the feeling I'll be eating it for a week."

He laughed again and helped remove carton after carton. Kung Pao chicken, spicy beef and broccoli, some kind of shrimp dish along with more chicken and beef appeared. Crab rangoons and spring rolls emerged, not to mention several containers of rice, both steamed and fried. He even produced fortune cookies and chopsticks.

"Or are you a fork kind of girl?" he asked, his eyes twinkling.

"Definitely chopsticks."

I grabbed some plates, napkins, and serving spoons. "Dig in. What can I get you to drink?"

"You got any beer?"

"As a matter of fact, I do."

I opened two bottles, handing one to him. He set it on the table and headed for the counter where he filled his plate to damn near overflowing.

"Wow, you must be hungry," I said as he took a seat. I filled my plate with plenty of Kung Pao chicken, fried rice, and several crab rangoons. I'd work on more later.

Josh shoveled food into his mouth. "Had to skip lunch. Mindy went home around noon saying she wasn't feeling well. She's gonna drop that kid any second now."

"Good for her! She told me she's more than ready to be a mother."

"I see the movers got here," he commented eyeing the four boxes in the corner.

"Sure did. They pulled in as the truck from Bell's pulled out. Perfect timing. I even got most of the furniture set in the right places. I still have some boxes to unpack, but it went smoother than I thought." I hesitated. "Did you get to talk to John Casey or Bill Jackson today?"

He nodded. "Got a file from John Casey in the car. I leafed through it. Not much there. If you're up to it, maybe we can go Atwell tomorrow and take a look at the newspaper archives."

"All right, but what did Casey and Bill Jackson have to say?"

"Not much. Casey wasn't happy, but forked over the copies. Chief Jackson wasn't helpful at all. Gave me some blather about confidentiality and investigations until I reminded him, this was a closed case. He finally said he'd check into it."

"Sounds like the same bull he gave me. Those investigation reports are making me very curious."

"They should. I think his predecessor was a bumbling idiot. A murder investigation may have been way over his competence level. I'm surprised he didn't call in the state boys."

"A territorial dispute?"

"Maybe."

He finished his food and went back for more, piling on a smaller amount this time. He also snatched another beer from the fridge.

"I don't remember much about Roy Wilson other than he was on the fat side and wore a mustache. Bill Jackson interviewed me after the funeral."

Josh ceased eating to stare. "He interviewed *you*? Why?"

I sighed. "I was in the house and could have seen or heard something, I guess. I later told my aunt I heard Mom and Dad arguing that night. At least, I assumed it was Mom and Dad and the night in question. Now, I'm not so sure. She immediately contacted the police. Anything to put Daddy in a bad light. I remember the sheriff coming out to ask me more questions, but I don't remember what I told him. I think Aunt Dee had urged me to say it was Mother and Daddy. I've always felt guilty about telling her."

He reached across the table to squeeze my arm. "No reason why you should. You were young and didn't really know what was going on."

"I knew Mother was dead, but that's about all."

"Why did your aunt hate your father so much?"

I wasn't ready to tell him that yet. Aunt Dee's thin, frail voice coming from her hospice bed still evoked anger in me.

"I don't think she felt a mere farmer was good enough for the great-granddaughter of a tycoon."

We polished off more of the food before finally calling a halt.

"I can open a Chinese restaurant," I said, shoving the last of the cartons into the fridge.

Josh grinned. "I guess I did go overboard, but everything sounded so damned good, I couldn't resist."

"I oughta make you take some home."

"But then I couldn't come here to eat the

leftovers."

I gave him a stern look, and then grabbed another beer.

"Come on into the living room. Tell me what you think."

He headed into the dining room and stopped in the archway. I followed, pausing next to him.

"Wow!" He walked into the room where he once again halted. "Great TV. Can't wait for football season."

"Spoken like a true man," I commented with a laugh.

"I like that black rug, too."

"Flokati, one hundred percent wool with three-and a half inch pile. It measures eight by eleven feet and is fabulous under the tootsies on a cold winter day." I was proud of that rug. It had cost an arm and a leg, but was worth every nickel.

"You, lady, have great taste. This farmhouse is over a hundred years old, yet the modern lines of the furniture don't seem out of place. Even the colors work with the walls."

My sectional was deep claret red. I don't care for microfiber upholstery or leather, so went with something more traditional. The chairs sported deep red and cream colored stripes. Contrasting cream and black throw pillows nestled against the seat cushions. The glass-topped tables were chrome and the lamps black ceramic.

And Josh was right, it all fit well with the light gold walls last painted some twenty-five plus years ago.

"I was pleasantly surprised, too. I figured my winter would be filled with cans of paint, but this seemed to work for now. Have a seat."

He gravitated to the end of the sofa across from the TV and lowered himself into the cushions. He found the button along the side, pushed, and sighed when the footrest popped up.

"Perfect. I am so going to be at your place on Sunday afternoons."

I chuckled and set my beer bottle on the coffee table, then sat in my favorite spot, the curving wedge with my feet curled under me.

"Now, about that file you have. Can I see it?"

He pushed the footrest back down. "Sorry, I got so carried away by that TV, I forgot. Just be a second."

He left and I chuckled again as he used the front door. He returned, resumed his seat, and handed me the file.

"It's mostly about his first meeting with your father as a suspect. I'll tell you this much—I think Casey was in way over his head, too. Where's the remote?"

I tossed it to him. "Yet he didn't suggest Daddy get a criminal attorney out of Atwell or even Sioux Falls?"

"He doesn't mention that," he said as he surfed the channels. "How many channels do you have?"

"Over five hundred. I bought the entire enchilada, including the Super NFL package that shows all the games. I like football, too."

"Oh God, I think I'm in love."

"Never had a guy love me for my TV and cable package before," I murmured.

Josh grinned while I turned my attention to the file.

It read like a screen play—cold, impersonal, unemotional. There was no heart, no soul, no nothing except black words on a white page. Casey began with the basics of name, address, age, and then the big question.

Mr. Casey: Did you kill your wife?

Mr. Bryant: No! Absolutely not!

Mr. Casey: Describe what happened that night.

I tuned out the various channels Josh paused on and read, hoping a few missing pieces would fall into place. I reread it four times before closing the file and chewing on my lip.

The prosecution witnesses had consisted mostly of law enforcement. The knife used had Daddy's fingerprints all over it. His clothing had been liberally splashed with Mother's blood. She had been stabbed in the back a total of six times. The body had been found with the knife still imbedded. The autopsy report was missing. I wished I could see it, although why I didn't know. There was also a time frame problem.

All in all, it was pretty damning evidence.

"This is it?"

"That's all. I think Casey will drag his feet on giving us anything more."

I mentioned the lack of an autopsy report.

"That would have been done at the coroner's office in Atwell. They may not even have it any more, although a copy should be in somebody's file. I'm sure it was pretty straightforward."

"I don't want straightforward. I want a clue somebody missed!"

"Callie, I'm sorry."

I mulled over what I'd read as tears welled. I blinked them away, tossed the file onto the sofa, rose, and ran into the kitchen. Getting emotional wouldn't help matters.

Josh joined me and drew me into his arms with a comforting hug. "Honey, I just don't know what to say."

I sniffed and took a ragged breath. "Mother was murdered on a Saturday night in August. I remember Saturday nights during the summer. A local band would play in the park gazebo. People sat on the benches or in lawn chairs to listen. What I *don't* remember is that night specifically. For instance, I have no recollection of Mother and Daddy arguing in the car on the way home like the report says, or of Daddy leaving again when he dropped us off."

"Maybe that was the argument you told your aunt about."

"Maybe. I just don't remember. But Daddy told Casey he went to Sweet Daddy's Bar and had a couple of beers. According to him, he got there around nine-thirty and left a little after eleven. Surely people at the bar remembered him. And who's this guy named Bennett? Daddy said he talked to him for quite a while. The bartender and Bennett can confirm Daddy was there!"

"I've never heard of him, and there was never any question that he wasn't at the bar. If I'm not mistaken, the prosecution claimed your father was drunk, got home, renewed the argument, and then killed her."

I shook my head. "Not true. That just wasn't Daddy. I never saw him drunk and he didn't have it in him to kill anyone. And apparently, none of the witnesses could confirm it either."

"Callie, your father left the bar around eleven. The call didn't come into the police until eleven-forty. It's a five-minute drive from the bar to the farm. That's thirty-five unexplained minutes."

I pulled away from his embrace and waved a hand in the air. "According to Casey's notes, Daddy came home, entered through the back door, and walked into the living room. Mother wasn't there. He assumed she had gone to bed, so returned to the kitchen for a glass of water, and then went upstairs using the back staircase. Only she wasn't in bed. He thought maybe she was sitting on the front porch, went back downstairs using the front stairs and found her in the foyer. He even admits touching her body. That's how he got blood all over him."

"There's still that time lag," Josh reminded me.

"He was probably in shock. Who knows how long he was with Mother before calling the cops?"

"This is just the beginning of our investigation."

My landline rang. I lifted the receiver from the old-fashioned wall phone. "Hello?"

Silence.

"Hello! Is anybody there?"

"Leave! Before it's too late," a voice hissed in my ear.

"Dammit! Who the hell is this?"

"If you don't leave, you'll find out."

Anger mixed with fear bubbled in my chest. "Go to hell!"

Josh snatched the phone from my hand. "Who is this?"

He scowled, replaced the receiver in the holder, and turned to me. "They hung up. What was that all about?"

I still hadn't shown him the note left in the mailbox.

"Just a second. There's something you should see."

I left to rummage through my purse on the dining room sideboard extracting the note before returning to the kitchen and handing it to him.

"I found this in the mailbox on Sunday morning. A follow-up phone call came later that afternoon."

As he read, his scowl deepened. He raised his gaze to me, a look of worry in his eyes.

"I don't like this. Not one bit. You haven't been here a week and already you've touched a nerve with someone. Did you tell Bill Jackson?"

"No. What can he do about it?"

"What about the phone calls?"

I gave him the gist of the short and not so sweet messages.

"Callie, you've put yourself in danger by asking questions. Maybe you should go back to Chicago for a while. Let *me* ask the questions."

I shook my head. "No. I told you the other night— no retreat. I don't care how long it's been. I have to remember and that's not going to happen on Dr. Halloran's couch."

"Then at least move into town. This farm is isolated."

"Not that isolated. I have neighbors a quarter of a mile away to the west and about half a mile to the east. And I am *not* moving. I'm wondering if Bob Kendall did this. He made no bones about me leaving town."

He shook his head. "This isn't about the real estate business. This is personal. Maybe I should stay the night."

"Not necessary. Only cowards do things anonymously. I'll be careful."

"Well, for Pete's sake, lock your doors. And take this to the police. Bill might recognize the handwriting."

"It's not handwriting. It's printed in block letters. He wouldn't recognize squat."

Josh glanced at his watch. "I should be getting home. Tomorrow all my news copies have to be in by noon for printing and ready for delivery on Thursday. Why don't you come by at noon? We'll have lunch at the Kozy before heading for Atwell."

"I'd like that."

I accompanied him to the back door where he paused. "Sure you don't want me to stay?"

The suggestion intrigued me, but I shook my head thinking about the Smith & Wesson upstairs. "I'll be fine."

"Goodnight, Callie. I'll see you tomorrow." He leaned down and gave me a substantial kiss.

My heartbeat accelerated as a warm glow spread from the pit of my stomach to the tips of my fingers and toes.

"And don't forget to lock up." He stepped back, smiled, and walked out the door.

I decided a steady diet of Josh Hendricks might not be a bad idea after all. Like Chinese food, an hour later I wanted more.

"And speaking of Chinese food…" I turned to the fridge, took out a couple of cartons spooning fried rice, Kung Pao chicken, and a spring roll onto a plate, then shoved it in my microwave which now sat on the counter near the stove.

I had just taken it out when the phone rang again. I hesitated as a knot of fear formed in my stomach. Then

I lifted my chin in a defiant gesture and answered.

"Hello?"

"Hello, Callie. This is Jessica Casey. John told me about the party and I just wanted to say we'd be delighted to attend. What time?"

"Around six. It's very casual—noshes and some adult beverages."

"Sounds like fun. Can't wait to see you again. Have a good one."

I hung up. See me again? I didn't remember her at all. Still, her voice had a neutral tone as if being careful of what to say. The stage was being set. Now, all I had to do was figure out the dialogue.

I ate in the living room while watching the History Channel. The file folder was still on the coffee table.

I suspected Josh had nailed it when he said John Casey had been in over his head. My question was why didn't he realize it? And if he did, why not bring in help?

Maybe tomorrow would give me a few answers.

Chapter Eight

I decided to head into town early to extend invitations for the party to Clovis Fisher and Emma Grandview, but my first stop was Kendall Realty. Bob was in and beamed when I walked through the door. I wondered if he was a coward.

"Callie, great to see you. Finally decide to sell the farm?"

Didn't this guy ever give up? "No, Bob, I'm in Wellington for good. I would, however, like to extend an invitation for you and Ruth to join me along with a few others for cocktails and hors d'oeuvres tomorrow night."

His eyebrows almost shot off his face. "A cocktail party?"

"I know it's short notice, but after being gone for so long, I'd like to give some of my parents' friends a chance to get to know me. Please say you can come."

His forehead wrinkled and he licked his lips, sure signs he was uncomfortable or about to lie.

"I'll talk to Ruth, but don't see a problem. What time?"

"Six o'clock."

He plastered his realtor's smile back on, no doubt plotting how to convince me to jam a "For Sale" in my front yard.

I hurried on to the Elite Beauty Salon.

"Oh, honey, I'd just love to come," Clovis gushed while patting her brassy hair all done up in Kewpie doll curls this morning. "What time?"

"Sixish, and bring your husband."

She giggled. "Honey, I unloaded Mr. Fisher years ago. But I do have a boyfriend. Okay if I bring him?"

I assured her it was and left for the Kozy. I found the proprietor chatting with Mrs. Comstock. Between Mrs. Comstock and Emma, they must have known everybody in town—dead or alive. I invited them.

Both women agreed to come, Miss Emma eyeing me as if she knew my motive.

"A party is just what we need. Might stir things up a bit."

I pretended ignorance. "Stir things up?"

She smiled and played the game. "You know—something new, something different."

Deciding to stop by my neighbors with invitations on the way home, I parked around the corner from the newspaper office at twelve-fifteen and hurried up the sidewalk. I wanted to look at newspaper files and go to the courthouse over in Atwell.

I burst through the door and stopped dead in my tracks. Mindy's desk was piled high with papers, some of which had found their way onto the floor. Josh was on the phone.

"Bob, I'm sorry, but I really don't know where the copy is. I'm sure Mindy has it somewhere in her computer. I just can't find it. Why don't you e-mail it again? How many properties are involved? Four? I'm sure that won't be a problem."

He hung up and the phone rang immediately.

"News-Sentinel. Hi, Arthur what can I do for you?

You didn't? That might be because the paper doesn't come out until Thursday. That's right, Thursday. Nice talking to you, too."

He hung up again and shot me a look, his expression bordering on panic. The phone, however, didn't allow him a moment of respite.

"Yeah, News-Sentinel, how can I help? Oh, hello, Mrs. Webster." He listened for a few seconds and rolled his eyes. "Mrs. Webster, I'm sure the photos you took of your family reunion were wonderful, but sending twenty-five of them in to be printed was a bit much. We only have room for a couple at a time. I understand it was a special occasion, but... Tell you what. Why don't you send in two of the best and I'll see that one gets the top of the page treatment in the next issue. I'll do two if I have the space. Okay? Thank you, too."

He hung up a third time and took the receiver off the hook.

"Quit smirking," he ordered running hand through his hair.

I couldn't help it. The laughter was choking me.

"I take it Mindy had her baby."

"Last night. A boy—eight pounds, six ounces. Dave Regis called shortly after I got home from your place. I didn't think handling her job would be a problem. I have no clue how Mindy's filing system works, Bob Kendall didn't receive a confirmation of some advertising copy for next week and I can't find it anywhere, old man Simmons complained he didn't get his paper this morning—which doesn't come out until Thursday, and Ida Webster is irate we didn't run any of her pictures in the last issue and demanding we do it in this one. How does Mindy cope with this?"

"A lot better than you, apparently. I take it we won't be going to Atwell today?"

"Not a chance in hell, but lunch I can handle. Why don't you take over here while I run over to the Kozy and get us something?" He glanced at the chaos on the desk. "Won't be gone but a couple of hours."

"Me? I know even less about how Mindy does things than you."

"Yeah, well, you look like the sensible, organized type." He moved out from behind the desk and hurried to the door. "I won't be long."

He was gone before I had a chance to protest. I did, however, laugh.

The laughter died when I looked at the desk again. I picked up the papers from the floor and tried to arrange them in neat piles before hanging up the phone. As soon as I did, it rang.

Heaving a deep sigh, I answered. "Good afternoon, News-Sentinel, how may I help you?"

"Mindy, is that you?" a woman's voice questioned.

"No, Mindy had her baby last night. I'm just filling in so Josh can breathe."

The lady laughed. "I can imagine. Don't kid yourself, Mindy really runs that place. Did she have a boy or a girl?"

I gave her the pertinent information before asking, "Now, what do you need?"

"My name is Janet Hastings and I live just east of town. I'm starting a new business—a kind of trash or treasure sort of thing—out of my barn and I was hoping to advertise in the paper. Any idea of what it costs?"

I didn't have a clue and told her so, but assured her I'd find out.

"In the meantime, why don't you write up some copy? Make it any length you want. We can edit once we know the fee structure. And include a photo of the business. E-mail me everything and I'll get back to you."

"That sounds like a good idea. I'll get right on it. I don't think I caught your name."

I hesitated, and then said, "Callie Bryant."

A moment of silence greeted my words. "Welcome home. I hope you're getting settled in."

"I am. Thank you."

"Well, guess I'd better be going. I'll send this as soon as possible."

After hanging up, I tried to separate the papers into related stacks for filing in between answering more calls. Some people asked about Mindy, so I gave them the good news. Others called to either complain about something or to request advertising information. I took names and numbers with the promise to get back to them. I also found Bob Kendall's advertising copy complete with photos in Mindy's computer file marked "Pending".

I glanced at my watch. Josh had been gone for over an hour. Either the Kozy was jammed or he'd run away. A few minutes later, he walked in carrying two Styrofoam containers. He stopped and stared at the semi-organized desk.

"Wow, I'm impressed. I can actually see the desk top." He put the containers down and pulled up a chair.

I lifted the lid and sniffed Chicken Alfredo in the main compartment. A salad with Italian dressing was in the second while the prerequisite green beans and a brownie rounded out the meal.

"Smells good. What took you so long?"

"Sorry," he mumbled through a mouthful of salad. "But I had to take a walk. I had no idea Mindy did so much."

"Kinda makes you want to give her a raise, huh?"

"She deserves it. I got in a little after eight with foolish visions of sending the layout and copy to the printer's by noon. Silly me. Now, I'm gonna be late. Around ten, the phones started ringing and by the time you came in, I was slammed. How did you do?"

I told him some of the calls dealt with advertising rates. In turn he gave me a printed list with the cost of everything from a few lines in the classified section to a full-page extravaganza.

"Circulation brings in peanuts, but the ads are keeping me afloat. This is a busy time of year. People are cleaning out their attics and basements. Yard and garage sales will flourish throughout the summer. I'm not surprised Janet Hastings is going into business. She's an enthusiastic picker."

"A what?" I asked.

"A picker. She goes to yard and garage sales, sometimes estate sales, buys items and resells them. Guess she figures it's time to set up shop."

"And people make money doing that?"

"From what I've heard, it can be lucrative. What's the saying? One man's trash is another man's treasure?"

I thought about all the antiques stuffed in the Chicago house and that great big empty barn on the farm. Hmmm. The idea had possibilities. Something to keep me busy, once I found Mother's killer, that is.

Lunch lived up to the Kozy standards and I finished nearly all of it.

Josh gathered the containers and dumped them into the trash before looking at me with speculation in his eyes.

"So, how do you like being a receptionist?"

I stared back, knowing what was coming. "Why?"

"I was thinking, you seem to know what you're doing, so why don't you fill in until Mindy comes back? I'd pay you what I pay her," he added hastily.

"And how much would that be?" He gave me a figure that wasn't half bad for Wellington. "I'll have to think about it."

"Think hard and quick. I need help here."

I laughed. I could see the relentless reporter tracking down a story, fearless when confronting felons, and leaving no stone unturned while searching for the truth, but a ringing phone and a file cabinet sent him racing out the door.

"All right, I'll help, but can we still investigate Mother's death? That might be tough with me stuck here behind a desk."

A look of sheer relief flooded his face. "No problem. If we have to go somewhere to dig up info, you can either put the phone into voicemail or forward calls to your cell. Trust me, today was not a normal day around here—at least, I don't think it was."

"It better not be or I quit. Now, go do whatever it is you do and let me get to this filing and returning calls."

I made good on my promise. In spite of what Josh had said concerning Mindy's filing system, I found it non-threatening and easy to follow. Janet Hastings had e-mailed her advertising copy with the exception of the photo. That would come later when she had her signage up. Her words were to the point and eye catching. I immediately e-mailed her back with the price.

The afternoon flew by. Josh spent the time on his computer doing heaven knows what while I answered the now reasonable call load.

At four-fifteen, the door opened and Lorna Bell walked in. She looked surprised at seeing me behind the desk.

"Goodness, Callie, what are you doing here?"

"I'm filling in for Mindy. She had her baby last night."

"Oh, that's wonderful! What did she have?"

By now, I had the vital stats on weight and name and passed them on. She ooh-ed and aah-ed for a few seconds before getting down to business.

"This is my copy for next week's edition," she said handing me a couple of sheets of copy. One dealt with the store in general and the other with specifics for the classified section.

"You know, Lorna, for just a few dollars more you can add a photo of the shop. Maybe an interior shot of the merchandise. Someone might see something they just have to have. Could bring in more business."

A look of panic swept across her face. "Uh, I'm not sure…"

I sensed this was the time to strike for that trust bond to form. Lorna obviously had no idea how to incorporate a photo into the ad. The fact she hadn't e-mailed it confirmed my suspicion she wasn't comfortable with computers.

"I have an idea. Suppose I drop by later this week? I have a really great digital camera—much better than my cell phone. I'll take the photo, download it to the electronic files here, and you'll be good to go."

She shifted from foot to foot and licked her lips. "That…that sounds wonderful, Callie. I don't know too much about how these electronic gizmos work. I really miss typewriters and carbon paper."

Oh my God, was she that out of touch? "Then it's a date. By the way, did my stuff arrive safe and sound?"

She brightened. "Oh my, yes. And it's lovely. I'm sure I won't have any problem selling it. I'll have your check ready by this afternoon. Is that all right?"

"No problem." If I'd still been in Chicago, I'd have demanded payment before the truck left my driveway, but this was Wellington and people trusted each other. I couldn't decide if that was charming or naïve.

"I'm so looking forward to your party tomorrow night. Haven't been out socializing in ages."

She left and Josh wandered out of his office.

"Are you sure about this party thing?"

"Absolutely. She and June showed up on my doorstep before I'd even unpacked. I want to know why."

"Idle curiosity?" he suggested.

"Maybe, but I think Lorna knows and retains every bit of gossip she's ever heard. I'll pick her brains."

"Just be careful. Your reappearance in Wellington has someone apprehensive. The letter and phone calls prove that. And you've made no secret you're beginning to remember things from that night. The killer either didn't think you were home or forgot about you. He may have been wondering all these years exactly what—if anything—you saw or heard. I'm thinking maybe your aunt whisked you away in the nick of time."

I hadn't considered that angle before. Had Aunt

Dee gotten me out of town for my safety? She'd never mentioned that possibility in her deathbed ramblings.

"I'll be very discreet with my questions."

He sighed. "Just don't push things, okay? You're already stirring things up. Any more notes or phone calls?"

"Nope."

"Dinner tonight?"

"Well, I do have a teensy bit of Chinese food left over."

"I was thinking more along the lines of Gruber's Steakhouse over in Laramore."

Laramore was west of Wellington some thirty miles and the county seat of Laramore County. Population-wise, it was slightly larger than Atwell.

"I don't remember having ever been in Laramore, and a thick, juicy steak sounds just fine."

"Good." He glanced at his watch. "Suppose we finish up here and head out? Tomorrow shouldn't be too busy—I hope—but the next day could be hell. The paper comes out on Thursday. I have to be in early to see my two delivery men get them on time."

"How early and does it include me?"

Josh grinned. "The copies are dropped off around four in the morning. I'm usually here by then, earlier if it's raining and I need to put them in those plastic baggies. Then Harlan and Ed deliver them—one covers the area south of town and one north. And no, you don't have to be here until eight or eight-thirty. I'm not picky."

"Glad to hear it. Now, I'll finish this filing, check e-mail one last time, and we can go."

The phone rang. I answered. "News-Sentinel, how

may I help you?"

"Buttering up Lorna and buying her lunch won't help," the voice whispered. "You don't belong here. How many warnings will it take?" The caller hung up.

My stomach churned. I swallowed and replaced the receiver with a shaking hand.

"Callie?"

"Another call." My voice quavered, but whether from fear or anger I wasn't sure.

"Here?"

"I imagine it's all over town by now that I'm subbing for Mindy."

"Son of a bitch! I don't like this. First your house and now my office. I'm calling Bill Jackson."

"I think investing in caller ID is a better bet. I doubt Bill can do anything."

He scowled and strode back to his office. "Doesn't hurt to try."

The fact the caller had mentioned Lorna sent a shiver up my spine. Was I being watched? Followed? Or had the caller been in the Kozy?

I picked up the phone and hit star-69. The last number received should have popped up. It didn't. It came up as unregistered. Probably a disposable cell phone. The phone on the opposite end rang forever. No one answered. Could Lorna have been the caller?

No, not with a disposable cell phone. I doubt she even has a cell phone. My resolve to find Mother's killer hardened.

Josh returned a few minutes later disgust on his face. "Bill says there's nothing he can do."

"The calls don't last long enough to trace anyway."

He ran a hand through his hair. "I'll report it to the

phone company. Give me a couple of minutes."

I drummed my fingers on the desk during his absence and thought. Plain Jane Lorna admitted to having had a crush on Daddy, but attractive cheerleader June, who must have known about her friend's infatuation, had been the one to pursue and date him. According to Lorna, June had hated both Sally and Mother, yet pretended to be their friends. Exactly how deep did the hatred for my mother go?

Had Mom seen June coming on to Daddy and called her out on it? Maybe even laughed at her? Could June in a fit of blind rage have grabbed the hunting knife and stabbed my mother? Then in revenge for rejection after rejection, let Daddy go to jail for it?

I put June Simpson at the head of my list of suspects.

Josh returned. "Well, it's been reported, but whether or not it'll do any good is anybody's guess. You ready?"

He locked up and we headed for Laramore.

The town had a similar layout to Atwell. Maybe it was latent pride at being an Atwell County product, but I didn't think this town had the same charm. I imagined there was one hell of a sports rivalry between the high schools.

Gruber's was nothing to write home about. The usual Western motif of cowboys and rustic decorations set the theme. I also could have done without the hostess greeting us with, "Well, howdy pardners."

On a scale from one to ten, the meal was a disappointing four with an underdone baked potato and a slightly overdone steak. I was too tired to care much one way or the other. We ate and headed back to

Wellington.

"I can't help but wonder what your brother would have thought of your plan," he said on the drive home.

Funny he should ask when it had been Denny's idea in the first place. Unfortunately, it was me, not my brother, who now lived on the farm. And I had made a promise. But I wasn't ready to talk about that yet.

"Given that Denny never considered Daddy guilty, I'd have to say he'd approve."

Back in town, Josh walked me to my Lexus, and then leaned down to kiss me. "Take care and I'll see you in the morning."

My lips tingled and I resisted the urge to trace them with my fingertip. I slid behind the wheel as he turned and walked back down the street.

The Wellington business district by night was deader than dead. Only the Kozy Kafe and Sweet Daddy's Bar showed any action. Down side streets, I glimpsed the glow of lights shining through windows of residences. I supposed if I wanted a night out, I'd have to endure Sweet Daddy's.

I yawned as I turned onto the gravel road toward my house. I was looking forward to a glass of wine, some TV, and an early night. After all, I was now a working stiff.

Ahead, a car pulled out of a driveway and moved quickly east, a plume of dust billowing behind it in the deepening dusk. Half a minute later, I turned into my drive. Dust still hung in the air on the road.

I parked and walked to the mailbox pausing before opening it.

"Don't be an idiot. Who the hell is afraid of a mailbox?" I muttered.

Shoving my hesitation aside, I opened it. A large bundle of mail bound with a rubber band greeted me. I yanked it out and went inside dumping my purse and the packet on the counter.

Inside, I poured a glass of wine and took it into the living room where I flipped on the television and surfed for a while before finally settling on the Food Channel. I called it a night at ten.

In the kitchen, I rinsed out my glass and made coffee for the next morning. I stared at the mail sitting so innocently nearby. "Oh, this is ridiculous. Open the damned mail."

Removing the rubber band, I flipped through the envelopes, discarding junk as I went along. It was near the bottom of the pile. Another plain, white, legal sized envelope with no writing on it. I swallowed. Uneasiness prickled along my arms and scalp. I ripped it open.

Why are you still here? Lorna Bell can't help you. Neither can Josh Hendricks. Leave now before it's too late.

The same printed letters. No signature. Anger replaced the uneasiness. I was not about to be bullied by some coward. As I turned to leave, my gaze fell on the table. The folder Josh had given me from John Casey was sitting near the edge. I'd been reading it again this morning and could have sworn I'd set it in the middle of the table while checking my e-mail and Facebook page.

I opened it. The pages were slightly out of kilter, as though someone had hurriedly riffled through them. I glanced at the back door and bit my lip. I'd walked right in when arriving home this evening. The significance of doing that hadn't hit me until now. I thought I'd locked up this morning. Had I forgotten? Given the note and phone calls, that was sheer stupidity. No, I'd locked it. I was sure. Which meant someone had a key, if indeed someone had been here. I put changing the locks on my mental to-do list.

I tidied the file, locked the door, and climbed the back stairs. It wasn't until I was in bed that I remembered the speeding car.

Had someone been here? Who? My mind flashed back to another plume of dust behind a car on the day I arrived in Wellington.

Bob Kendall? Why would he be so interested? And how worried should I be?

Chapter Nine

I nervously paced the dining room, stopping to tweak the corner of the antique pink damask tablecloth to straighten a wrinkle. Maybe this party hadn't been such a great idea after all. Josh was in the kitchen setting up the bar. I'd taken the afternoon off to get the house ready. He'd been nice enough to run my errands to the liquor and grocery stores. I also showed him the new anonymous letter. He was not happy.

"Goddammit, Callie, someone *is* following you. This is serious. Call Bill Jackson now."

"And tell him what? I haven't been threatened directly. And I've said this before, the words are printed, not written. Anyone could have sent it. Isn't that what he told you when you called?"

Josh scowled. "I'd say the words, 'before it's too late,' are pretty threatening."

"And if he finds the author, he or she could simply say they only meant I'd be unhappy to learn Daddy was the killer."

He sighed. "Have you received any more phone calls?"

"No." I told him about my suspicions someone had been in the house last evening.

"And you're just now telling me? Call Bill. Now!"

"Josh, I can't swear I didn't move the folder myself. And I'd just turned onto the road. The car could have come out of several driveways."

"What kind of car?"

"I don't know. It was getting dark and the dust obscured the taillights. If I get any more letters or phone calls, I promise I'll call the police." I ran a hand through my hair. "Can we just forget it for now? I'm having a cocktail party."

Was Josh right? Was I tilting at windmills, choosing to believe the good and ignoring the bad? It had all sounded so simple a few months ago—return to Wellington, find the killer, and exonerate my father.

The reality is so much harder than the vision. I didn't expect so much animosity from someone who prefers to deal in anonymous letters and phone calls. But then, I wasn't sure what I'd expected.

My watch told me my guests would arrive shortly. I made my way through the living room to the foyer.

My biggest concern about this party was getting people to open up—to talk. I wanted to see their reactions to being in the house in a social setting. But first I needed to establish something for them to react *to*. The foyer, the scene of the crime, was the answer.

I'd bought a five by seven foot Oriental rug similar to the one that had been there twenty-five years ago. Rather than have it in the middle of the room, I put it in front of the door, leaving those faint but discernable stains visible to anyone who entered.

That was my second problem—getting country-bred people to enter through the front door instead of the kitchen. I flipped the switch on the wall. The old-fashioned alabaster chandelier glowed with a soft yellowish color. I also turned on the porch lights. The back porch lights were off.

"Josh," I called out. "Could you do me a favor?"

"Sure, what do you need?" He joined me in the foyer.

I opened the front door wide. "Would you mind directing the guests to enter this way?"

He stared at me, and then around the foyer. His glance included the discoloration in the middle of the room.

"Going for the jugular, huh?"

"Yes. I want to see how they react."

"Nothing like making your guests feel uncomfortable the minute they arrive."

I ignored his sarcasm. *He doesn't understand. Not completely.*

The first car swept into the driveway, its headlights cutting through the deepening dusk.

Let the games begin.

Josh walked out onto the porch and waved. "Hi there! Come on in."

Clovis and her boyfriend trotted up the steps and entered. I hadn't expected good taste in clothing to be high on Clovis's list of priorities, and I was right. I wouldn't call a long-sleeved, turtle-necked, spandex mini-dress in leopard print with matching four-inch heels flattering for a woman her age. A dozen or so bangle bracelets clanged like cow bells every time she moved, and I couldn't imagine how she had the nerve to wear shoulder-length feather earrings. Her hair was swept into an elaborate updo complete with ringlets across her forehead. She paid no attention to the floor.

"Are we the first here?" she asked in a cheerful voice.

"You are indeed," I answered in the same cheery

tone.

"This is Eddie Masterson. He lives over near Castor."

"Pleased to meet you, Eddie."

He grinned and shook my hand like a pump handle. He was tall and skinny with a grin that stretched from ear to ear. His brown toupee didn't match his gray hair.

I directed them with a wave of my hand. "Drinks are set up in the kitchen. Food's on the table. Help yourselves."

"Come on, Eddie. I'm thirsty."

They moved out as Lorna walked in.

"My goodness, going formal tonight. Front door and everything," she said, her gaze darting around the room. She glanced down at the floor, and then averted her eyes.

"It's the big city coming out in me," I replied with a laugh.

The Entwistles and the Grays, my neighbors, arrived next. Neither had lived here when Mother was killed so I didn't pay any attention to their reactions. I said hello and directed them to the goodies.

They were followed by my childhood friend, Gina, and her husband, Kyle Anderson. They had taken over the family farm down the road on her parents' retirement. It was a friendship I looked forward to renewing.

John and Jessica Casey showed up a few minutes later. John looked at the stains briefly before turning his head away, too. Jessica's gaze also gravitated to the stains. She looked away and held out her hand when John introduced us.

"Welcome home, Callie."

"Thank you. Good evening, John."

He nodded. "Callie. Thanks for inviting us."

Mrs. Comstock and Miss Emma arrived together. Both looked at the floor, and then at me. Miss Emma raised an eyebrow.

"Yep, gonna be an interesting night," she said.

June and Roger Simpson were right behind them. June stared at both the rug and the floor before looking away with a shudder.

The Kendalls arrived last. Ruth gave me an air kiss on each cheek.

Bob greeted me with a smile. "Callie, great to see you."

Both of their smiles faded when they spied the stains. They gazed at each other before Bob shrugged. I directed them to the buffet and bar.

"Hail, hail, the gang's all here," Josh murmured, coming in from the porch. "What's next?"

"We mingle."

I took a deep breath, disappointed no one had reacted much to the stains. On the other hand, I wasn't sure what they could have said.

I moved amongst my guests sipping from a glass of wine and nibbling on hors d'oeuvres discussing what all Iowans discussed: the weather, the crops, the price of corn and soybeans, and if the University of Iowa would have a good football team come fall.

"Having a good time?" I asked Clovis. She and Eddie were making the spread a dinner stop. Their plates were filled with plenty of everything.

"Honey, I'm having a ball. And don't you look nice, too. Like something right out of the fashion magazines, right?"

Ruth and Lorna stood next to Clovis. "Yes, indeed," Lorna commented.

I'd chosen to wear a pair of navy silk slacks with a bright yellow silk tunic. Glitzy high-heeled silver sandals adorned my feet. I'd kept the accessories to a minimum. I wasn't really much of a jewelry person, but had compromised tonight on sterling dangle earrings and a garnet and rhinestone bracelet that had belonged to my mother.

"Very stylish," Ruth intoned. She shifted her gaze to the bracelet. Her eyes widened. "How pretty."

"It belonged to Mother. The clasp is faulty, so I rarely wear it, but for some reason, tonight I wanted part of her in the room with me."

Lorna also stared, but said nothing, no doubt thinking a large part of my mother was already in the foyer.

I moved on playing the part of the perfect hostess, one skill Aunt Dee had drummed into me at an early age.

I cornered June Simpson at the dining room table. It was time to get down to business.

"I'm so glad you could come, June. I know you were great friends with Daddy."

"Your father was just wonderful, Callie. So kind and giving." She piled some shrimp onto a plate.

"And Mother?"

She didn't make eye contact. Instead, she added a spoonful of macaroni salad.

"I don't think your mother ever felt really a part of Wellington."

Ruth came up to the table, picked up a plate, and selected several stuffed mushrooms and an assortment of cheeses. June sent her a sidelong look.

"Some people never fit in, I guess. That was a shame because your mother was so nice. Very down to earth. Not the least bit snobbish considering she came from money."

Ruth's fingers tightened on a serving spoon at the not so subtle put down by June before smiling at me.

"May I compliment you on the food, Callie? It's wonderful. You obviously have good taste. Most people would have served up those dreadful frozen concoctions." She slid a malicious glance at June. "And your clothing looks to be from the best boutique on Michigan Avenue. You definitely don't look like you live on a farm."

June clenched her jaw and spooned more sauce onto her shrimp. Josh's information about the two of them not getting along was spot on. I hoped a catfight wasn't in the immediate future.

I didn't wait to find out, but moved on into the kitchen where Mrs. Comstock and Miss Emma sat at the table each nursing a glass of amber liquid.

"I'm so glad you ladies could make it tonight."

Mrs. Comstock waved her glass in the air. I had a feeling it wasn't her first of the evening.

"Thank you for inviting me."

"Did you know Mother and Daddy well?" I asked replenishing my wine.

"Not your mother so much. She kept to herself, but I taught English at the local high school. Your father was a very good student. And so athletic! He played just about any sport that came along. As I mentioned last week, your grandmother and I were close." She drained her glass, reached for the nearby scotch bottle, and poured. "She lived with Eric and his first wife, Sally, but moved into an apartment in town when he married your mother. She claimed it was for convenience's sake, but I don't think she and Grace got along so good."

"Maybe you should lay off the booze, Ellie," Miss Emma said. She patted my arm. "Drop by the café sometime next week and we'll talk."

Those blue eyes had the look of having seen a lot.

"I'll do that."

Back in the dining room, a wobbly Clovis approached the food with a fresh plate. I couldn't tell if her gait was due to the stilettos or an excess of liquor.

"You finding everything all right, Clovis?"

She smiled, her eyes not quite focused. "Sure am, honey."

A slightly popped Clovis gave me the opportunity to probe.

"I just want to thank you for being such a good friend to Mother. I'm sure she looked forward to seeing you every week."

She loaded shrimp, stuffed mushrooms, finger sandwiches, and cheese on her plate.

"She was so nice. And a good tipper, too. You wouldn't believe how cheap some of the women around here can be. I liked chatting with her."

I sighed. "I'm so glad you were one of the last people she talked to before she died."

Clovis didn't miss a beat and added on more food.

"I just knew something wasn't right, you know what I mean? Those last few weeks, she just wasn't her normal self."

"How so?"

She stopped, popped a shrimp in her mouth, and chewed.

"She wasn't as chatty as usual. Seemed sad about something. Of course, it wasn't until after the…well, *after* that I realized why."

"And?"

"Well, after the funeral it was all over town that your daddy was having an affair and that she'd finally had enough. When she asked for a divorce, he went into a rage and killed her. Not that I believed that for a moment, you understand," she added hastily. "I mean, I didn't know your father at all. Mr. Fisher and I came here from Sioux Falls a couple of years earlier, but not one of my customers suggested they thought he was guilty."

I managed to pick through her pronoun use and nodded. "Yes, he was a gentle man."

"Of course, once he was arrested and put on trial, a few had doubts."

"Oh?"

She shoved a stuffed mushroom into her mouth. "June Simpson and Ruth Kendall said the evidence didn't lie or some such nonsense."

"What a shame John couldn't convince the jury of Daddy's innocence."

She snorted, picked up her wine glass, and drained it.

"I can tell you this, that prissy wife of his was madder than hell at the verdict."

"Jessica? Why?"

"Because she thought a not guilty verdict would make her husband a power broker in the county. She had political ambitions for him." Clovis patted the ringlets on her forehead. "Bitch. She wants everything to be perfect and done her way."

That probably explained why she no longer allowed Clovis to cut her hair.

I escaped the dining room and headed for Jessica Casey who sat in a chair talking to one of my neighbors.

"Having a good time?" I asked.

"Yes, lovely, thank you," Mrs. Gray said with a smile.

"Tell me, what really brought you back to Wellington, Callie? I'd think Chicago would be more your style," Jessica asked.

I wondered if she and John ever talked, and then gave her the now familiar spiel about living the simple life.

"I just hope you aren't planning on opening old wounds. Small town minds can remember a long time and take even longer to forgive. I'd hate to see someone who's worked hard for something taken down by renewed gossip."

Apparently, she and John did talk. Her tone suggested I get the hell out of Dodge. *Kinda like the letter writer and caller. And Bob Kendall.*

Mrs. Gray rose with an uncomfortable expression on her face. "If you'll excuse me, I need to speak to my husband. Nice party, Callie."

"Mrs. Casey, I have no intention of causing trouble."

Her blue eyes stared hard. "If so, then why did you want the notes on your father's trial?"

"I'm hoping they will help me understand a tragic time of my life."

"My husband, out of a sense of friendship and loyalty to your father, took on his defense. Some in this town never forgave him for losing. He's running for County Judge in November. I'd hate to see that snatched away at this late date. He's earned it. Don't rock the boat."

She stood and made her way toward the dining room.

Well, can't get any more blunt than that. I could see Jessica with a disposable cell phone and slipping letters into my mailbox. Maybe now was the time to corner my father's attorney.

I didn't have to corner John Casey. He sought me out near the archway to the foyer several minutes later.

"Nice party, Callie. I assume you've read the trial notes Josh demanded."

"Yes, I did, and he asked for them at my request."

"Let it go. A lot of time has passed and stirring up old wounds won't change the outcome of something that occurred twenty-five years ago."

The warnings from both he and his wife caused the old, familiar anger to push its way into my chest. Even their words mirrored each other. They'd probably discussed things on the way over. I also added him to the list of possible harassers.

I curled my fingers around my wine glass. "Maybe not, but I'm hoping it will help me remember and put my mind to rest. Please excuse me."

I turned sharply and ran into Bob Kendall standing behind me. He steadied me and glanced at John who sidled past into the living room.

"So, have you given any more thought to selling?"

"I won't sell, Bob. It's my home."

He looked into the foyer with a frown. "Suit yourself, but I'd at least have the floors refinished."

He turned and walked away, his comment leaving me stunned. The expression on his face had bordered on angry. Maybe I'd gotten a reaction to the stains after all. The plume of dust from the other night flashed through my mind. *Another candidate for the list?*

By nine o'clock people drifted toward the door. I was the gracious hostess to the end, accepting thanks and giving the same.

Lorna paused in front of the Kendalls on her way out. The Caseys stood nearby. She lifted my arm and gazed at the bracelet.

"I remember seeing this a long time ago. I'm sure your mother must have loved it. Was it a gift from Eric?"

"I think so. Thank you so much for coming, Lorna. I'll be in to see you next week. We can have a nice long chat while I show you how to operate a computer and digital camera."

She left, as did Bob and Ruth. The Caseys followed. Both couples had frozen, disapproving expressions. Miss Emma assisted a slightly rocky Eleanor Comstock down the porch steps. The headlights flashed by with halogen-like brightness while alternating with the red glowing taillights. Clovis and her boyfriend were the last to leave.

"First in, last out! Great party, sweetie. Drop by the shop soon and we'll work on those highlights."

"Will do."

In the distance, thunder rumbled. I hoped everybody got home before the bad weather broke.

"Storm's coming," Josh said as he closed the door.

"I'll help you clean up. Maybe by the time we're done, it'll be over."

I didn't mind storms. Kinda liked them. All the lightning, thunder, and rain. I loved watching the forces of nature clash to renew the earth. I remembered Daddy once telling me how lightning replenished the nitrogen in the soil making it perfect for growing corn. Odd how I could remember something like that, but not the important events of that fateful night.

I turned and headed for the living room.

Josh strolled up presenting me with a glass of wine.

"Have a seat, honey. You look exhausted."

I sank into my corner of the sectional and sipped gratefully. "I'm beat to hell and back."

"The point is, did you learn anything useful?"

"Some, but not nearly as much as I'd hoped. How about you? Did you hear anything of interest?"

"I spent most of my time with the guys. Your neighbors haven't got an axe to grind. They moved here after the fact."

"Except for Gina Anderson. She and I were the best of friends when we were kids. She invited me for lunch next week. What did the other men have to say?"

"Bob Kendall and John Casey probed into why you'd returned. Neither of them looked convinced when I gave them your answer about the simple life."

I snorted. "I told them the same thing when I first got here."

"Obviously, they don't believe you. Both, however, were more concerned about any rumors I may have heard regarding future opponents for the mayoral and county judge positions. Naturally, each wanted the paper's endorsement."

"Naturally," I drawled. "Bob didn't have a whole lot to say to me, other than rather crassly commenting I get the foyer floor refinished."

"What did you expect? You set it up as a shock element."

I shrugged. "Maybe, but John Casey suggested I not pursue any further information about the trial. His wife wasn't nearly as subtle. She out and out told me to not rock her husband's political boat."

"I can see that. Such a windfall would move her up several rungs on the social ladder. Ruth's superiority would be seriously challenged."

"Lots of undercurrents," I murmured.

"Did you get the reactions you wanted?"

I shrugged. "No one suddenly cried out, 'I did it. I'm guilty.' Do you think the letter writer was here tonight?"

"I don't know, but it wouldn't surprise me."

"Bob, John, Jessica—all could have done it."

"I can't see Bob or John doing something like that. Anonymous letters feel more female." Josh plucked the glass from my fingers. "Did you get enough to eat?"

"Not really."

He disappeared into the dining room. Off to the southwest, lightning flashed. The thunder rumbled closer. Raindrops plopped lightly against the windows and on the front porch roof.

I thought about what Josh said. The letters could have been written by the so-called other woman—if the rumors regarding Daddy's affair had been true. And had she been in attendance tonight? Possibly.

He returned a few minutes later with a heaping plate and a full glass. "Shrimp's almost gone, but there's enough of everything else to keep you eating for a couple of days."

I dug in while he cleaned up the leftovers and the kitchen.

This evening hadn't been the stunning success I'd envisioned. Maybe people were wary of my motives and had used the party as an excuse to watch and question *me*. Oddly enough, even in her inebriated state, Clovis provided the best information. In spite of their protestations to me, both June and Ruth had thought Daddy guilty—even if it was after the trial.

Jessica Casey just plain pissed me off. I wondered what her relationship had been with my parents. Did she know and like Mother? Jessica struck me a mild snob. Did she suck up because of the Conrad name? And if the rumors *were* true and Daddy *was* having an affair, could it have been with her? Of course, I didn't believe Daddy was cheating on Mother, but I wondered if Jessica had tried to seduce my father and been rebuffed. John Casey struck me as less than exciting.

This is a small town. Everybody knows everybody else's business. If Daddy had an affair, surely those rumors would have surfaced before Mother's death. No one is that discreet.

Even though I didn't receive any concrete information about Mother's death, I did enjoy making contact with my neighbors. The Entwhistles invited me to their Memorial Day barbeque, and Mrs. Gray suggested we have a shopping spree in Atwell soon. I accepted both with enthusiasm. Small town life was growing on me.

The storm moved in with the lightning and thunder coming in closer intervals. The rain increased in volume. I finished my food and rose to join Josh in the kitchen. Putting the remains of the noshes in containers in the fridge didn't take long.

The storm moved directly overhead. Lightning sizzled, and thunder boomed. Rain pounded, the sound not unlike a load of gravel being dumped on the ground. The wind picked up speed, shrieking through the branches of the trees.

The phone rang. I looked at Josh who raised his eyebrows.

"Don't answer."

"I will not be afraid to answer my own phone!"

I picked up the receiver with trembling hands.

"Hello?"

Silence for a heartbeat, then a whispered voice said, "If you know what's good for you, get out of town."

Another flash of lightning struck nearby as static crackled in my ear. I hastily hung up. The lights flickered and died. The crashing of thunder almost, but not quite, drowned out the sound of breaking glass and the loud report.

Josh snatched the magnetic flashlight from the side of the refrigerator and switched it on. "Stay here!"

I ignored him as we rushed into the living room. The strong beam homed in on one of the front windows. A pane was completely smashed, the shards littering the floor. Rain sluiced in.

Josh trained the flashlight around the room, and then sucked in a sharp breath. "Son of a bitch!"

Stunned, I followed his line of sight to the wall opposite the windows. There, about a foot below the ceiling was a neat round hole.

"I thought I told you to stay put!" he snapped.

I pushed him aside and stared. "Dammit! Someone shot out my window!"

He strode through the foyer and fumbled with the lock on the front door before yanking it open and stepping out onto the porch.

I was right behind him. Might not have been the smartest move, but since the electricity was out we wouldn't be silhouetted. Besides, the shooter had probably hightailed it out immediately.

Lightning still flashed and thunder reverberated. I could see next to nothing through the almost impenetrable gray sheets of rain lashing down. Could that be the red glow of taillights far off to the east? I wasn't sure.

Josh pulled his cell from his pocket and dialed. "This is Josh Hendricks. I'm over at Callie Bryant's and someone just took a shot at her house. Yes, I'm serious. I told you she's been getting anonymous letters and harassing phone calls. In fact, one came through just before the shot. Thank you." He hung up. "Someone's coming right away. Let's get inside."

The lights snapped back on as we reentered the house. In the living room, the damage looked a lot worse than it had by flashlight.

I swallowed and wobbled my way to the sofa where I sat with a thump.

"What did the caller say?"

"Told me to get out of town."

"Sounds like good advice."

I shook my head. "No way. I've got someone damned scared."

"You've got someone determined to kill you."

We waited as the minutes slowly ticked past. I sat silent and numb, my brain refusing to work. Had someone meant to kill me or just scare the crap out of me? Most likely the latter and it worked.

The rain had slackened along with the lightning and thunder. The storm was moving on. A car pulled into drive and up toward the back door. Reinforcements had arrived. I hurried to the kitchen and let Chief Bill Jackson in. Another officer accompanied him.

"Whew," he said shaking raindrops from his hat. "Some storm. Callie, this is Carl West, one of my deputies. Now, tell me what happened."

I gave him the details about the party, including the letter and phone calls.

"Any problems at the party?" he asked.

"No, none."

He stalked into the living room where I pointed out the slug still in the wall. He dug it out, looked at it for a moment, and then slipped it into a small Ziploc bag.

"Well?" Josh demanded.

"Looks like a forty-five. Any idea why someone would do this, Callie?"

Josh answered for me. "She's been asking questions about her family and the night of the murder. Everyone knows. Somebody isn't too keen on that."

The chief stared at me. "And the phone calls?"

"Just whispers to get out of town."

"Where are the letters? Better let me have them."

"About time," Josh muttered.

I walked into the dining room, retrieved the messages from one of the sideboard drawers, and handed them over.

He pulled one from the envelope and read it with a

frown. "Not likely to get much from them, but I'll try. Unless the sender has been fingerprinted for some reason, anything we find will stay unknown."

With a simple, "I'll be in touch," the chief left.

"Got any cardboard around?" Josh asked. "I'll put some over the broken pane. It'll keep insects out until you can have it repaired."

"Lots of boxes still on the back porch."

I swept up the broken glass while he worked. Thirty minutes later, the window was semi-fixed. "I can see how this played out. The shooter, car headlights off, uses the rain to mask any sound. He stops out front, makes the call, shoots, and then takes off."

"Maybe." My voice quivered. "It could have been kids."

"In the middle of a thunderstorm? Get real."

"Even though it's a school night, kids could be out with nothing to do. They swipe daddy's gun, see the lighted windows, and let off a round. Then they get scared and take off."

"Callie…"

"I don't want to talk about it."

He sighed. "I'm staying tonight, and don't give me any arguments."

The thought of Josh staying here gave me a sense of safety. It also made me realize I didn't want to stick him in my old bedroom. I'd known him less than a week, but wanted him all the same. Then common sense took over.

"All right. You can sleep in the back bedroom."

He stared at me and smiled. "That sounds far enough away to resist temptation."

I didn't respond, but led him upstairs.

Perhaps this party hadn't been as uneventful as it first appeared. Had something scared the killer into taking action before I could remember?

Chapter Ten

I rushed out to the car at the ridiculous hour of seven forty-five. Today was my first real day on the job. Yesterday didn't count. I'd been too busy with party plans to do much more than answer the phones and file a few papers until I left at noon. Today, however, I didn't want to screw it up by being late.

Josh had been gone when I woke up at five-thirty. He'd left a note on the kitchen table thanking me and saying we'd talk later.

Jerking open the car door, I slid behind the wheel, twisted the key, and hurried out of the driveway. I looked forward to spending the day with Josh and even though the job was temporary, it gave me something constructive to do besides think about Mother's death and Daddy.

I had just turned onto the highway into town when a movement from under the passenger side seat caught my attention. I spared a quick glance, but saw nothing.

Probably a piece of paper blown around by the wind.

A second later, the movement repeated itself. I looked down again. This time a long, skinny tail poked out—long, skinny, and naked. Too long for a mouse.

I sucked in a deep breath. My passenger had to be a rat. I hate rats. I'm scared to death of them. Furtive, disgusting creatures!

Then the whole rat appeared, made a nasty noise, and leaped onto the seat near my purse.

I screamed and stared into its beady eyes. My hands tightened on the wheel. The little bastard looked ready to leap into my lap. My throat closed and my breaths came in short gasps. I paid no attention to my driving. The right side tires left the road.

Snapping my attention back to the windshield, I saw the ditch rapidly approaching. I slammed on the brakes, but it was too late. The car nose-dived.

I didn't waste any time, but unfastened my seat belt, shoved the door open, and tumbled out. The rat followed, disappearing like a gray ghost into the brush.

I stood on the side of the road a few feet away until my breathing returned to normal, then grabbed my purse and sorted through it for my phone. I called Josh.

"You're not going to believe this, but I'm in a ditch just north of town."

"A ditch? What happened? Are you hurt?"

"I'm fine," I said, and explained what had occurred.

"A rat? You've got to be kidding. No, never mind, I'm sure you're not. Stay put. I'll call Ed Sanders towing service and be right out to get you."

He hung up and I waited. A car passing by in the other direction stopped to ask if I was all right and needed a ride. I told the driver help was on the way.

A few minutes later, Josh showed up. He gave me a brief hug and stared at my car.

"Are you sure you're okay?"

"Yes, fine. I just feel kind of stupid. I hate rats. They scare me to death."

"How the hell did a rat get into your car?" he asked

again frowning.

"I have no idea. I suppose there are enough of them around what with the corn crib and barn, although I've never seen any evidence of them in the house."

"Did you leave a window open?"

"I think I had the passenger side down a few inches. I forgot to close it before the storm last night. Luckily, the wind came from the west, so the seat didn't get wet, just damp."

"Still doesn't explain how it got in."

The tow truck arrived. Within minutes, my Lexus was back on the road with only a few scratches on the bumper.

While I inspected, Josh told the tow truck driver what had happened. "I just don't understand how a rat could get in."

"Well," the man drawled. "Rats are athletic little buggers. You said the window was cracked. Did you park under a tree or near a bush?"

"No, I parked close to the back door."

"If I remember right, you got an enclosed back porch. Could be he was on the roof, jumped down to the car and found his way inside, maybe to get away from the rain last night."

I didn't think it likely, but said nothing and slid behind the wheel.

"Are you sure you're all right?" Josh asked for the umpteenth time.

"Other than feeling like a fool, I'm fine. Let's go. I'm late and my boss might dock me pay."

He laughed, thanked the tow trucker driver, and followed me into town.

My mind worked overtime on the short drive. My

window had been open no more than two inches and while a rat could easily squirm through, I hadn't parked that close to the porch. And my car had been unlocked.

Given the letters and phone calls, I wondered if this was another warning. A country person, even one living in town, would know how to humanely catch and release a rat. In spite of my fears someone had been inside the house, I'd slept soundly, so never heard if anyone had come into the driveway. Maybe knowing Josh was just down the hall helped.

And if it had been later in the morning, the traffic would have been heavier. I could just as easily have veered to the left and had a head-on collision resulting in more than a few scratches to my bumper.

I shivered at the implication. The ante had been upped.

****

I tidied Mindy's desk, rose, and then hurried back to Josh's office. This morning's incident still preyed on my mind. If the rat had been planted, then I had a bigger problem than just proving Daddy's innocence.

"I'm about to leave for lunch and Bell's. I promised Lorna I'd take some photos. Are we still going to Atwell this afternoon?"

He nodded. "I've set it up with the newspaper. Things that old aren't in their electronic files, so we'll have to either view microfilm or the actual paper."

"What about the *News-Sentinel's* files?"

"I'm not sure anything is still around. The newspaper offices used to be over on Campbell near the railroad tracks, but the building burned to the ground about fifteen years ago. I've been keeping everything on the computer. The guy I bought it from did the same after the fire."

The news was disappointing, but then I didn't expect this journey to be easy.

"Well, I'm off. I'll try to be back by one."

He nodded with a worried look in his eyes.

"I'll be discreet, Josh. Lorna has no idea of my motives. I want her to think of me as a friend."

"Yeah, just don't forget, if your father didn't kill your mother, then one of his or her so-called friends did."

On that sobering piece of advice, I left for Bell's.

The morning had been fairly quiet with the usual complaints, like not receiving a paper or an error in an ad. Josh had thoughtfully left a copy on my desk and I'd spent part of the morning looking through it.

The *News-Sentinel* was a good newspaper. Josh had kept the information topical to the community. National or world events were absent unless they affected Wellington. As a weekly paper, printing breaking news was not an option. The economic news and how it related to farmers and small town America was about it.

An editorial on supporting the city council's decision to spend money on the July Fourth fireworks display took center stage. I remembered those. Held in a large field just south of town, they'd been the highlight of summer. We'd sit on a blanket and watch the multi-colored explosions in the sky with awe.

"Whoa, peanut! That one was a beauty, wasn't it?"

Peanut, Daddy's pet name for me. A lump formed in my throat. And Mother had laughed and clapped her hands after every boom and bang—just like a kid.

She'd loved fireworks. Denny was usually off with his friends doing the things boys do and trying to stay out of trouble.

I swallowed and blinked tears from my eyes, glad Josh supported finding room in a tight town budget for something everyone could enjoy.

I also read four letters to the editor—three supporting the editorial position on farm subsidies and one from an irate woman who demanded something be done about the storm drain on her street.

Whoever set up the advertising copy did a good job. It was attractive and easy to read. One of the largest was a half page ad from Kendall Real Estate showing four properties for sale in the area complete with pictures.

I ate quickly at the Kozy before heading for Bell's. I pushed open the door and immediately saw my parents' furniture prominently displayed near the front. Lorna was on the phone behind the counter.

"Yes, yes, I just got in a nice nineteen-inch console TV the other day. It works and would look great in that apartment. All you need is a cable hook up. Why don't you come by this afternoon sometime after two? See you then."

She hung up and smiled. "I think I may have just sold your old TV. Jean Cowan is re-furbishing one of her apartments over on Jackson. She rents them out furnished, and is always looking for a good deal. I'm hoping she'll take a few more things from your place, too. Oh, and before I forget, here's your check."

I took the slip of paper and tucked it into my purse, then extracted my digital camera. It took sharper pictures than my cell phone.

"Thanks, Lorna. I'm sure the furniture will sell quickly. It's in great shape. Suppose I take a couple of photos to go with your ad copy for next week?"

I snapped some photos of the sofa, loveseat, and my old wrought iron glass topped kitchen table, the four chairs, and matching baker's rack before going outside for an exterior shot, then had Lorna view them on the screen.

"You know, I think I like the ones that show the interior—especially the table and baker's rack. With any luck, I'll have most of your stuff sold soon."

"Good choice. See how easy that was?" I laughed and patted her on the arm.

"I wish I understood all this digital and electronic nonsense," she said with a sigh.

"It's not hard at all. I'll show you. You do have a computer, don't you?"

"I do, but all I can do on it is write stuff and print it out."

"We'll get you a digital camera. I'll teach you how to upload photos and download all kinds of things off the Internet. We'll set Bell's up on Facebook and get you a simple website. I'm sure it'll increase your sales."

An appreciative expression crossed her face. "Thank you, Callie. You're so nice. Not like..." she paused and bit her lip.

"Not like who?"

"Not like a lot of people I know."

I patted her arm again and left.

"How was your lunch? Get your photos?" Josh asked when I returned.

"Yes. Anything going on here?"

"Naw, just the usual. Even got another new

subscription from a man over in Crossmore. That's a small town east of here. You ready to go read old news?"

****

We drove into Atwell, parked near the *Courier,* and made our way to the archives with the microfilm. Here, we struck our first substantial information. The entire trial had been covered by one Daniel Harper, now the managing editor.

Daddy's trial hadn't taken long and mirrored what I'd read in John Casey's notes. John Casey had not been even close to a good defense attorney, but then I was highly prejudiced against him. Seeing the words in the actual black and white of a newspaper made me sick to my stomach.

"You all right?" Josh asked when I sat back in my chair.

"Not really. I didn't expect to react this way. I thought I'd be more clinical, unemotional about the printed word."

He turned off the machine and rewound the microfilm. "Let's get out of here. Maybe hearing it from a live person will be easier to bear."

We left the archive room and headed for the main newsroom and a chat with Daniel Harper. Luckily, he was in and able to see us.

"Nice to meet you, Miss Bryant. Good to see you again, Josh. Of course, I remember the trial. It was my first big assignment as a reporter."

"What was your take on it?" Josh asked.

I folded my hands in my lap and kept quiet.

"The prosecution had a good case. Fingerprints on the knife, a time gap from when Eric Bryant left the bar to when he called the cops, and their frequent arguments, all added up. Even where the knife was kept worked against him."

"And where was that?" Josh asked.

A distant memory flashed through my mind. "In a scabbard hanging on the wall on the far side of the back porch."

"In plain sight?"

I shook my head and worried my lower lip. "It was visible, but not in your face. I don't think Daddy used it much."

"So, the chances of a stranger knowing its location would be slim," he noted with a frown. "On the other hand, a friend…"

"What was your take on the defense?" I asked the editor, interrupting Josh.

Harper sighed. "Not the best choice of attorneys. Brought up the subject of the defendant going to the bar in the first place, leaving the door wide open for the prosecution to ask why."

"And because my father was an honorable man, he admitted he and mother had had an argument on the way home from the concert."

He nodded. "Means, motive, and opportunity. He tried to argue that someone could have known where the knife was hanging, but the jury dismissed it as unlikely. The only smart thing John Casey did was during pre-trial when he argued against admitting hearsay about your father having an affair into the record."

"Especially since the prosecution couldn't produce the so-called third party," I said.

"That's about it, although the rumors were out

there."

Josh shot me a speculative look, and then said, "Casey didn't try for a change of venue?"

"Nope."

"So, he was in way over his head. Can't imagine why your father hired him in the first place," Josh muttered.

"Guess we'll have to ask John Casey. Mr. Harper, you were there. Do you think my father did it?"

"Is that what this is all about? Proving your father innocent?"

I squeezed my folded hands together harder. "Yes."

The man took a moment to gaze out of the window. "To be honest, I was never sure. He was grief-stricken over the loss of his wife and bewildered that anyone would think he could have done it. He had an air of honesty—of openness—about him I liked."

"And yet, the evidence was there," Josh added.

"The evidence was there. The blood, the fingerprints, the time gap, the argument, it was all just too much to ignore."

Josh rose and extended his hand. "Thanks, Dan, we appreciate your input."

I also stood. "And thank you for taking the time to answer my questions."

"Miss Bryant, are you thinking of trying to get the case re-opened?"

"Well, in order to do that, I'd have to find the real killer, wouldn't I? Goodbye, Mr. Harper."

We left the room with him staring at us, a surprised expression on his face. I wondered if he'd start digging again, too.

I may be opening one hell of a can of worms.

Chapter Eleven

"Did you know your father was supposed to be having an affair?" Josh asked as we headed back to Wellington.

I stared straight out the windshield. "Not until the other day when Ruth mentioned it."

"Ruth Kendall? Did she say who the other woman was?"

"No. But apparently Aunt Dee told her about it."

"And how did she know?"

"Ruth claimed Aunt Dee said Mother had called her a few weeks before all upset at finding out."

He spared me a glance before refocusing on his driving. "Odd."

"What's odd?"

"That your mother wouldn't have confided her suspicions to her best friend, Ruth."

"Maybe Mother was too embarrassed to admit she couldn't hold her man."

"And do you believe he was having an affair?"

"It's bullshit."

"Callie, your parents argued frequently. Isn't it possible your father strayed?"

"No. Daddy loved Mother. He wouldn't cheat any more than he would kill."

"Honey, you were only seven. Would you have understood?"

I lifted my chin and took a deep breath. "Maybe not, but Ruth is wrong and so was Aunt Dee. From all I've heard, Mother could sometimes be suspicious and a little out there. My aunt probably told the prosecution about the phone call just to get him deeper into trouble."

Josh had the good sense not pursue this line of conversation further. He changed the subject.

"I can do some Chinese leftovers tonight if you're up to it."

"Well, goodness knows I have enough of them."

"Let's drop by the office and see if there are any messages. I'll stop at the convenience store for some more beer on my way."

A couple of messages had been left concerning advertising space. I returned the calls with the rates while Josh dealt with a few items left in his private voicemail. By five-thirty, we were done.

I pulled the cartons of Chinese food out of the fridge and set the table. Josh arrived with a cold six-pack a few minutes later.

The food tasted just as good the second time around and we did some serious damage to the leftovers. I cleaned up as Josh headed for the living room. A minute later the TV popped on.

Josh sat in the reclining portion of the sectional his attention focused on the baseball game. I curled up next to him. Tonight, I craved the warmth of his body, the human contact. His arm snaked around my shoulders drawing me closer.

It *had* been a rough day. I don't know what I expected to find in the old archives. Some slice of new information, perhaps? I'd kept my emotions concerning

Daddy tucked away for years. I wished I had the trial transcripts or the police reports. Maybe a witness said something John Casey had missed—a tiny comment that would be a revelation.

Some witnesses—a bartender and a bunch of bar flies. They'd tried to help Daddy, but had merely helped put him in prison.

I hadn't thought reading about the events would be so disturbing. But they were and I was at rock bottom. A tear trickled down my cheek. I sniffed and brushed it away with the back of my hand.

Josh squeezed my shoulders. "Are you all right?"

I sniffed again and wiped away another tear. Soon I wouldn't be able to keep up with them.

"No, dammit!"

The floodgates opened and I sobbed like a five-year old.

He kicked the recliner back into position and pulled me onto his lap.

"Aw, Callie, don't cry. Please. I know you pinned your hopes on finding something concrete to prove your father's innocence, but we may still come up with something."

I cried harder into his shoulder unable to speak. He let me howl all the while murmuring soft words of comfort and rocking me to and fro. Eventually, the storm passed.

"Feeling better?" he asked.

I nodded and struggled to sit up. "Sorry. Don't know where that came from. I haven't cried like that since I got the news about Denny's death. I need a tissue."

Rising, I made my way into the kitchen and

grabbed a couple, blowing my nose and wiping the tear residue from my cheeks. When I turned, Josh stood in the doorway.

"Maybe it would be a good idea if you dropped this whole idea."

"Of proving Daddy innocent? How many times do I have to say this? No way!"

He opened the fridge and took out another beer. "How old were you when he died?"

"Twelve. Aunt Dee broke the news right after dinner. She said she was sorry to tell me Daddy had died a few days earlier and was buried in the Wellington Cemetery next to his first wife."

"She didn't let you go to your dad's funeral?"

I shook my head. "Nope. Neither Denny nor I made the trip. He was at military school. I remember when he next came home he refused to talk to Aunt Dee. As soon as he graduated, he joined the Army. We didn't see him much after that."

"So, she kept his death a secret until after the funeral, but made sure he wasn't buried near your mother, too. Your aunt sounds like a cold woman."

"She was. And Mother's casket was moved from Wellington to the family plot in Chicago as soon as Daddy was sent to prison, or maybe when he died. I'm not sure which. I never thought to ask how Daddy died, but a few years ago Denny contacted the authorities. I'd always envisioned a heart attack or something romantic like a broken heart. Turns out he was murdered by another inmate over a magazine."

It was the ultimate irony: Daddy convicted of a murder he didn't commit, murdered while in jail.

Josh set the beer bottle on the counter and took me

into his arms.

"I'm so sorry, honey. So very sorry."

He lowered his head until his lips met mine. The kiss was gentle, consoling, and then quick as match fire, ignited into a searing flame.

Heat licked along my nerves. My legs trembled and a rush of desire swept from the pit of my stomach to scorch my entire body. My arms found their way around his neck. The kiss deepened, our tongues dancing like an ancient mating ritual. I moaned deep in my throat.

Josh's hands slid down to my derriere where he squeezed and pulled me hard against his body. His erection stabbed my lower abdomen. The fires within burned hotter. I wanted him, and I wanted him now.

He broke off the kiss and rested his forehead on mine.

"Callie, if you want me to stop, step back now." His voice was thick and raspy.

I pulled his head down to mine and renewed the kiss. He picked me up and headed for the living room, continuing to kiss throughout the house and up the stairs. I pointed to the master bedroom. We entered and set me down by the edge of the bed.

I stepped back. My heart pounded and my breaths came in gasps. We stared at each other for a moment, then proceeded to rip our clothes off.

Josh reached out to caress my cheeks before moving on down to my throat and finally my breasts.

I did the same, my fingertips stroking his smooth, sculpted chest. When my fingers encircled his erection, he groaned and laid me on the bed. Then his lips claimed mine again.

The lid blew off. We thrashed and rolled like a pair of animals in heat. No words passed our lips. We stroked, pinched, licked, and bit as much skin as possible. He pinned me to the bed and nestled between my legs.

"Now," I moaned. "Now!"

"Not yet, baby. Not yet," his panting voice answered.

With my body squirming and undulating, he let his lips trail down my body. Beginning at my throat, he moved on to my breasts, his tongue laving and his teeth nibbling on the erect centers.

I pumped my hips, silently demanding to be taken. He ignored me and moved on to explore my navel. I moaned and gasped. The fire in my body threatened to consume me. By the time he got to the junction of my thighs, I had no coherent thought remaining. I cried out and pumped harder when his tongue tickled that most sensitive of spots. I was close to going over the edge. I wanted him inside me and I wanted him now.

"Josh, please!"

He laughed and kissed the inside of my thighs, then rolled off to fumble for his clothes on the floor. I stroked his throbbing shaft. His groan told me he wasn't too far away from the pinnacle either. I couldn't stop my body from moving. Like a spring tightening to the breaking point, I was ready to snap.

"Hurry, dammit," I moaned.

He laughed again, tore open the little foil package with his teeth, and quickly sheathed himself. I opened my legs for him. He knelt between them and slid in with one sure, hard thrust.

I almost flew off the bed. Ripple after ripple of

pleasure shock-waved throughout my body. Wrapping my legs securely around his waist, I met him thrust for thrust. Awash in a sea of sensation, I let myself go. The heat intensified like a volcano until finally erupting.

Hard spasms from my gut rocked me. I screamed Josh's name and lunged with all the strength I had left. I prayed it would never stop. Then he uttered a loud, harsh cry and jammed deep inside me. My waning orgasm renewed as his shaft pulsated.

His panting breaths seared the skin of my neck. I also sucked in as much oxygen as I could. Finally, he rolled off and collapsed onto his side.

The world ceased its frantic spinning and he moved the rest of the way onto his back, but kept his fingers entwined in mine.

"Wow," he whispered.

"Yeah."

He turned his head toward mine. "I knew I was in deep trouble the day we had that first lunch. Back at the office, all I could do was think about you. The more I tried to shove you into the back of my mind, the more you kept coming back. Drove me nuts."

I chuckled. "Funny, I thought the same about you the day you knocked on my front door. You were a distraction I didn't need, but wanted anyway."

He propped himself up on an elbow, his eyes the color of liquid silver gazing at me. A fingertip traced a line from my temple to my chin. He followed it up with a kiss.

The fire wasn't as squelched as I thought. It rekindled, the tiny flames licking at my nerves again. My fingers played with the hair at the nape of his neck. The kiss deepened and he groaned. Something that shouldn't jabbed at my thigh.

He broke contact and looked down. "This isn't supposed to happen again so fast."

"Yeah, but it did." I laughed and pushed him onto his back, then straddled his hips. "Let's make the most of it, shall we?"

He grinned and pulled my head down to his. The night was far from over.

****

I stared across the kitchen table at Josh as he spooned cereal into his mouth. He took a sip of coffee, made eye contact, and grinned like the Cheshire Cat. I pulled down the peel of a banana and snapped off a huge bite.

"Hmmm, are you deliberately using symbolism this morning?" he asked.

"Could be."

"Should I say ouch?"

I swallowed and bit off another chunk. "Maybe."

Last night had been one of those a girl writes about in her diary, complete with a lot of exclamation points. How often had we made love? Three times? Four? I'd lost count. Didn't matter anyway. It was definitely a night to remember.

He finished his cereal and leaned back in the chair.

"You're an enigma."

"How so?" I ate the last of the banana and sipped some coffee.

"During the day, you come off as calm and in control. Last night you turned into a heat-seeking missile. Who are you really—Dr. Jekyll or Mr. Hyde?"

"Why do I have to be either? Wasn't one of them evil? I'm not evil."

"No, but you're bound and determined to uncover evil."

I sighed and put my cup down. "Josh, this is important. My parents were ripped from me by someone who's been walking free for a quarter of a century. It's time justice was served."

"I still don't like it."

"I do. Sooner or later, somebody will slip up, and then I'll have the killer."

"You'll also have a buttload of trouble." He glanced at the clock on the wall and rose, a look of irritation on his face. "I've got to go home, change clothes, and get to the office. I'll see you there."

I waved goodbye as he swung out of the driveway. One good thing about country living was that my neighbors were far enough away not to be curious about a strange car parked overnight next to my house.

An hour later, I entered the newspaper office.

Josh stood at my desk writing a note. "Oh good, you're here. I'm late."

"Where are you going?"

"Atwell. The minutes from the monthly city council meeting were available today. I read them online this morning, and then called one of the councilmen to do an interview. Can you cope?"

"Sure, no problem."

He grinned leaned down to kiss me briefly on the lips, and then left.

The *News-Sentinel* phones were not as busy today, but e-mails stacked up fast with people sending in ad copy. Businesses from all over the county advertised. I could see how Josh made money on the paper. The printing was done by a company in Atwell in exchange for a free half page ad every week.

It was almost five before Josh returned.

"Hi. How did it go?"

"Fine. Got a nice interview."

"Would you like to eat at my place tonight?" I asked. "I can stop at the grocery and get something on the way home."

I hoped my invitation would be accepted and that dinner wouldn't be the only thing on the menu.

He shook his head dashing my hopes. Was he regretting last night? I hoped not. With just a small nudge of encouragement, I could see this relationship deepening. I wouldn't mind that, but did Josh lean in the same direction?

"Can't tonight. The Wellington City Council is meeting to discuss the road repair budget, a permit for the development of a piece of land south of town into a home improvement store, a possible stop light at the main intersection in town, and who knows what else. These meetings sometimes get lively. Want to come?"

Listening to a bunch of small town politicians arguing about a stoplight didn't fill me with enthusiasm.

"I don't think so."

He chuckled. "I understand. To be honest, I don't want to go either, but it's my job. I could always stop by when the meeting's over and tell you all about it."

"You could indeed. I'll keep the lights on."

He smiled and winked before leaving. His gesture gave me hope.

I tidied up my desk, put the phone on voicemail, locked up, and headed home where I popped a frozen dinner into the microwave and poured a glass of wine.

Josh arrived shortly before ten. In the kitchen, the refrigerator door opened, and then closed. A moment later he entered the living room, plunked himself into the recliner portion of the sofa, and kicked back, the remote in his hand. A second later, the TV popped on. He sighed and took a long swallow from his beer bottle. Some women might have been pissed at his actions—no hello, how are you—no conversation at all. I found it comforting—like an old married couple that didn't need words to communicate.

"So, how was the meeting?" I finally asked.

"The usual. About seven people showed up to oppose the home improvement store, including Lorna's brother who now operates the family hardware store. He claimed it would put him out of business. Bob Kendall pointed out it would bring in more tax revenue than Mahon's Hardware. It got lively for a while until the Council finally approved it."

"Let me guess, Bob Kendall owns the land to be developed."

Josh grinned. "He does, and that was brought up. One of the protestors suggested he had a conflict of interest and shouldn't vote. Bob replied that he didn't care who built there, he had several irons in the fire."

"So, did he vote?"

"Nope, but it didn't matter. All those possible taxes for a small town couldn't be trumped." He took another swig from the bottle and frowned. "Bob pulled me aside after the meeting. He suggested that you were causing trouble, something the town doesn't need. I once again gave him the answer you give everyone about living the simple life and trying to understand a tragic time in your life. He flat out said he didn't believe it. Urged me to use my influence to get you to sell out."

"Bastard."

"That's what I almost called him, too. Instead, I told him you had a mind of your own."

"And what was his reaction?"

"He glared at me, said there'd be hell to pay sooner or later, and walked away. I have to say I agree with him on that."

"I can't back away now, Josh. I'm in too deep."

"I worry about you out here by yourself, especially after the shooting. I could move in for a while. A man in the house could be a deterrent."

"I'll think about it." I glanced at the TV, and then at the remote. "Are you really interested in a baseball game?"

His finger hit the off button. "Uh-uh. I'm thinking about another sport."

My voice dropped to a low, sexy growl. "Kinda along the lines of gymnastics?"

His right eyebrow rose and a smile tugged at his lips. "I'd love to see you do a double somersault dismount in the lay out position."

"Let's give it a try."

We ran up the stairs and into the bedroom.

Much later, I listened to Josh gently snoring. My euphoria hadn't subsided yet. I hadn't attempted the double somersault dismount, but had the lay out position down pat. I lay wide-awake savoring the satiated feeling of making love and thinking. Try as I might, I couldn't get the reality of murder out of my head.

I appreciated that Josh didn't like my plan to prove Daddy's innocence. But it had to work. I had to find the real killer—for Mother, for Daddy, for Denny, and for me, because if my plan failed, then I was left with an alternative that had stuck with me for years and I didn't want to believe. That Daddy had been guilty as hell.

Chapter Twelve

"Callie, Callie! Wake up! Stop screaming!"

Josh's voice penetrated the terrifying haze shrouding my mind. Someone shook me like a rag doll. My eyes finally snapped open. I was sitting upright in bed with Josh kneeling on the mattress next to me. The fog cleared.

Sweat drenched my skin. My breaths came in short, sharp bursts. Nausea churned in my stomach. I pushed him away and ran for the bathroom where I threw up.

Josh joined me a few seconds later. He turned on the water and soon a cold cloth wiped my neck and face.

"Are you all right?" he asked in a soft tone.

"You mean for being bent over a toilet, buck naked, and puking my guts out? I don't think so. At least you grabbed your boxers."

I straightened, rinsed my mouth out, made my way back into the bedroom where I grabbed a t-shirt from the dresser drawer, and pulled it over my head. I sat on the bed and tried to regain control.

"That was one hell of a nightmare," he said sitting next to me.

"This one was a real beaut."

"Want to tell me about it?" He tucked a stray strand of hair behind my ear.

"Give me a second to remember it all."

I gathered my thoughts and took a deep breath.

"I'm at a party, only I can't find any of the partygoers. I wander from room to room. I can hear laughter and conversation, but no one's around. It's like they're moving too fast while I'm always one room behind. Does that make sense?"

"I guess so. Go on."

His sympathetic voice gave me courage to recall every detail—a new phenomenon for me.

"Finally, I come to a room that's pitch black. I don't want to go in, but something keeps pulling me forward. Then I see a staircase and climb. It seems to go on forever, but I finally reach the top. There's a little girl up there who keeps saying, 'Help me. Help me.' When I ask her what's wrong, she just shakes her head and disappears. Could you get me a glass of water?"

Josh nodded, went into the bathroom, and returned with a small paper cup. I drained it in one gulp before continuing.

"I turn to go back downstairs when I hear a loud crash, voices, and someone sobbing down below. I look over the banister, but can only see faint shadows in the dark room along with flashes of light. Then suddenly, everything is quiet. I slowly descend, only when I reach the bottom, the floor is covered in a sea of blood. It's up to my ankles and rising. I guess that's when I started screaming. I was screaming, wasn't I?"

"Blood-curdling. Scared me to death." His arm snaked around my shoulders and squeezed. "Have you had this dream before?"

"No, never. Some parts are a variation on a theme, but what astonishes me is that I can remember all the details with clarity." From outside the window, a bird offered up the first song of the day. "What time is it?"

"Almost five."

"Might as well get up. I won't sleep anymore."

"Why don't you grab a shower? I'll go down and make coffee."

While I showered and dressed, I tried to scrub the dream from my mind. I'd spent enough years in therapy to understand most of the symbolism. I didn't want to think about it. Not now. Not when I was so unprepared. The problem was I couldn't keep from doing so.

Downstairs, Josh had the coffee made and was pouring me a cup as I entered the kitchen.

"Feeling better?" he asked.

I sipped the hot brew cautiously and nodded. "Still can't stop thinking about it, though."

We sat at the table.

"Okay, let's talk about it then. It's not surprising the venue was a party. You just gave one."

"I'm sure the shot fired through the window had something to do with it, too." I took a deep breath. "I know enough about the searching part to understand I'm looking for a solution to a problem."

He nodded. "And the fact you can't quite catch up to the partygoers means you're close, but no cigar. The dark room and staircase could represent the foyer here. The darkness may indicate that it was the scene of the crime."

"Possibly. And I'm pretty sure the child is me. The blood is obvious along with the voices and other noises."

"Callie, you said that your psychiatrist could never determine what, if anything, you heard or saw the night

173

your mother died."

"That's right. He said something about my psyche refusing to let go. He thinks I may have seen my mother's body and been so traumatized I simply went back to bed and blocked it all."

He frowned and gulped most his coffee. "Suppose you didn't just see the body. Suppose you heard noises, got up, and actually saw the murder."

I shook my head. "I've gone over that a million times in the past. Each scenario is slightly different. I've willed myself to remember, but nothing comes through. I may be dreaming about things I heard in conversations before we left for Chicago. I just don't know."

"If you did see something, then it's something so horrifying not even deep therapy or hypnosis can release it."

I stared him in the eye. "You mean like leaning over the banister and seeing my father plunge a knife into my mother's back?"

"I'd hate to think so, but it's something you need to consider."

I started to sip again, and then stopped with a gasp. "Oh my God, what if those flashes of light in my dreams are the living room lights flashing off the blade of a descending knife?"

Josh frowned, a frightened expression on his face. "It could mean you *did* witness your mother's death."

I pushed my chair back and rose abruptly taking my cup to the sink. He followed and took me in his arms.

"Callie, I'm sorry you have to go through this."

"Josh, what if I'm crazy?"

His fingers tightened on my shoulders as he shook me gently. "Don't even think that."

I twisted away. "I can't help it. What if I am? What if it's a family trait? What if my father was having an affair, asked for a divorce, and got so angry, he snapped and killed my mother? Oh God, you were right. That party was a big mistake."

He pulled me back into his arms. "Not necessarily. I watched people, too, and I can tell you Bob Kendall and John Casey were both nervous. They watched *you* most of the evening. Plus, I believe the more we learn, the more likely your dreams are based in reality. We simply have to open the door and find out the truth."

I clung to Josh's warmth. More than anything I wanted to believe right along with him.

"Maybe everyone is right. Maybe I should sell the farm, go back to Chicago, and forget about trying to find a killer."

"On the surface, that makes sense."

"But I came here with a mission, and if I turn tail and run now, I'll always wonder. For the rest of my life, I'll always think about Daddy. I'll always ask the question, who killed my mother? And I'll always have the nightmares. I've started this. I have to see it through." *And I promised Denny.*

He hugged me close to his chest.

"Then we'll see it through together. I'll run over to Des Moines next week and see if I can unearth the transcripts from the appellate court."

"I can go to Atwell and get copies of the newspaper coverage. And maybe I'll be more aggressive and try to find the witnesses. If they're still around, I might be able to ask my own questions."

He smiled and kissed me hard. "You're right about one thing."

"What's that?"

"Never tell a reporter no. Now, I want to know, too." He glanced at the clock on the wall. "I usually go into the office for a couple of hours on Saturday to check e-mail and read what's online. Why don't you get a few more hours sleep? When I'm done, I'll come back and we can go fishing. You're a country girl. You must like to fish."

"Daddy used to take me to Miller's Lake often. We'd catch sunnies, bluegill, and the occasional catfish. Even bass. I'd love to go. I noticed some old poles and reels in one of the outbuildings."

"Don't bother. I have several. Why don't you make us lunch? I'll pick you up around noon. How's that?"

"Sounds great."

He kissed me goodbye and left.

The chances of me falling back asleep were slim. While the nightmare was not forgotten, I managed to push it to the recesses of my mind and concentrate on the day to come. I helped myself to a second cup of coffee and made a light breakfast of cereal and fruit.

Finished, I headed upstairs to make the bed and see if I had any appropriate clothing for a day of fishing. My gaze fell on Mother's bracelet. It was still on the nightstand where I'd left it after the party. Maybe I should take it to a jeweler and have that clasp fixed. For some unknown reason, I suddenly wanted to wear it.

I found a pair of old jeans and a long-sleeved shirt in my closet—the perfect fishing attire, along with beat up sneakers I'd forgotten to toss out before moving.

Saturdays in Wellington started early. Dim

memories of running numerous errands hovered in my mind. I was usually with Daddy and my brother. This was Mother's special pampering day at The Elite.

I had to cruise up and down the streets a couple of times before finding a parking spot near Sweet Daddy's. During one of my sojourns into town, I'd noticed a jewelry store on the other end of the street. As I strolled down the sidewalk, people nodded and greeted me. In spite of the recent events, I reciprocated in a cheerful tone. This was home and maybe, just maybe, the inhabitants were getting used to Callie Bryant being back in town. Then I recalled the shooting. *Well, most of them anyway.*

Carson's Jewelry was nestled between a shoe store and a small book exchange. I pushed open the door and entered. A short man in his mid-sixties was behind the counter writing prices on tags. He looked up with a smile.

"Well, well, Callie Bryant, it's good to see you. I'm Phil Carson. What brings you here?"

"I need some repair done on a bracelet. Can you oblige?" Goodness, I slipped into country lingo.

"Sure can. Whatcha got?"

I fished in my purse and withdrew a box containing the bracelet, handing it to him.

"The clasp is faulty. I rarely wear it, but when I do, I live in fear I'll lose it. Can't imagine why I haven't had it done before now. It belonged to my mother."

He removed the item from the box and held it up to the light. The red and white colored stones set in wide silver links glimmered in the light from the front window. For a moment, they sparkled like fire. Then Mr. Carson set it on a black velvet pad in front of him.

"You say this was your mother's?"

"Yes. Until last night, I hadn't worn it in years. Can you fix it?"

He held it up again and frowned.

"Yes, yes, I can fix it. No problem there." His voice had a questioning quality as he turned it over in his fingers to view the back. His frown deepened. "I see there's an inscription, 'To my beloved,' on one of the links."

"Sweet sentiment, isn't it?"

"Yes, very sweet."

He scratched the back of his neck and didn't make eye contact. I guessed handling something from a murdered woman made him uncomfortable.

"Did you sell the bracelet to Daddy?" I asked to ease the awkward moment.

"No, no, I didn't, at least I don't think so, although it does look familiar." He finally looked at me and smiled. "It's a nice piece. I can fix the clasp and have it back to you pronto. I'll even put a safety chain on it so if it does come loose again, it won't slip off your wrist."

"Thank you, but there's no hurry. I can come in sometime next week and pick it up. Like I said, I don't wear it often."

He carefully returned the bracelet to the box and wrote out a ticket for the work. I thanked him again and left.

Strange little man. Odd that he'd find a possession from a dead woman disturbing. After all, antique jewelry was once worn by people who had died. Maybe the circumstances made him uneasy.

I wandered down the other side of the street window shopping until coming to the Kozy Kafe.

Through the window, I spied Josh having a cup of coffee. I entered and walked up to him nodding to Bob Kendall, John Casey, and another man I didn't recognize at the next table.

"Mind if I join you?"

Josh grinned. "Be my guest. What are you doing here?"

"Had to run a couple of errands."

The waitress hurried over to the table.

"Just coffee," I told her.

She nodded and left.

"Ready for that fishing trip?"

"Of course, look at my clothes. And I'll bet I catch more fish than you, so there!"

He laughed. "An afternoon on the water at Miller's Lake is just what the doctor ordered. Warm sunshine, a cloudless sky, and lots of relaxation."

"And you, of course, are the doctor. I still haven't called about getting the window fixed. Know anyone?"

"I'll call Nathan Winger when I get back to the office."

"Thanks. The sooner, the better. I'll fill in the bullet hole with toothpaste until later."

The conversation at the next table stopped abruptly.

"Toothpaste?"

"Old renters' trick. Hides nail holes, especially in white walls."

"But your walls are gold."

"It'll still look better than a black hole."

The waitress brought my coffee and slapped the check on the table. Josh immediately picked it up.

"How about a fish dinner tonight?"

"You clean 'em, I'll cook 'em," I promised.

"You got a deal."

"I understand the movie of the week at the theatre is a comedy. Wanna go?"

He stared as though suspecting I didn't want to be in the house. "That sounds like fun, too."

Chairs scraped on the floor as Bob, John, and the other man rose to leave. John and Bob stopped next to me.

"Nice party the other night, Callie," John said.

"Thanks, John." I stared at Bob. "Hope everybody had a good time."

"Lovely, thank you," the real estate guru of Wellington replied checking his watch. "I have a showing in Jasper this afternoon. I'll talk to you later."

The two men moved off. Both had been polite, but that was about all. I'm sure my conversation with them at the party still stuck in their heads. I wondered how soon news I had a bullet hole in my wall would be common knowledge.

Josh and I left the Kozy together where he walked me toward my car.

He discreetly kissed my forehead as we stopped on the corner. "I'll see you at noon."

"I'll be ready, complete with a basket of goodies for lunch."

We waved goodbye and went our separate ways. Maybe a day of relaxation would help put the disturbing events of the past few days out of my mind.

****

I hefted the cooler filled with leftover cheeses, assorted lunch meats, mini rolls, condiments, and the remaining pastries Clovis hadn't chowed down. I'd also included several bottles of water. The damned thing weighed a ton.

I hope the boat doesn't sink.

Josh pulled into the drive a little after noon. I was so eager to begin the afternoon I almost leaped out of the door.

"In a hurry?" he asked with a twinkle in his eye.

I handed off the cooler to him and laughed. "You betcha. I haven't been fishing in years. That particular pastime never crossed my aunt's agenda. I can remember Daddy baiting my hook and taking fish off. He'd laugh at me for crying because the worms would die."

He chuckled. "Does this mean I'm going to have to bait your hook and remove the catch?"

"Not unless you teach me how. By the way, are we boat or shore fishing?"

"Shore. I don't own a boat. I like to lie back under the shade of a tree."

"In other words, a lazy fisherman."

He grinned and heaved the cooler into the trunk. I spied several poles complete with reels in there already.

"Looks like we're good to go," I commented opening the passenger side door of his car.

"You are eager, aren't you?"

I didn't answer. I'd rather be out of the house where I couldn't see that cardboard covering the windowpane. The man Josh had called couldn't make it out until Monday.

Miller's Lake straddled the Atwell-Sampson County lines some ten miles northwest of town. On summer weekends families would flock to its cooling waters. Daddy had taught me to swim here, although I could still hear Mother reminding us to be careful. She wasn't a good swimmer and never ventured further out than a few feet.

Fishermen preferred the eastern shore. Here the tree line was closer to the water and the reeds were custom made for fish to hide.

Josh pulled off the dirt road and parked on the berm. He carried the cooler and a blanket while I followed him with the gear and another smaller cooler down a short path through the trees to the lake. A large oak and several hickories provided dappled shade. By the time summer rolled around, this particular part of the shoreline would be cool and inviting—even more than now.

"This is lovely," I said.

"We're far enough toward the north end that most people ignore it. The water gets pretty shallow in this area, so the boaters don't come in too far."

As he spoke he spread out a blanket and set the coolers off to the side.

"Well, Miss Bryant, shall we begin?"

For the next three hours we fished, ate, talked, and generally relaxed. The second cooler contained several containers of worms and a few artificial baits. My childhood squeamishness regarding baiting my own hook vanished, even though it took me a while to get the hang of taking a fish off the line.

I reveled in relaxing and being with Josh. Yet when we'd first arrived, a feeling of being watched had me looking into the woods on more than one occasion. A light breeze rustled the leaves reminding me of something or someone treading lightly along the narrow path.

Eventually, I got used to the noises. My heebie-jeebies dissipated. The warm air and the food made me sleepy. I yawned and reclined on the blanket, my hands beneath my head. The branches overhead laced with late spring leaves allowed a peek of the blue sky. Not even a cloud drifted by. I closed my eyes and sighed. This was the life. Chicago seemed like another lifetime, and I'd only been here a little over a week. The unpleasantness of the last few days still lingered, but I was determined not to let it spoil the day.

I awoke to a pair of lips caressing my forehead.

Josh leaned back and grinned. "Awaken, Sleeping Beauty."

"Goofball," I replied, my hand bringing his head down to mine.

We necked like a couple of teenagers. Heat rose from the pit of my stomach to warm every inch of my body. I wanted him and I wanted him now.

"Wanna get nekkid?" he whispered.

"Oh, yeah."

His fingers found the buttons of my shirt and slowly undid them. I hadn't bothered with a bra today. His hands immediately fondled and stroked as his lips slid down my throat to suck on that pulse point near my collarbone.

I moaned, never wanting him to stop. My heart hammered and my breaths came faster as anticipation of making love on the isolated shore of a lake escalated.

His tongue and teeth were exploring my nipples when the putt-putt of an engine interrupted the pleasure.

Josh sat up and I quickly covered my breasts with my shirt.

"Guess we aren't as alone as I thought," he said.

"No, but I know where we can be."

He smiled that sexy, lopsided grin. "Then I suggest we pack up and head for your place."

As I folded the blanket and gathered up the gear, Josh rearranged the coolers. The remaining worms were dumped on the ground to live another day. He spread most of the ice from my cooler to his, and then added several baggies of cleaned fish.

"When did you do that?"

"While you were sleeping. I figured the fishing part of the day was done, and you did promise that if I cleaned them, you'd cook them."

"It's a little early for dinner."

"I'm sure we can find something to do until then."

We packed the car in record time and hurried home, pulling into the driveway a little after five. Neither of us gave much thought to anything except getting inside.

I burst through the back door and into the kitchen, setting the food cooler on the table. Josh was right behind me. He slapped a change of clothing on the counter and jammed the fish into the fridge.

"I see you came prepared," I said indicating the clothes with a thrust of my chin.

"I was a Boy Scout."

"Race you to the shower. First one there calls dibs."

"I suggest we become conservationists and save water by showering together."

"Deal!"

Laughing we charged up the back staircase and ran down the hallway to the bedroom. I entered and stopped dead in my tracks, gasping in shock. Josh ran into me.

"What the hell…" he exclaimed.
The room was in shambles.

Chapter Thirteen

I went cold, and then hot as an adrenaline rush sent my heart into overdrive. My breathing almost stopped. My knees wobbled. I grasped the doorjamb to stay upright.

Every drawer was either open or ripped out and overturned, the contents dumped in piles with the drawers tossed aside. Even the books in the bookcase were scattered across the floor. Through my shocked fog, I heard Josh calling the police.

I slowly walked into the room, my gaze taking it all in. The first thing I noticed was my jewelry box, the one I'd had since childhood, was gone. The boxes where my better pieces were kept lay among the ruins, empty. I turned toward my closet where the door gaped wide. My clothes had been disturbed, but not ripped from the hangers. Every shoebox, however, had been opened and dumped.

Then a horrible thought occurred. I whirled, pushed past Josh who was still on the phone, and ran for my old bedroom. I pulled open the nightstand with shaking fingers. Relief washed over me. The Smith & Wesson was still there. My ultra modern platform bed didn't have nightstand drawers, merely an open space for storage.

Thank God, I didn't move the gun. The thieves must have figured this room was unused.

Josh hurried down the hall. I shut the drawer as he stopped in the doorway.

"Are you all right?" he asked.

I nodded. "Just in shock, I think. Why would somebody do this?"

"I don't know, but the police are on the way. I don't suppose you know if anything's missing?"

I brushed past him and returned to my room where I surveyed the place again.

"My jewelry, that's all." I paused as another thought hit me. "Oh my God, the TV!"

We raced down the front stairs and into the living room. Nothing had been disturbed. The LED still hung on the wall and the entertainment goodies remained in their places.

In the kitchen, I noticed my purse overturned on the floor. I hadn't taken it with me to the lake and, since I had other things on my mind, didn't notice it when we'd returned. A quick inspection showed my wallet was missing. I spied my cell phone behind one of the table legs. At least the thief wasn't calling Paris or Rome on my dime.

The initial shock had worn off and was replaced with anger. I kicked one of the kitchen chairs in frustration. I was angry. Angrier than I'd been in a long time.

"Goddammit! I lived in Chicago for twenty-five years and never had something like this happen. I'm here a lousy week, get threatening letters and phone calls, my window blasted out, and now some asshole comes along to rob me. I expect this kind of bullshit in the big city, but not Wellington."

Before Josh could answer, a police car pulled into

the drive. The deputy I'd spoken with when I first arrived emerged and walked toward the back door. He entered the house, nodded to Josh, and then looked at me.

"Are you all right, Miss Bryant?"

"No, I'm not all right! I feel violated!"

"I understand. Show me the bedroom."

"Why don't you wait down here? I'll show Pete the crime scene," Josh offered.

"No way. It's my house, my bedroom, and my shit scattered all over hell's half acre."

I stomped past both of them to the back stairs and climbed. They followed. I entered the room and paused to wave my hand at the mess.

"There it is. Do something."

He remained calm to my angry words. "Anything missing that you can see?"

"My jewelry box and a few pieces I kept in boxes in a drawer. The only good thing is whatever the thief took he won't get much for."

"How much would you say the jewelry was worth?" He used the toe of his well-shined shoe to poke at and lift a couple of sweaters.

"In the jewelry box? Probably less than two hundred bucks. It was inexpensive costume stuff. I had a few nicer things in the boxes in the drawer. Those items might have been worth another three hundred. I'm not big on jewelry. The only things I wear on a regular basis are small earrings and a watch. Thank God, I still have the heirlooms and expensive items in my lawyer's care in Chicago."

"And this is the only room ransacked?" he asked.

"Yes. Oh, my wallet is gone, too."

"How much was in it?"

"A little over a hundred dollars. And my credit cards, of course, plus my driver's license. Now I have to go through the hell of replacing them."

Josh, silent until now, finally spoke. "I take it you're going to dust for fingerprints."

"Yeah, I have a kit in the car."

"You? No forensics person?" I asked.

"In Wellington? No. Atwell has two people who do that work. For a major crime scene, we call in the state boys."

"I'd say somebody has a lot of guts," Josh said. "Callie's car was in plain view in the driveway."

Officer Young shrugged. "Whoever it was, took a chance, knocked on the back door, and when no one answered, went in. I take it the door wasn't locked."

I shook my head. Anticipating an afternoon with Josh, I'd hurried to pack the car and forgotten. Given the events of the past week, it was an incredibly stupid thing to overlook.

"As you said, this is Wellington, but you'd better believe this place will look like Fort Knox from now on," I told him in a grim tone.

I didn't mention my equalizer upstairs in the nightstand drawer. From now on, it would be within easy reach.

"How long were you gone this afternoon?"

Josh gave him the details of our day while I gazed at the carnage. My anger faded. Sadness crept in. Tears welled in my eyes. Daddy had given me that jewelry box for my sixth birthday along with a special ring to fit my small fingers. It was just blue-colored glass and Mother had coated the inside of the band with clear nail polish so my finger wouldn't turn green. Now it was gone.

I blinked hard before the tears spilled over. I would not give this…this violator the satisfaction of making me cry. I'd see him hung by this thumbs—or a couple of more sensitive pieces of anatomy—first.

"Officer, how long before I can clean this mess up?"

He snapped a small notebook he'd been writing in shut and stowed it in his pocket.

"I'll dust for prints now, but in my opinion, I doubt we'll find anything of use. And even if we do, the perp will have to have a record somewhere for comparison. And speaking of comparisons, I'll need your fingerprints so we can eliminate those that should be here."

We trooped downstairs to the foyer, and then the living room.

"I don't get it," I said to Josh as the deputy left to get his kit. "Why ransack my room, take some inexpensive jewelry, but leave the TV and the rest of this stuff behind."

"Maybe whoever did it was on foot. He took the small, easy to sell or pawn stuff, and split. It's your credit cards I'm worried about. You need to contact the issuers immediately."

I sighed, suddenly exhausted. This was not how I imagined the end of my day.

Officer Young returned with a box and a camera, fingerprinted both me and Josh, then went upstairs to make more of a mess.

Josh joined him while I scrounged my address book from the sideboard drawer and made phone calls to the various credit card agencies. Thank God I only had three, two of which I rarely used.

"Well, so far, so good," I commented when the men returned to the kitchen. "Nobody's tried to use anything yet. Any thoughts on who did this?"

Peter Young sighed. "Could have been a vagrant. Planting season is over. Most of the extra hired help is moving on. One of them could have come up asking for work, realized you weren't home, and took advantage of the situation. Could have been kids, too."

"So, in other words, Miss Bryant isn't likely to see any of her stuff again," Josh commented.

"We'll see. We'll put out the word to pawn shops, but there aren't many in the area. I'm sorry this happened. I'll be in touch if we find out anything."

"Does Bill have anything yet on the shooting or the letters Callie gave him last night?"

The deputy gave him a strange look. I had the feeling this was the first he'd heard of it.

"No, nothing yet to my knowledge. You'll have to ask him."

He left and Josh pulled me into his arms.

"I'm so sorry, Callie."

For a moment I let the tears well again before blinking them away.

"It's not the mess or the value of the items stolen. It's the sense of being violated and the memories that are now gone. Crap, even my wallet had pictures of Mother, Daddy, Denny, and Aunt Dee in it." I sniffed and pulled away. "I assume there's even more of a mess to clean up now."

"I'm afraid so. I'll help."

The bedroom was indeed more of a mess. Black

powdery residue covered every surface. While I returned the drawers to the dresser and vanity, Josh scrubbed with soap and water. The urge to wash the clothing scattered about was overwhelming. The thought of someone's dirty fingers pawing through my underwear made me gag. I heaped all of it in a pile. I'd take it to the basement and do a load immediately.

I came back upstairs to find Josh in the kitchen wringing out the dishrag he'd used to clean.

"Let's go out and get something to eat. I won't hold you to the fish cooking thing."

Reluctant to leave the house again, I shook my head. It was a sharp contrast to earlier in the day when I didn't want to be here.

"No. I don't have the stamina to do that. The fish won't take long and I can find plenty to go with it. Go watch TV while I act domestic."

Dinner was as simple as I could make it—beer battered fried fish, frozen French fries, steam-in-the-bag broccoli, and salad made from pre-packaged lettuce. I actually worked to cut up the tomatoes.

It was close to nine o'clock by the time we'd done the dishes and put everything away.

Josh came up behind me while I rinsed the last of the soapsuds down the drain. His arms encircled my waist, and he kissed the top of my head.

"Would you like me to stay the night?"

"Of course I would, but tonight isn't the night for it. I've just been burglarized. This coupled with everything else tells me I need to face being alone in the house. The sooner I do that, the sooner I can come to grips with things. I know I'm not sounding logical, but do you get what I'm saying?"

He nodded. "I get it, but I worry."

"I'll be fine. I'll keep my phone next to the bed and if I hear something suspicious, I'll call nine-one-one immediately."

"Nine-one-one here will connect you with Atwell. Program the local police station's number into your phone now."

He gave me the information along with the local emergency volunteer fire department number.

"I suppose this will be the lead story for the *News-Sentinel's* next edition."

"Sure will, along with an editorial on how crime can strike anywhere at anytime." He looked at me with a smile. "You going to church tomorrow?"

"Yes. And this time I might take you up on that cafeteria thing."

He kissed me hard and long. "Are you sure you'll be all right?"

I rested my hand along the side of his face and thought of the Smith & Wesson. "I'll be fine. Believe me, the doors will be locked tight. Besides, whoever did this is in the next county by now."

"Okay, but if you change your mind, give me a call and I'll be here in a few minutes." He leaned down and kissed me again. "See you in church."

I waved as he left and wandered into the living room where I turned on the TV. Channel surfing on a Saturday night didn't produce anything of interest. I finally settled on—appropriately enough—*Cops* reruns. I stayed tuned throughout the news and part of *Saturday Night Live* before clicking the off button. Throughout the evening my gaze wandered from the boarded up window to the as of yet unrepaired hole in the wall.

I sucked in a ragged breath. It was after eleven. Time to face the night. I double-checked all the locks on the doors and downstairs windows trying to ignore the cardboard pane. To be on the safe side, I set up a booby-trap of pots and pans on the table under the window. The window repair on Monday morning seemed a long ways off.

Upstairs, I retrieved the Smith & Wesson from the drawer and placed it on my nightstand next to the bedside lamp along with my phone. Finished with my nighttime routine, I turned out the light and slid beneath the sheets.

I inhaled several deep, cleansing breaths, willing my muscles to relax. Every night sound from leaves rustling in the breeze to frogs croaking to insects chirping drifted in the open windows. I imagined each of them as something sinister. I transferred the gun from the nightstand to under the unused pillow on my right comforted by the feel of cool steel.

My equalizer. *Come and get me, asshole.*

A distant train whistle further comforted me as I drifted off to sleep.

****

Lorna met me at the foot of the basement steps of the church recreation hall for the coffee hour after the service.

"Is it true someone broke into your house?" she asked in a shocked tone.

"I'll say, but how did you know?"

"Oh, Sarah Michaels is the dispatcher at the police station. She took your call. What did they get?"

I gave her a shortened version of the event. "I'm not holding out a lot of hope of getting anything back."

She shook her head. "I can't believe it. This is Wellington, not some big city."

"Crime happens everywhere," Josh said handing me a cup of coffee. "I'm just glad Callie wasn't home when this guy knocked on her door."

Lorna's eyes went wide as the implications struck her. "Oh good heavens, a woman alone. You could have been hurt. Well, you can be sure I'll lock my doors from now on."

"Why would you lock your doors?" June asked as she joined us.

Lorna relished retelling the news to her friend.

June frowned. "How odd the thief would pick on you. I guess he must have thought that being from the city you had lots of expensive items."

The "why me" hadn't struck me before. Letters, phone calls, and a shot in the dark not withstanding, I assumed this was a random act. Why would a thief target me?

"Maybe because I'm the new kid on the block?" I suggested.

"Never thought of that angle," Josh said. "Still, it's sad we all have to think about this happening, even in Wellington."

"Think about what happening?" Bob Kendall asked as he and Ruth joined the group.

Once again Lorna, like a town crier, enjoyed revealing the news.

Bob turned a wary gaze on me. "Anything other than jewelry taken?"

I shook my head. "No, thank goodness. I suppose I should be grateful the thief didn't have a vindictive streak in him. In Chicago, my entire house would have been vandalized and everything smashed."

"I always lock the doors at our house," Ruth said. "It discourages the riff-raff that come and go at planting and harvest times."

"Not all itinerant workers are thieves," June said in a stiff tone.

During the discussion regarding farm hands, I nibbled on a chocolate chip cookie and finished my coffee. The Kendalls drifted on to chat with other people. I looked at Josh who raised his eyebrows in a silent question. I nodded. I was ready to get out of here.

Lorna had been unusually quiet, sipping her coffee with a frown on her face.

She finally looked up with a serious expression. "If you all will excuse me, I have to get home. Callie, I'm so sorry. Not a very nice welcome home, is it? I assume that lovely bracelet you wore the other night is also gone. How sad to lose things with emotional ties."

"I'm not a big jewelry fan. I was wearing my only good pair of earrings and my watch, both graduation gifts from my brother and aunt. Luckily, I'd taken the bracelet in to get the clasp fixed."

"How fortunate," June murmured.

"Callie, are you ready to go?" Josh asked.

I set the cup on a dish tray and nodded. "Yes, I think so. Lorna how about we get together on Wednesday evening after work? I can show you how to use the computer and the social networking sites to the fullest. And I have a friend in Chicago who can set up a nice website for Bell's."

"That sounds lovely." She cast a glance around the rest of the group. Bob and Ruth had rejoined us and also appeared ready to leave.

"Suppose we have lunch tomorrow? Let me check my schedule first. I'll call," Ruth suggested. "Do you play bridge?"

"I can, but haven't in a long while."

"Perhaps we can also have lunch one day," June insisted cutting a sharp glance toward Ruth. "I'm on several town committees. You'd make a wonderful addition to the groups."

"Sure. Just give me a call."

Suddenly, I was the most popular girl in town. We said our goodbyes and moved outside.

"Josh, how come nobody's mentioned the shot fired, especially since I mentioned it in the café yesterday? They know everything else that goes on in this town."

"Because I didn't call the police station. I called Bill Jackson directly. And he and his deputy would be closed-mouthed about it. Come to think of it, I'm not sure Pete knew about it when I asked yesterday. I guess the word hasn't spread yet from whoever overheard you in the Kozy. Do you want to have lunch at Wanamakers?" Josh asked.

"Would you rather indulge in fried chicken with everything at the house?"

His grin said it all. "My mouth is already watering. I'm surprised you know how to cook. Didn't you have a cook in Chicago?"

"Yes. But being an independent-minded type, I watched her making dinner and often asked questions. I notice you didn't leave much of the fish on your plate last night."

"Damn good fish."

"Cook's batter recipe, which incidentally was

never used at our house."

"How did you sleep last night?" he asked as we walked to my car.

"Badly. Every noise outside was magnified, but the important part is I did it on my own. I'll be fine from now on, just more aware."

I opened my car door and slid behind the wheel. "Give me a few minutes head start. I need to stop at the store and buy things."

"I need to go home and change out of this suit. See you soon."

With my errands complete, I pulled into my drive and approached the back door with trepidation. My heart rate accelerated and I swallowed a nagging lump of fear stuck in my throat. Would I find a repeat of yesterday or would all be intact?

I unlocked the door and entered, setting the groceries on the counter. A quick glance at the dining and living rooms showed everything in its place. I climbed the front stairs with trembling legs. The bedroom was just as I'd left it. Breathing a sigh of relief, I stripped off my Sunday clothes and got comfortable in a pair of jeans and a collared pullover. It would take a while for the fear to completely go away.

I performed one last task before heading for the kitchen. I slid my hand under the pillow and touched the cold steel of my Smith & Wesson.

Good. Still there. *Hope I never need to use you.*

I walked rapidly down the hall to the back stairs. I had once again neglected to retrieve the mail yesterday. Taking a deep breath, I marched down the drive to the mailbox. *And there better not be an anonymous letter today.* There wasn't—just a few flyers.

I breathed a sigh of relief. Josh would be here in a few minutes. It was time I showed him how valuable an asset a rich girl from the big city could be when transplanted to the country.

As I unpacked the groceries, I wondered if Josh knew how much he was beginning to mean to me. He was a complication I hadn't counted on, but one I welcomed—with open arms.

Chapter Fourteen

I walked down the sidewalk to Carson's Jewelers with a spring in my step. Dinner last night had been a huge success. For once, leftovers didn't exist.

"Lady, you may be a keeper," Josh had said with a twinkle in his eye.

My heart lunged with an extra beat. "Oh, yeah?"

He kissed me hard and long. "Definitely."

Naturally, he stayed the night. I had to chuckle remembering his expression when his head hit the pillow—the one with my protector under it.

"What the hell?" he asked pulling it out and staring. "What's this?"

"A Smith & Wesson .38 caliber, snub-nosed titanium revolver."

"I can see that. What are you doing with it?"

"Protecting myself."

"Do you know how to use it?"

"Of course, I know how to use it. I might not be the best marksman in the world, but I can hit what I aim at—I hope."

He rolled his eyes. "I'm surprised it wasn't stolen, too."

"It was in the other bedroom. The thief didn't bother looking there."

"Callie, I'm not sure this gun is a good idea."

"I'm not going to be a victim." The words "like my

mother" hung in the air. "You never know, someday it may save my life."

I took the gun from his fingers and placed it on the nightstand, then pulled off my shirt and unhooked my bra. Both fell to the floor.

"Now, are you interested in *that* gun or in these six-shooters?" I asked pointing at my breasts.

He grinned and yanked me onto the bed. We hadn't talked much after that.

I pushed open the door to Carson's and breezed in. Phil Carson stood behind the counter.

"Ah, Miss Bryant, you're in bright and early this morning."

"I was hoping my bracelet was finished."

He smiled. "Had it done quickly. Not much of a problem. The catch was sprung, that's all. Let me go get it out of the safe."

I waited while he disappeared into the back of the store. He returned within a couple of minutes and laid the bracelet on a black velvet pad. The stones sparkled under the strong hi-intensity light above it.

"I cleaned it up for you. Would you care to try it on?"

I held out my wrist while he fastened it. A few quick shakes showed no signs of it coming undone.

"Wonderful. Thank you so much, Mr. Carson." I undid the catch and handed it back to him.

He placed it in a jeweler's box, and then in a plastic bag.

"Heard you had a spot of trouble the other day out your way?"

"Yes. Thank goodness the bracelet wasn't among the victims. It's one of the few things I have that belonged to my mother. The good stuff is still in Chicago."

"If I were you, I'd get this into a safety deposit box as soon as possible."

"I hadn't really thought about that."

He eyed me with a frown. "It's a good idea with something this valuable."

"Valuable?"

"Yes, I'd say its worth somewhere between five to six thousand dollars."

I gaped. He had to be kidding.

"What? You mean these stones are real?"

"Oh, yes—rubies and diamonds set in fourteen carat white gold." He shook his head. "Funny, I now remember that bracelet. Not sure if I sold it or just did some repairs. Ah, time. How it destroys the memory. Can't recall details from that long ago."

Oh my God, I'd had a valuable piece of jewelry tossed into a box in my vanity drawer for years and never suspected. I needed to get this over to the bank right away.

"Thank you, Mr. Carson. How much do I owe you?"

I paid up, stashed the bracelet in my purse, and headed for the bank immediately. I didn't breathe again until my newly rented safety deposit box with its solitary contents was secured in its cubbyhole.

I walked into the newspaper still mulling over the news. Josh poked his head out of his office door.

"Call Ruth Kendall."

"Yeah, in a minute," I mumbled.

"You okay?"

I told him about the bracelet.

"No kidding? And you never knew? Didn't your aunt give you a heads up on it?"

I sat down behind the desk slowly. "You know, I don't remember Aunt Dee even giving it to me. It just always seemed to be in my jewelry box. Could be she didn't know its value either. Maybe she assumed Daddy had given it to Mother and therefore, was costume jewelry. I'm still stunned he could afford anything like this. Or maybe Mother brought it with her from Chicago."

"Well, at least it's in a safe place. Want to read the editorial I wrote on your break-in? The burglary is getting front-page space. Sorry you won't be the headline. That's reserved for the city council's decision to sell off the land for a home improvement store."

Even though he said it with a straight face, I had to laugh.

"Aw, shucks, there goes my fifteen minutes of fame."

He grinned and ducked back into his office. I called Ruth Kendall.

"Callie, I know this is short notice, but would you like to come over for lunch today?"

"Sure. I can spare some time around noon."

She sighed as if holding a breath. "Oh, good. We can chat about your mother and Wellington. You know where I live?"

"I'll find it. See you at noon."

I hung up and stared at the wall opposite me. She wanted to talk about Mother and Wellington. Good. If she and Mother were such good friends, Ruth might know about her relationship with my father other than the supposed affair he was having.

The phone rang. I answered to find John Casey on the other end.

"Callie, Serena just told me about the burglary. I'm so sorry."

"Thank you. They didn't get much, but it's maddening all the same."

"Strangers in your house, touching your things. I understand. Jessica's parents in Des Moines were robbed several years ago. It took months for her mother to get over it." He cleared his throat. "Exactly what did they steal?"

"As I said, not much. Mostly just inexpensive jewelry. Some nicer pieces are gone, too, except for Mother's bracelet. That was being repaired at Carson's."

"Well, thank goodness you're all right. If there's anything I can do, don't hesitate to call."

I assured him I would, but didn't see how he'd be of any help.

The morning slipped by quickly. Josh gave me the directions to the Kendall house on the east edge of town. While driving, I tried to form questions to ask and comments I'd make.

This could be a very important lunch.

****

The Kendall home was a large rambling two and a half story Victorian set on a huge lot. The driveway looped around in a semi-circle. I pulled up in front of the porch steps and stared. Cream with white trim, black shutters, and a red door, it screamed, "I belong to the most important people in town."

I climbed the steps and rang the doorbell. A few seconds later, Ruth answered.

"Callie, please come in. I'm so glad you could make it on such short notice."

I entered a perfectly appointed foyer. To the left, rose a staircase and to the right, a large parlor loomed through an equally large archway. At the foot of the stairs, another smaller room housed a piano. From what I could see, most of the furnishings were in the style of the house and just as old. It reminded me of where I'd grown up in Chicago.

"Thank you so much for inviting me. What a lovely home."

Ruth smiled. "Thank you. It once belonged to Cyrus Wellington, the founder of the town and its first mayor. He also owned the bank at one time." As she talked she led me from the foyer down a hallway to a dining room. "Please have a seat. Lunch is ready. I like to keep things simple for lunch, so I hope lobster bisque with a shrimp salad is all right with you."

Was she kidding? Lobster bisque and shrimp salad as a luncheon menu in Wellington? Somehow, I just didn't see that being served at the Kozy Kafe.

"Sounds wonderful."

The dining table was set for two complete with water goblets and wine glasses. I sat gazing at the expanse of the remaining table that could seat at least twelve.

Ruth disappeared through a doorway and returned less than a minute later with two bowls of steaming soup. She placed them on the table, and then from a pitcher on the sideboard, filled the water glasses. She disappeared again and reentered with a wine bottle.

I was rather surprised she was doing this herself. I'd envisioned a maid or servant of some sort. But then, this was Wellington, not Cleveland or Chicago.

"Hope you like Chardonnay," she commented filling the wine glass, too. "I like a glass with lunch, don't you?"

"On special occasions." I sipped and nodded. "Very good."

Ruth took her seat. I spooned the bisque into my mouth. It was delicious.

"This is wonderful. Could I have the recipe?"

She laughed lightly. "I'll ask Mrs. McGreevy. She made it."

"You don't cook?"

"Oh, I've learned how to make some dishes over the years, but for special occasions, I call her in. She also comes and cleans the place once a week. The house is huge and I just don't have the time. I hope you got the mess from the break-in cleared up. I swear I can't think of who could do such a thing. I heard they got all your jewelry, the TV, and the silver."

"The TV and family silver are all right, but they did get the jewelry, except for Mother's bracelet."

"You mean that lovely thing you wore the other night? Why didn't they take that I wonder?"

"Because it wasn't there. I'd taken it in to Phil Carson to fix the clasp." I didn't enlighten her as to what Phil had told me or that it now sat in a safety deposit box at the bank.

"Well, thank goodness for that."

I ate for a few minutes before asking, "So, you were good friends with my mother?"

"Oh, yes, she often came here for lunch, especially during the school year when your brother was in school. She'd sometimes bring you with her, but I don't suppose you remember that."

I had no memory of lunching with Ruth Kendall and told her so.

"Oh, the housekeeper of the moment usually looked after you, so your mother could enjoy lunch uninterrupted."

"What was Mother like?" I inserted a wistful tone to my voice.

"She was warm, funny, and very out of place here in Wellington. I think that's why we hit it off so quickly. We were both city girls and not native-born Iowans. The other women in town resented our sophistication. Luckily, I had been here a few years and could show her the ropes. She eased into the Garden Club, and a couple of bridge clubs with no problem. We even organized a book group—you know, where you read a book, and then once a month, gather to discuss it."

"Yet she was unhappy."

Ruth sighed. "She just never quite fit in, and I can tell you, she really hated the farm. I know she refused to have anything to do with the chickens, the cow, and she loathed the hogs. She felt isolated out there, especially during the winter. To make ends meet, your father would sometimes take a couple of part time jobs in town or in Atwell. The only thing that kept her here was Eric. Grace hated the farm and Wellington, but loved him in her own way."

This was not what I had been led to believe. Aunt Dee had been emphatic that Mother had hated Daddy in the end.

Now was the time to probe. "Until she discovered he was having an affair."

Ruth rose, not answering, removed our empty soup bowls, and returned to the kitchen. She came back with two large plates of shrimp salad on a bed of mixed greens complimented with raspberry vinaigrette. She set the plate in front of me and resumed her seat.

"I hope you like this. Mrs. McGreevy does a wonderful job with seafood."

I forked a portion into my mouth. "It's delicious." If Ruth thought she was going to ignore my question, she had another think coming. "Do you know who he was supposed to be having the affair with?"

She sighed. "Why go over things that happened long ago? What possible good can it do?"

"Because, I think I need to know. Was Daddy in love with the other woman? Is that why he supposedly killed Mother? My memory of that night was almost obliterated—if there was anything to remember in the first place. And Aunt Dee never breathed a word about an affair to me. She didn't like Daddy, so I can't believe she wouldn't pass up an opportunity like that."

Ruth stared into her plate, then picked up the wine glass and sipped.

"Please help me out here, Ruth. I can't believe Daddy would have an affair. He adored Mother."

"He may have adored her, but you've heard of the saying, 'Happy wife, happy life.' Your mother was not happy, and when she wasn't happy, she could make life miserable for anyone around her. She loved him, but nagged a lot, and became suspicious of his absences from home."

"So he found solace with another woman. That's taking a chance in a small town. No one keeps a secret that explosive." I leaned forward. "Tell me, Ruth."

Ruth didn't sip her wine this time, but took a sizable swallow. "I don't know for sure. Your aunt told me about it the day of the funeral. She asked the same question, thinking that because Grace and I were so close, I'd know."

"And?" I prompted.

"Well, he and June Simpson were an item at one point in time. Some say she never got over him marrying first your brother's mother, and then Grace. Plus June flirted with him every chance she got. At first, I think it amused your mother. Then it became an irritant."

This fit in with what Lorna had told me.

"So, you think he finally succumbed to June's charms?"

She shrugged. "Maybe. I try to avoid June whenever possible. She's one jealous bitch. She hates me because I have better organizational skills and can handle the responsibilities of various clubs and committees."

"Who else?"

"You didn't hear this from me, but Lorna Bell was always sweet on your daddy. She'd sometimes stare at him with puppy dog eyes and never missed an opportunity to touch his shoulder or squeeze his arm while talking to him. And he often came into the store, ostensibly to see Rich or something. Who knows? Maybe he was seeing Lorna."

"With Rich there?"

"Richard Bell was a dolt and had lunch at the Kozy every day at noon sharp. If Eric was seeing Lorna, that would be the time to do it."

I finished my salad and the wine, and wondered if

anyone else loomed on the horizon. I didn't need to ask. Ruth supplied the name.

"And then, there was Clovis Fisher."

I almost choked on the last drops of Chardonnay sliding down my throat. "Clovis!"

"There were times when the lights were on at the beauty shop long after the closed sign went up in the window."

I was shocked, but dismissed Clovis immediately. If Daddy had an affair, it sure as hell wouldn't be with Clovis. Beside, I had the impression Clovis had never kept a secret in her life.

"And the list keeps on growing. This is surprising for such a small town."

"Small towns aren't much different from big cities. They contain people, and people are human." She finished her wine. "I guess, I should also mention Jessica Casey."

"John's wife?"

"They were going through a rough patch in their marriage about that time, and I think they separated for a short while. I'm not sure of the timing on this. It could have been before your mother died."

She rose and cleared off the plate, then returned with the wine bottle.

"More wine?"

I shook my head and glanced at my watch. I'd been here a little over an hour, but it felt like days.

"No thank you, Ruth, I have to be heading back to the newspaper. Mindy does more than Josh imagined."

She laughed. "Yes, I can believe that. We women always do more, don't we? And men just accept it. It would only be fair for them to have to walk in our shoes for a week. Maybe then, they'd appreciate us more."

She walked me to the door. "Thank you so much for coming, Callie. Perhaps you'd like to join my bridge club. I have two other women who are waiting to make up another table."

I didn't like bridge, but pretended interest. "That sounds lovely."

"Maybe I'll even get you to join one of the town committees."

"I'm not sure I'm ready for that," I replied with a laugh. "Thank you so much for having me. Next time I'll play hostess."

She waved good-bye from the doorway as I drove away.

On my way back to the office, I mulled over the conversation. I had four names of possible lovers for my father. I scratched Clovis off the list. According to both Lorna and Ruth, June Simpson topped the bill. Could Daddy, with an unhappy wife, have turned to his high school flame for comfort?

And what about Lorna? I'd already deduced most of what Ruth had told me. Could a sympathetic, touchy-feely woman he'd known all his life have seduced him into an affair?

Jessica Casey was the surprise. I remembered her veiled animosity at the party. If Ruth was right, and she and John were separated, could she have enticed Daddy into something just to get back at her husband? Had John known? Is that why he'd offered to defend Daddy? Had he deliberately lost the case?

Anger bubbled in my chest. *For your sake, Mr. Casey, I sure as shit hope not, because if I find out you did, there will be hell to pay.*

And there was always the possibility of a woman in Atwell capturing his interest. And any of them could write an anonymous letter or make a phone call.

As I walked into the newspaper, a sudden thought came to me. I was on a mission and suspicious of everyone. There was one name amongst Mother's friends that was missing—Ruth Kendall.

Nothing like the woman who has an affair with her best friend's husband.

I had opened the door to my past and discovered a nest of snakes. I hoped I didn't get bitten.

Chapter Fifteen

Tuesday was turning out to be one of those days. First of all, I was dressed and ready to head for the newspaper when I stopped to read my Facebook page. While doing that, I managed to dribble coffee down the front of my blouse, which required a quick run upstairs to change. Naturally, I couldn't find another that went with the pantsuit I wore. Cursing, I changed into a whole new outfit.

I blamed Josh for my predicament. He'd kept me up until after three in the morning. The great sex was worth it, but lack of sleep promised a sluggish day.

As I finally exited the house and into my car, rain splattered on the gravel driveway.

"Damn," I muttered, fishing around under the passenger seat for my umbrella.

"Damn, damn, damn," I said out loud to the rapidly increasing shower when I couldn't find it.

As I drove the two miles into town, the shower turned into a deluge. I had to park two blocks away from the newspaper office and wait until the rain lessened.

Fifteen minutes later, I shoved open the *News-Sentinel* door and walked in a good half an hour late.

Josh appeared in the doorway to his office. "Thank God you're here. The phone's been ringing off the hook. You look like you swam in this morning."

"Couldn't find the umbrella, couldn't find a place to park, and I hate sitting around in wet clothes."

I dumped my purse on the desk and tried to shake some of the moisture from my hair.

Josh chuckled and walked over to kiss me on the cheek.

"So you're a little damp. You won't melt, will you?"

"Apparently not, although I feel like the Wicked Witch of the West right now. Why are the phones ringing off the hook?"

"It's Tuesday. Advertisers are calling in last minute changes, customers are requesting extra copies delivered, and I'm having a problem with the layout."

I waved him back to his office. "Go do your thing. I'll take care of this."

My crummy mood vanished as the morning advanced and the rain disappeared. The phones weren't nearly as busy as Josh had made out and by noon had returned to normal.

The toast I'd had for breakfast didn't last long and my grumbling stomach suggested it was time to do something about it.

"Josh, I'm going to the Kozy. You coming?" I called out.

"No thanks. I've got a little more rearranging to do before sending the copy in. Bring me back some meatloaf, okay?"

"No problem."

I snatched my purse from under the desk and glanced out the window, glad to see the rain was still held in check. The phone rang before I made it to the front door.

Sighing, I turned to answer. "Good afternoon, *News Sentinel*, how may I help you?"

"Uh, is Josh available?" a male voice asked.

"He's busy at the moment. May I take a message?"

"This is Fred Carson, Phil Carson's son. It's really important I speak to him."

I put the caller on hold and called out, "Josh, Fred Carson's on the line. Says it's important."

"I'll take it. Go ahead and get your lunch."

I transferred the call and slipped out the door. The sidewalks were still damp from the morning rain and the gutters ran with the residue. The heavy overcast suggested Mother Nature wasn't done with us yet.

The Kozy was almost full. I chose a small table for two tucked away in the back corner. A chicken salad sandwich, potato chips, and iced tea sounded perfect—topped off, of course, by a slice of Miss Emma's apple pie. The latter was served by Miss Emma herself.

"Hello, Callie. Just wanted to say how much I enjoyed the party the other night."

I indicated the empty chair across from me. "Have a seat. Can you spare a few minutes to talk?"

"Don't mind if I take a load off."

She sat as I dug into what I knew would be the best apple pie I'd ever eaten.

Emma leaned her elbows on the table and cupped her chin in her hands, then smiled.

"So, I understand, you and Josh are becoming quite the item."

I almost choked. "Why do you say that?"

Her smile widened. "You were seen having dinner over in Larramore last week, Homer Whitson saw the two of you canoodling on the shore while he was out fishing on Miller's Lake last Saturday, and Josh's neighbor, Iola Swanson, says his car hasn't been parked in his driveway at night much the last week or so."

"Never underestimate the power of small town gossips," I murmured.

She laughed. "It's what keeps us going. I'm glad for Josh. Not much left to pick from here in Wellington."

I ate another bite of the delicious pie and sipped some of my iced tea through the straw. Miss Emma was here. I was here. Why not ask a few questions?

"Speaking of gossip, I understand my mother had to put up with her fair share of it."

"Everybody's interested in the newcomer. Human nature."

I fiddled with my fork, scraping some of the pie filling out of the crust.

"I also heard that Daddy might have been having an affair. Any idea who the lady was?"

Emma snorted. "Don't you believe everything you hear, Callie. Your daddy was a wonderful man, but your mother almost drove him crazy with her constant complaints. Nothing around here was good enough for her, especially once you came along. She wanted something more for her daughter."

"Something Wellington couldn't offer?"

"She never forgot she came from money and the big city. Never let the rest of us forget it, either."

Her tone suggested she hadn't liked Mother all that much. "What about Denny?"

"Your brother wasn't her child. All her affection went to you."

"You think she was going to leave Daddy?"

She shrugged. "Maybe. Don't know for sure. She didn't talk much about personal things."

"Not even to Ruth Kendall? They were good friends and Ruth said Mom loved Daddy in spite of being unhappy here."

"Ruth was the closest thing to sophistication available in Wellington, and I do know the four of them got together often."

Odd, I couldn't see Daddy having much in common with Bob Kendall.

"Toward the end, your mother withdrew. Oh, she went through the motions of smiling, saying hello, and such, but I could tell by the look in her eyes that she wasn't happy."

"Do you think Daddy suspected she might bolt and killed her? Was he having an affair because he was unhappy himself? I've heard all kinds of things—from him being a tomcat to being drunk when she died."

Emma leaned forward. "Callie, if your father was having an affair, I can't imagine who the woman might have been."

"I understand June Simpson and he were high school sweethearts."

"Honey, Eric Bryant liked a pretty face, that's for sure, and if Sally hadn't died, your mother would never have entered the picture. The honest truth is June Simpson never measured up to either Sally or Grace. And I don't believe for one moment your father killed anybody."

"So somebody got away with murder," I said staring her straight in the eyes.

"Sure seems that way." She glanced down at my plate and shoved her chair back. "Finish your pie,

Callie. I've got to get back to work."

I ordered Josh's meatloaf to go, and then did as she requested, mulling over her words.

Had Mother been ready to head back to Chicago? If so, Aunt Dee, even on her deathbed, had never mentioned the possibility—any more than she had mentioned a phone call about Daddy having an affair.

The waitress brought the bill and Josh's lunch. I paid and left. The more I heard, the less I liked my mother. She sounded like a spoiled, selfish, little rich girl. Funny. Growing up, I couldn't remember Aunt Dee ever saying much about her younger sister. Most of her venom had been directed toward Daddy. Until she lay dying, of course. Confession cleanses the soul or something like that. I wished I had asked Denny about his relationship with Mom. The thought had never occurred to me that the two of them might not have gotten along.

I sighed as I entered the office. This was turning out to be more complicated than I'd thought.

"Josh, I'm back." I walked back to his office and found him busily pounding away at the keyboard. I set the Styrofoam box on his desk. "Here's your lunch. Are you still at it? I thought you'd have that in by now."

"So did I, but I have to write a front page obituary."

"Obituary? Who died?"

He paused to shuffle through some papers next to the computer. "Phil Carson."

Surprise rolled through me. "Phil Carson! What happened? He was fine when I saw him yesterday."

Josh shook his head. "That phone call as you left was Phil's son, Fred. Seems Phil was the victim of a hit and run in Atwell last night."

My surprise deepened. "Oh no! Poor Phil. He was a nice guy. What kind of hit and run?"

"Pedestrian. Phil was leaving a friend's house after his usual Monday night poker game. As he was crossing the street to his car, someone hit him."

"Do the police have the driver in custody?"

He shook his head. "Not as far as I know. I left a message with the Atwell police for more details."

I walked back to my desk visualizing Phil Carson's face as he'd returned Mom's bracelet. He'd struck me as a genuinely nice person who enjoyed what he did. He'd spent a lifetime selling and repairing jewelry, some expensive, most not.

The door opened. I raised my head to see Mindy, complete with a stuffed diaper bag slung over her shoulder and clutching a baby carrier in her hand.

"Mindy! Good to see you. Is this the little fellow?"

She laughed and set the carrier on the desk. "Sure is."

The baby was adorable. His eyes were wide open as he tried to stuff his fist into his mouth.

"Oh, Mindy, he's so cute. You do good work."

"Thanks. We're kind of fond of him, too. And so far, he's been a perfect angel. Sleeps when he's supposed to and does all the rest on a regular basis—if you get what I mean."

I chuckled. "I do. Glad to see you're out and about already."

"I'm moving slow, but staying at home every day is driving me nuts. Where's Josh?"

"Right here," he said striding from his office. "Let's see this creation up close and personal. May I?"

To my astonishment, he unbuckled the safety belts and lifted the baby into his arms, cradling and rocking him.

"Isn't da baby da cootest in de whole, wide world," he cooed in baby talk.

I gaped as Mindy giggled before saying, "I wish I had this on tape."

"Oh, shut up. I happen to like babies. Totally innocent with no opinions or prejudices yet formed. Shame they have to grow up into adults."

"You handle him like a pro," I said in astonishment.

"I have three older sisters, all with kids of their own. Here, you hold him."

Before I could open my panic-stricken mouth, he thrust the baby into my arms.

"Oh my God, I've never held a baby before."

"Just support his neck in the crook of your elbow and keep your arm under him. See? Not so hard, is it. You look kinda natural."

I shot him a glance that clearly suggested he was a liar. Luckily, the latest addition to the Wellington population didn't cry or fuss, which would have totally sent me over the edge.

The phone rang and Josh leaned over my desk to answer. "*News-Sentinel*. Hendricks here… Oh, hi, Matt. Thanks for getting back to me. Let me get this in my office. Hang on." He transferred the call. "It's Matt Douglas over in Atwell about Phil. I'll be back in a couple of minutes."

Mindy took the baby and placed him in the carrier. "Matt Douglas? The Atwell chief of police?"

I nodded and told her about Phil Carson.

Her eyes went wide. "Oh no! How awful. He was just the sweetest man. Never had a bad thing to say about anybody. I hope they've caught the person who ran him down."

"I guess that's what Josh is finding out now."

"Don and I bought our wedding bands from him. He knew what we could afford and didn't try to press us into something more expensive. His wedding gift to us was a lovely pair of silver candlesticks."

"Oh! Gifts! That reminds me, I have some gifts for the baby still in my trunk. Can you hold down the fort while I run and get them?"

"Sure."

I left and hurried the two blocks to my car, retrieved the package, and trotted back. As I reentered the office, Josh was done with his call and tickling the baby under the chin with his finger.

I handed the shopping bag to Mindy, who immediately opened the goodies, ooh-ing and aah-ing over each item before thanking me profusely.

"My pleasure. I had fun shopping for him." I turned to Josh. "What did the police have to say?"

"No witnesses to the actual hit. A couple around the corner walking a dog saw a dark car speed past with its lights off and disappear. That's about it. Driver was probably drunk. The poker game had ended and Phil was one of the last to leave. Damned shame."

"He's going to be missed, that's for sure," Mindy said.

"I take it he was a long-time resident," I asked.

"Lived here all his life. Inherited the store from his father. Also sat on the city council for a few years. The last time I talked to him, he was looking forward to retiring. He was proud that Fred was going to be the third generation to sell jewelry in Wellington. A damned shame," he repeated. He paused and looked at me. "Uh, Callie, while you were gone, Mindy and I talked. I don't know how to tell you this, but you're fired."

"What?"

Mindy laughed. "I wouldn't put it that way, but I meant it when I said I was going nuts at home. Babysitting duties can be divided between the more than willing grandmothers, and if I have to, I can bring Mikey here for a day." She stared. "You don't mind being jobless, do you?"

"Of course not. I just filled in for a while, although what I'll do with all the spare time I'll have is a question mark."

Mindy exhaled as though holding her breath. "I'm sure you did a wonderful job."

"Better than your boss," I murmured tossing Josh a glance.

"Hey, I was doing just fine."

"Yeah, I'll just bet," she said with a laugh and hefting the carrier. "I'll see you tomorrow morning, Josh." She left with a wave.

"So, now that I'm on the unemployment line, I guess I have more time to devote to other things. Are you coming over for dinner tonight?"

He shook his head. "Can't tonight. I have to cover a debate for an Atwell city council seat. Will you be all right on your own?"

"Of course. You know that according to Miss Emma, we are the latest in the gossip pipeline, don't you?"

"We are?"

"Seems we've been seen together a lot lately. Some fisherman saw us—what was the word Emma used—oh, yes, canoodling out at the lake on Saturday, and one of your neighbors made mention that your car is not often in the driveway overnight anymore."

He laughed. "Small towns, you gotta love 'em. Now, I have to finish that obit and send in the new layout. Why don't you finish up the filing and head home?" He kissed me hard on the lips. "I'll call you tomorrow."

I picked up some papers to file and sighed. I'd gotten used to working here. Of course, now I could concentrate on clearing Daddy's name.

An hour later, I finished for the day and headed back to my car. Across the street, the Bell's storefront awning dripped from a recent shower. On impulse, I crossed and entered the shop. Lorna stood at the counter, a batch of papers in front of her. She looked up and smiled.

"Hello, Callie."

"Hi, Lorna. I know I'm a day early, but if you're free, I was wondering if I could buy you dinner tonight, and afterward maybe show you how to deal with the computer."

"Oh, I'd love that, but could I take a rain check? I've got a garden club meeting tonight. We're planning for our annual "Garden of the Year" awards in August. Maybe tomorrow night? I'd like to talk to you about something important, too."

"Important?"

She shook her head, her forehead furrowing as if working on a problem. "I haven't got time to go into it right now. Could it wait another day? I need to check a couple of things first."

"Tomorrow night is fine. That's what we originally had planned. I might not be able to do dinner, but I could stop by after hours. What time do you close?"

"Five."

"No problem. It shouldn't take too long to show you the ropes."

She rolled her eyes. "You don't know me. Can't teach an old dog new tricks."

I laughed. "Don't sell yourself short. Sometimes the so-called old dogs learn faster than we think. See you tomorrow."

The rain caught up with me again on the short drive home. I dodged the drops as they rapidly grew in both size and intensity. The temperature had dropped and the evening promised to be one of those cold, wet affairs that sometime occur in springtime Iowa.

It was chilly, but not enough to warrant turning on the heat, so I changed into a pair of jeans, a lightweight sweater, and thick socks. I also decided dinner would be soup and a salad.

After eating and cleaning up, I stood in the kitchen already bored without Josh around. Neither TV nor reading appealed tonight. I wandered down the hallway to Daddy's office. Maybe now would be a good time to go through the drawers and cubbyholes.

The rain drummed against the window as I eased into the old swivel chair and ran my fingers over the bumpy grooves of the closed roll top. Memories rushed through my mind so fast I could barely grasp the images. Daddy writing in an old-fashioned ledger book. Me on his lap pretending to help. Him on the phone talking to various people about seed, hogs, cattle, and prices. I also remember him and Mother arguing about money.

I pushed that last thought away and opened the desktop. Two hours later, I had several piles of twenty-five year old receipts, paid bills, and assorted letters. I even found that last ledger, the final notation jotted down the day before the murder, and made a mental note to drop by John Casey's office tomorrow and find out about the tax situation. Aunt Dee had never mentioned any of it nor did I find correspondence to clarify things after her death.

Finished with this task, I closed the office door and stood in the hall, unsure of what to do next. A trip to the attic? Those Hummel figurines had to be someplace. Besides, what else did I have to do?

I grabbed a large flashlight from the work area on the back porch, and made my way upstairs. The attic door and steps were between my and Denny's old rooms. The hinges protested with a loud screech when I opened it. I flipped on the switch at the foot of the stairs. Dim light glowed from above. I turned on the flashlight anyway and climbed.

The space wasn't as disorganized as I'd feared, but it was stuffed full of boxes. Luckily, they were neatly lined up against the walls under the sloping roof. The rain hammered just a few feet above my head.

The beam caught something near the tiny window to my left. Tears welled as nostalgia clogged my throat. I walked over and stroked the heavy string mane of a rocking horse. I also spied my old dollhouse, a Christmas gift when I was maybe five or six. I could still remember the awe as I'd stared at it that morning so long ago.

Later, I'll go through all of this later.

Heaving a sigh, I turned and walked over to the first box under the eaves. All were clearly marked as to the contents. I pulled the sealing tape off one marked "dining room dishes," opened it, and unwrapped a teacup. I remembered it as being the pattern of the china in the hutch. Several other boxes held more of the same. Another box with the words "silver" sat next to it. Inside, I discovered a beautiful tea service and my great-great grandmother's sterling silver, the felt lined wooden box still protecting the five piece settings for twelve after all these years. The silverware alone had to be worth ten or twelve thousand dollars.

I moved those boxes to the top of the steps. The sooner I got them into the hutch, the better.

The next box was labeled "china figurines." I dug through several inches of old wadded up newspaper before finding a small figurine. I shined the light on it and saw a Hummel. Mother's collection had been extensive. She'd kept them in the large curio cabinet in the bedroom.

As a child they had been forbidden territory, locked up and the keys stored on top out of the reach of tiny, fascinated fingers.

Lightning flashed followed a few seconds later by the rumble of thunder.

I shook my head and returned to my task. An hour later I'd opened most of the boxes. Denny's sports trophies, more Hummels, and books—lots and lots of books—were all that remained of my parents. I'd haul them down tomorrow morning to see which I'd keep and what could be tossed.

Back downstairs, I washed the dust from my hands and poured a glass of wine. I sat in my corner of the sectional and stared at the blank TV.

Boxes. That was it. Eight years of marriage condensed to cardboard containers. I wondered who had packed everything. Certainly not Aunt Dee. She would have hired someone. And why didn't she ever send for any of it? The dollhouse would have been a nice touch, helping to ease the pain of missing my parents and being uprooted from all that was familiar.

And does it really matter now?

I shook my head and took another sip of wine. Yes, it did matter, but getting nostalgic and morose wouldn't change anything. "Remember the past, but don't dwell on it, Callie," my psychiatrist had said. "Move on." Of course, Dr. Halloran was also the one who told me not to force forgotten memories to return.

"Yeah, a lot he knows," I muttered. Right now, I needed those memories.

To get my mind off my problems, I turned on the TV. Fifteen minutes later, I turned it off again and eyeballed my reading device sitting on the coffee table. No. Tonight, nothing appealed.

I drained my wine in several continuous swallows, then set the glass on the coffee table and rose. Off to the east, lightning still flashed and thunder occasionally rumbled, but the rain here had stopped.

Time to call it a night.

I turned off the light. Outside, a car slowly drove past. I held my breath, half expecting another gunshot. The driver moved on. I breathed again, but just barely. Was I being watched? And had the watcher noticed the absence of Josh's car in the drive?

I climbed the stairs and stared out the bedroom window into the darkness for several minutes. All was quiet. I wished Josh was here. My hand hovered over my phone. *No, you can do this. Do not let this person win again.*

Much later I awoke to the fading moan of a train whistle.

Chapter Sixteen

I slept in, not cracking an eyelid until close to nine o'clock. I'd had a restless night waking up every hour or so to get up and look out the window. Deep sleep hadn't claimed me until after four.

The gloomy weather still hung around, and low overcast skies suggested the rain would continue. I dressed in jeans and a long sleeve t-shirt, then made my way downstairs. Breakfast sounded like a good idea.

I left the bacon sizzling in the pan while I went outside to collect the Atwell newspaper. I'd subscribed yesterday after hearing about Phil. I had to admit that one thing I did miss from Chicago was the *Tribune* being delivered daily.

Back inside, I flipped on the radio and listened to farm reports, sports, weather, and the world news. I set a large plate of bacon, eggs, hash browns, and toast on the table, poured a cup of coffee, then opened the paper.

Phil Carson's obituary was the headline, complete with a photo of him obviously taken several years ago. I read it along with the sketchy information Josh had also obtained from the Atwell police. I shook my head as I ate.

Phil's death was so senseless. A driver, too drunk to remember to turn on his headlights, had mowed down a pedestrian and kept on going. It was only a matter of time before the police caught up with the guy.

The car must have sustained considerable front-end damage. I stopped eating and sat back.

I assumed Phil had been in a residential neighborhood. Had the driver been to a nearby bar? And if so, how far away had it been? Didn't anybody see this clown weaving or speeding down the streets before he hit an innocent bystander?

The phone rang, almost scaring me to death. Other than the harassing phone calls, I don't think anybody had called me on it since I'd moved in. I scrambled from my chair to answer. Would I hear a breathy whisper?

"Hello?"

"Callie, this is Gina."

I breathed a sigh of relief. My childhood friend was making good on her promise to call.

"Sorry to bother you so early, but I had the time and thought I'd call."

"Gina, how good to hear your voice, and it's not early at all."

"Ah well, I wasn't sure how citified you'd become. For all I know you sleep 'til noon every day."

"I did a bit this morning. Must be the rain, but my country roots are taking hold again. I was hoping we could get together for lunch or something."

She laughed. "Great minds think alike. That's why I'm calling. Would you like to come over tomorrow? It wouldn't be anything fancy, just soup and a sandwich or salad."

After a steady diet of the Kozy and Ruth's rather opulent meal the other day, soup and sandwiches with my former best friend sounded like a reprieve from the calorie witches determined to plant pounds on my hips.

"Gina, I'd love it. What time?"

"Noon all right with you?"

I assured her noon was fine and hung up. The two of us back together after so many years. I looked forward to this lunch.

I finished my cooling breakfast and the paper at the same time. As I washed the dishes, rain pattered against the window guaranteeing a day indoors. With that task done, I poured another cup of coffee and tried to find something to do. The past week of working for Josh had been fun. Now at loose ends, I realized I was bored—so bored I spent the rest of the morning cleaning a relatively clean house.

Josh called at noon. "How did your night go? Is everything all right?"

I didn't mention the slow moving car or my fears. Besides, I had no proof it was anything other than a slow moving car.

"Everything's fine. You checking up on me?"

"I just had to call my former receptionist and invite her to dinner tonight."

I laughed. "I accept although I'm supposed to meet with Lorna at five to help her learn a few computer ropes."

"That could take a lifetime."

"I'll just give her the basics of attachments, downloading, uploading, how to do photos and such. I may even set Bell's up with a Facebook page, and point her in the right direction for a website builder. It shouldn't take too long. How was your day?"

"Long," he grumbled.

"Aw, poor baby. I'm looking forward to my fifteen minutes of fame article along with the editorial. Also, the obituary on Phil Carson. The Atwell paper today had a good one."

"The Atwell paper? Are you flirting with the competition?"

I chuckled. "Only for the daily news. Have you heard any more from the Atwell police?"

"Talked to them a little while ago. They haven't found the car yet."

"You'd think somebody would notice a car weaving or something. If nothing else, a speeding car makes noise."

"Funny you should mention it. Apparently, the couple with the dog said they heard nothing like that. All was quiet, then a sudden engine noise, a squeal of tires like a car taking a turn too fast, and bam—impact. It blew a stop sign at the corner and raced away."

"How odd."

"The couple also had the impression it was some type of luxury car, not the usual sedan."

"Maybe the person doesn't live in Atwell. Could have been from someplace like Center City or Sioux Falls. That would explain why they can't find the car. It's probably in somebody's garage."

"With the owner wondering how and when it got damaged," he said in a disgusted tone. "If he takes it to a repair shop, someone might notify the cops."

"Did the police tell you all this?"

"Some. I talked to Fred Carson this morning. By the way, the funeral's been set for two o'clock Friday at Gearhart's Funeral Home."

Gearhart's. Mother's had been there. I vaguely remembered sitting between Aunt Dee and Daddy staring at the casket, not completely understanding the circumstances. Oddly enough, I didn't recall Denny although he must have been present.

Nearby in the background a baby cried. "Ah, it sounds like Mindy brought Mikey this morning."

Josh chuckled. "She's out to lunch and I agreed to keep an eye on him. Looks like naptime is over. Hope she gets back soon to feed the little bugger. Come to the office when you're done with Lorna. We'll go someplace fun."

"In Wellington?"

The baby's cries escalated into screams. "Yes, in Wellington," Josh said raising his voice. "I gotta go. See you later."

I laughed hard when he hung up. Josh and a baby. Strange, but after his handling of Mikey yesterday the image wasn't unbelievable. I'd bet he changed a mean diaper, and could probably deal with a bottle— assuming Mindy wasn't breast-feeding. He was out of luck there.

****

The rain had been on again, off again all day. At the moment it was off, but low-scudding clouds still swept the sky. After talking to Josh earlier, I decided it was time for another chat with John Casey. This time I made an appointment. I slid into a parking spot just down the street from his office. The dashboard clock read two-fifty. I was ten minutes early. No matter. Maybe his receptionist, Serena, would be in a talkative mood.

She looked up as I entered. Her expression changed from welcoming smile to that deer in the headlights look.

"Good afternoon, Serena, how are you today?"

"Uh, good afternoon, Ms. Bryant. I'm fine, thanks."

"Ms. Bryant? That's awfully formal."

"Just being professional. If you'll have a seat, I let Mr. Casey know you're here."

She gestured toward the waiting area, lifted the phone receiver, and announced my presence to her boss. Her attention was immediately claimed by her computer. She was definitely not talkative. I'm sure John had instructed her to keep her mouth shut around me.

John emerged from his office with a tight smile on his face.

"Callie, please come in."

He stepped back and I entered. He followed, closing the door behind him.

"Have a seat. What can I do for you?"

I sat and crossed my legs. "I was going through my father's desk yesterday and came across some twenty-five-year-old receipts and such. I wondered about the taxes on the farm. Who pays them? I assume someone is filing. I don't want a visit from the IRS."

He smiled. "Not to worry. Your aunt left the running of the estate in my hands. I contacted a CPA in Atwell who does all the tax work. The acreage is leased to area farmers. Do you want to continue with this arrangement?"

"Yes. I believe Aunt Dee had everything set up in a trust for Denny and me. I got regular payments."

"That she did. With your brother's death, the entire estate came to you. It's a revocable trust. Do you wish to continue it that way with me as executor?"

I didn't one hundred percent trust John Casey. My

suspicions regarding his handling of Daddy's defense still needed answers, but he was the only game in town unless I wanted to shift matters to an attorney in Atwell.

"Yes, of course. You're familiar with the set-up and I have no complaints with how things have been done." I paused and smoothed my hand down my pant leg. "You know, I was kind of surprised to find all those things in Daddy's desk. The rest of the house had been packed away. I found a bunch of boxes in the attic."

"At your aunt's request, I called in a moving company from Atwell to pack things up right after you all left for Chicago. I knew I'd need the information in the desk and told them to leave it."

"I see. Well, everything seems to have been packed away quite well."

"Ruth Kendall supervised the actual packing. I believe Jessica also helped. Both were determined nothing went missing. At that time, we weren't sure when or if you would return. If things needed to be shipped to Chicago, then the work would be done."

"I wonder why Aunt Dee never had any of it shipped."

He shrugged. "She never said. I guess by the time she adjusted to two children in the house, she forgot. Besides, she had the money to buy you anything you wanted."

"But not needed," I said with a sigh thinking of the dollhouse.

He glanced at his watch. "Is there anything else I can help you with?"

"Actually, yes there is. What became of the witnesses for the defense in Daddy's trial? I'd like to talk to them."

He shifted in his chair and frowned. "I'm not really sure. It's been a long time. A couple have died and others have moved on. I doubt if they could supply any new information at this late date anyway."

He looked more pointedly at his watch this time. As if on cue, his phone rang. He snatched up the receiver like a drowning man would a life preserver.

"Yes, Serena. Please tell him to hold. I'll be right with him." He stared at me with a smile. "Sorry, Callie, I've got a client with a problem."

I got the hint and rose. He wasn't going to cooperate with me at all. I was on my own.

"Thanks for your time, John."

I swept out of the office closing the door behind me. Serena refused to make eye contact preferring to fiddle with some papers on her desk. I decided to be friendly.

"So nice to see you again, Serena. Maybe we can finally have that lunch next week."

A quick glance at her phone showed no lines lit. The phone call was a sham, just as I suspected.

Serena's eyes glazed as she fumbled for an answer. "Oh, well, gosh, let me see, I'm not sure of my schedule. Can I give you a call?"

"Sure, you do that. Be seeing you soon."

I walked out slightly pissed off that the eager, friendly woman of a couple of weeks ago was now avoiding me. I blamed Casey for that. He'd probably threatened her with dismissal if she talked to me.

"Bastard," I muttered under my breath as I stood on the sidewalk. He wouldn't be getting my vote come election time.

It was too early to see Lorna and while the thought of passing the time with Josh was pleasant, I feared my presence might make Mindy uncomfortable. I strolled down the street window shopping until a light drizzle forced me into the Kozy. Bob Kendall was leaving as I entered.

"Hello, Callie. What brings you out on this rainy day?"

"Oh, I needed to discuss some tax issues with John."

"I see. Does that mean you're staying?"

I wanted to heave an exaggerated sigh, but refrained. "Yes, Bob, I'm staying. In fact, I spent part of last night in the attic opening boxes that haven't seen the light of day in a quarter of a century. John said Ruth and Jessica helped pack things away. Must have been a tough job."

He shrugged. "I don't remember offhand, but given how close Ruth was to Grace, it must have been hard. What did you find in the attic?"

"China, my great-great grandmother's silver, a few collectables, Denny's sports trophies, and some old toys. A lot of the boxes are loaded with books. Eventually, I'll get things sorted out."

"Well, if you do decide to go home, let me know."

How could the man be so persistent in the face of my repeated statements that I was here to stay? Persistence served him well as a realtor, but his constant prodding chipped away at my patience—not that I had that much to begin with. I also decided that if *he* ran for mayor, my vote would go to the other guy even if his name were Donald Duck.

"This is my home, Bob." I spied Mrs. Comstock at

a table for two. She waved and motioned me to come over. I waved back. "Nice to see you. Give my best to Ruth."

I walked away toward my grandmother's friend.

"Have a seat, Callie."

I pulled out the chair and eyed the half-eaten slice of cherry pie and coffee.

"That looks good."

"I try to indulge my addiction to Emma's pies several times a week."

At this hour the Kozy wasn't busy. A waitress sidled up immediately. I ordered the same as Mrs. Comstock.

"You chose a gloomy day to come to town," she said, sipping her coffee.

I explained about Lorna.

She chuckled. "Good luck with that."

"I think you said you were a teacher?"

"High school English and literature for over fifty years. Guess I must have tried to cram gerunds, pronouns, and sentence structure, not to mention Shakespeare and other classics into the heads of most of this town." She may have spoken in a jesting tone, but pride glowed in her eyes.

I laughed. "You said at the party that Daddy was a good student. I can believe that. I remember we always had books around and him reading them."

The waitress brought my pie and coffee. When she left I leaned forward.

"So, tell me about other people. What were they like in high school?"

She forked another bite of pie into her mouth. "Well, Sally Renfro, your brother's mother was a fairly good student. I can remember the day after class when she and June Simpson got into it. June and your daddy were an item and when Sally moved here, she stole him away. Ah, teenage angst. Nothing like it to liven up a day. I had to separate them."

"You mean it got physical?" I cut off a bite with my fork and popped it into my mouth. Best damn cherry pie I'd ever eaten.

"June shoved her a couple of times, and Sally was ready to deck her when I got between them. Told them to take their arguments off school property."

"Wow. I guess Sally won since she married Daddy."

"Now, John Casey was one of those serious types who may not have liked his assignments, but did them anyway. Bob Kendall never turned in a term paper or book report on time. Always had an excuse. And when he did turn them in, I could tell he'd had someone else write them."

I had to laugh. Bob Kendall cheating didn't surprise me. "What about Lorna?"

"Poor girl never had an ounce of sense. She mooned over boys constantly, and every time she chose a book for a report, it was always some sappy romance. I can still recall her anguish over the fates of Cathy and Heathcliff in *Wuthering Heights*. Never liked that story myself."

"I heard she was sweet on Daddy, too."

"She was sweet on just about every boy in town at one time or another. Don't know why she settled on Rich Bell. He came close to being the most boring man on the face of the earth. I'm surprised the store is still open. Rich took care of the business end of things while

Lorna just hung around talking to customers. Called it customer relations or some such nonsense."

I let Mrs. Comstock ramble on as I finished the pie and coffee. She gave me the lowdown on people I didn't know, but I let her talk. I figured that if Lorna was a clueless, out of touch businesswoman, my computer teaching would be in vain. Lorna would maybe learn a few things, but most would be forgotten the minute I walked out the door. I agreed with Mrs. Comstock. Bell's probably wouldn't be in business much longer unless its owner came into the twenty-first century.

"Well, dear, I've chewed your ear off long enough. Rain's stopped. Time for me to head home. Good luck with Lorna. See you soon."

She gathered up her purse along with an umbrella and ambled up to the cash register to pay. The waitress stopped by asking if I wanted a refill on my coffee. I declined, paid, and also left.

With half an hour until my meeting with Lorna, I changed my mind and decided to stop by the newspaper. As I turned the corner, I almost collided with June Simpson.

"Oh, June, I'm so sorry."

She glanced up at me with a frown. "Hello, Callie. Sorry, I can't stop to chat right now."

Her abrupt tone surprised me. "That's all right. Maybe we can get together for lunch one day next week."

"Why? So you can pump me for information about your parents?"

My surprise deepened at her aggressive tone. "Pump you?"

"That party last week was a ruse to get us to open up. I've heard you've been talking to damn near everybody in town about your mother's death. Well, I have nothing to say about it. Now, if you'll excuse me, I have to see someone."

I stood gaping as she strode down the street. I wondered if what she'd heard had also included some not so flattering references to her, Sally, and my mother. With a shrug, I walked on down to the paper, pushed open the door, and entered. The bell above the door tinkled to alert Josh. Mindy's empty desk suggested she'd called it a day.

Josh came out of his office. "Hello, gorgeous. How was your day?"

I strolled over to him and planted a kiss on his lips. "Until now, boring. How was Mindy's first day back?"

"She packed it in at three. I think today was more tiring than she was willing to admit."

"So, what's this fun time we're going to have tonight?"

"I was going to suggest the Pizza Palace followed by a round of miniature golf, providing the rain holds off."

"Hmm, I guess that is a fun time in Wellington. Maybe we should bring the pizza home, open a bottle of Chianti, and watch TV or something."

He raised an eyebrow. "Or something?"

"I'm sure we can figure it out."

He leaned down and kissed me hard. The faint, clean scent of his morning aftershave still lingered enough to smell good. His lips ignited a tiny flame in the pit of my stomach. Maybe I could put Lorna off for another day.

Before the kiss escalated into something a lot more interesting, the phone rang.

He stepped back. "Damn."

I laughed as he answered.

"News-Sentinel. Oh, hi, Fred. Any more information on your dad?"

My ears perked up at the question.

"Yeah? No kidding, I was wondering about that." Josh paused to listen for several seconds. "Well, I'll do what I can, of course, but I'm not sure the Atwell police will be too thrilled… Uh-huh, what time? I guess I can make it. Just keep in mind that the car may not be taken in for repairs right away and even if it is, whoever fixes the damage might not report it, especially if it's in a town fifty or more miles away… Okay. I'll do my best. See you on Monday." He hung up with a frown.

"I take it that was about poor Phil."

He nodded. "Fred confirmed something I wondered about. The house Phil was at is in a residential neighborhood. Stores and any bars are at least ten blocks away."

So our minds had thought alike on this. "Does that mean the driver was lost or just too drunk to find the right street?"

"I'm not sure. He wants me to investigate and bug the cops for information. With no sign of the car, he's afraid they'll give up on it too soon. He also wants to meet with me on Monday night for an update. I'm just not sure I'll have anything to tell him."

"Sounds like he's mad."

"Furious, and with little confidence in the police."

I glanced at the clock on the wall. "I'd better go on over to Bell's. The sooner I get his over with, the sooner I can eat, drink, and be merry."

Josh grinned. "I'll phone in the order with a pick up time of say an hour or so from now, lock up here, and then meet you at Bell's. Maybe between the two of us, we can speed up Lorna's education."

I left, turned the corner, and sauntered down the street toward the green and white awning outside the furniture store while mapping strategy in my head. If Lorna wrote down all my instructions, she shouldn't have too hard a time remembering it all. The navigation would confuse her at first, but eventually, she'd learn. Everybody did.

The storefront was dark, the 'closed' sign in place. I knocked and waited, then knocked again when Lorna didn't appear. Finally, I pushed the latch. The door opened. A glowing light emanated from a room off a hallway in the back, the feeble beam causing the merchandise take on strange shapes and casting odd shadows.

"Lorna, I'm here," I called making my way past the clutter of end tables and chairs.

When she didn't answer, I called again in a louder voice, "Lorna? Are you here?"

A chill of uneasiness made me shudder. I followed the hallway, found the back room, and paused in the doorway.

Lorna was sound asleep, her head planted on the desk with her right arm and hand inches from the phone. I wanted to laugh—until I saw the bright red stain under her head.

Chapter Seventeen

Blood slid down the walls behind the desk in gooey streams. A chunk of clotted brain matter detached and fell to the floor with a splat.

My hand clapped over my mouth to stifle a scream. The pie I'd just eaten rose in my throat. My heart pounded so hard it damn near burst from my chest. Swallowing, I backed up until I could go no further, the wall stopping my shaky retreat.

I stared at Lorna's body, but didn't see it. Instead, my vision went dark, and then exploded in flashing red and white lights. I saw a body on the foyer floor, heard voices, and someone sobbing. As quickly as they came, the nightmare images dissipated.

Now, I did scream—if the breathless, gasping sound gurgling from my throat could be called a scream. I whirled and ran down the hall. I had to get out of here. Did the killer hide in the shadows? Fear wiped out all rational thought. I tripped over something and fell hard to my knees, then picked myself up and ran again. The clutter of furniture and shadows in the store became an obstacle course to prevent my escape. I ran into a table, and then a chair, overturning it in the process. Something crashed to the floor, shattering. Escape was the only thing on my mind.

The bell above the door tinkled. I looked up. A man was silhouetted in the entryway. This time my scream was the real thing.

"Callie, relax. It's me."

Josh's voice barely registered in my panic-stricken brain. I could do no more than scream again.

"What's wrong?" He strode into the room and pulled me into his arms. "What's going on? Where's Lorna?"

Finally, I found my voice. "In there," I said with a gasp, pointing toward the back of the store.

He released me and ran down the hallway, then returned immediately. He lowered me into a nearby chair.

"Sit. Breathe deep." He whipped out his cell and called the cops.

I obeyed his instructions. Now that Josh was here, I was better able to cope.

He ended the call and cursed, then walked quickly to the front of the store where he flipped on the lights. The clutter became furniture arrangements. The menacing shadows receded. A shattered vase lay on the floor near an overturned table.

"Oh, my God," I whimpered.

"Looks like she was shot. Are you all right?"

"No, I'm not all right! I just found a body! Who the hell is all right after finding a body?" Daddy's face floated before my eyes.

Sirens screamed down the street and two Wellington police cars screeched to a halt outside. A few seconds later, Chief Bill Jackson and Officer Young entered, guns drawn.

"Nobody move," Jackson ordered.

"Oh for Pete's sake, Bill, put the gun away. It's a little late for that. In the back room. It's Lorna Bell."

Both officers hurried to the back. Outside, curious citizens stood on the sidewalk whispering and pointing.

Within a minute, the men returned, the chief with his phone against his ear. Young exited and made his way to one of the cars where he removed a roll of yellow crime scene tape. He waved the crowd back proceeding to string the tape between the light posts and the awning supports for the store.

Bill Jackson finished his call and turned to us. "Okay, what happened?"

"I…I had an appointment with Lorna at five o'clock. I was supposed to teach her some computer skills."

I was amazed. My voice sounded reasonably steady as I told him about finding Lorna.

"Did you see anyone leaving the store or a stranger hanging around?" he asked.

"Chief, just about everyone in Wellington is a stranger to me, but no, I saw nothing like that. Was she shot?"

He nodded. "Won't have the full story until the forensic team from Atwell gets here, but it looks like whoever shot her stood just inside the doorway. Nailed her in the forehead."

I remembered the position of her hand and arm and related it.

"She must have looked up, seen her assailant, and tried to call for help," Josh said. "I wonder why no one heard the shot."

"There's a pillow on the hall floor—you know, kinda like those things women put on couches. Killer must have used it to muffle the shot, plus there's fluff from the stuffing all over the office floor."

I'd been too panicked to notice any pillow stuffing, but *did* remember tripping over something as I ran. My fingers touched my knees and I winced at the little dart of pain.

"So, you think the killer thought the place was closed for the night, and when he found Lorna panicked and shot her?" Josh continued.

"I don't know what to think yet, Josh, and this is an official police investigation, so I'd appreciate it if you didn't print anything."

"And I'm a reporter with a duty to the public to give them as much information as possible. For all any of us know, this is just part of the recent crime spree in town."

"Crime spree?" the chief sputtered.

"Yeah, crime spree. Or are you forgetting the window shot out at Callie's last Wednesday night or that her home was burglarized on Saturday? My God, what if she'd been home? Would the burglar have shot her, too?"

I shuddered, not wanting to think about that.

"And why are you here?" Jackson asked in a cold tone.

"I was going to assist Callie in helping Lorna. I stopped to close up the office while she went ahead."

The two men glared at each other until the chief finally turned to me.

"Is there anything you can add, Ms. Bryant?"

"No, not that I can think of at the moment. The place was dark, the 'closed' sign was displayed, but the door was unlocked. Since she expected me, I thought Lorna had done it deliberately. I guess that's how the killer left—right out the front door. It was starting to drizzle again. I guess any passersby were in a hurry and didn't notice."

"There's a back door at the end of the hallway," he said. "That's how merchandise was delivered. My guess is the killer came in and left the same way."

"Was that door locked?" Josh asked.

The chief ignored him, but continued to stare at me. "Is there anything else you can tell me?"

I shook my head.

"In that case, why don't you come into the station tomorrow morning around nine—both of you? You can make formal statements then. Take the night to sleep on it. You might remember more."

An ambulance pulled up out front. The crowd had not gotten any smaller. The EMTs entered followed by a short, rotund man in slacks and a golf shirt.

"Hi, doc," Jackson said to the newcomer with a nod. "She's in the back room."

"Who's that?" I whispered to Josh.

"Doctor Craig. He lives on the west edge of town."

"Bet this is a first for him."

Even as I spoke, a memory of a kindly older man dispensing lollipops to me after booster shots surfaced. No name came to mind, but the image was clear.

The chief turned back to me. "Now, Ms. Bryant, do you remember hearing anything unusual after you entered the store?"

I sighed. God, I was tired. All I wanted was a good stiff drink and Josh.

"No, chief, I heard nothing. It was quiet as a tomb." I shivered at my choice of words. "Can I go home now?"

The chief closed the notebook he'd been writing in

and nodded. "Yes, go on home. Just don't forget to come in tomorrow."

Josh spoke up as he turned to leave. "By the way, chief, I believe both Callie and I requested the police reports on her mother's death. So far, neither of us has seen them."

Jackson turned back with a scowl. "This is an open investigation. I have a murder on my hands. I don't have time to sort through old reports of closed cases."

"That was a murder, too."

"The killer was arrested and put in jail."

"No," I said. "My father was arrested and sent to prison where he died an innocent man."

"I am not going to go over this with you now," he said, his voice rising. "Now, get out of here—both of you."

Josh helped me from the chair. "Chief, I'm sure someone in your office can find those reports. If I don't have them by the close of business tomorrow, I'll be in Atwell Friday morning getting a court order."

The chief didn't answer and we left. Ducking under the yellow tape, the crowd parted like the Red Sea. No one spoke. The silence was almost as scary as the scene in the back room.

"Can you drive?" Josh asked as we hurried down the sidewalk.

"Yeah, I'm fine. I need a good stiff drink."

"Oh crap, I forgot all about the pizza." He glanced at his watch. "Should have picked it up half an hour ago. Are you hungry?"

"Oddly enough, I am. Why don't you go get it? We can reheat it. I'll meet you at my place."

"I'll be about half an hour. I'm going to stop off at

home and pack a bag."

"Why?"

"I'm moving in. Something's going on in this town and I don't want you out there alone."

My independent nature wanted to protest, but deep down, I wanted Josh. His presence represented safety. And I needed all the safety I could handle.

"All right. The whole town's talking about us anyway. Might as well fuel the gossip fires."

"I'd say Lorna's murder will be the main topic of conversation for a while."

A shiver raced down my spine. Josh was right. Something *was* going on in this town.

****

I snuggled next to Josh on the sectional while draining the last drops of Chianti from my glass. I had killed the bottle. Three beer bottles graced the end table next to Josh. The empty pizza box sat on the coffee table. Only a small bite of crust and a few crumbs remained. A large duffle bag was upstairs in the bedroom, the contents now hanging in my closet and sitting in my dresser drawers. I liked seeing them in place. Even the male toiletries in the bath looked good—and permanent.

The TV was tuned into a baseball game, but neither of us seemed to watch. I couldn't. All I could see was Lorna—and the blood. I shivered.

Josh's arm pulled me closer. "Are you all right?"

"I suppose." I turned my head to look at him. "I blacked out, you know."

His startled gaze met mine. "Blacked out? When?"

"When I saw the blood. Suddenly everything went dark. I saw a body in the foyer along with those red and white flashes. I also heard voices and someone sobbing. It only lasted an instant. Then I ran."

"Flashes—as in your dreams?"

I nodded. "I was obviously remembering another night a long time ago."

"Your mother. You think you may have witnessed the murder?"

I shrugged and swallowed. "I'm not sure. I've never been sure. But if I saw her killed, why didn't the killer see me and do something about it?"

"Callie, you may never remember it all without an expert guiding you."

"Dr. Halloran felt I'd gone as far as he could take me. He wanted me to consult with some doctor in New York. I said no. I've been in therapy for years. Enough is enough. Any remembering will have to take place here."

Josh frowned. "I don't like the whole feel of this. It's like trying to put together a jigsaw puzzle with half the pieces missing."

A bit of conversation popped into my head. "Josh, when I met with Lorna yesterday, she said something interesting. I forgot about it until now."

"What was it?"

"I'd gone into the store to ask if she wanted to work on the computer that night. She said no, she had a garden club meeting and suggested tonight. Said she needed to talk to me about something anyway—something important."

"Any idea what?"

I shook my head. "Not a clue. I didn't think too much about it at the time. I assumed it had to do with computers since she said she wanted to check out a few things—you know, like maybe she wanted to surprise me with some knowledge. But now that I look back on it, she seemed confused—like *she* was trying to put the pieces of the puzzle together, too."

Josh and I stared at each other, his worried expression mirroring my feelings of fear.

"Oh my God, Josh, what if Lorna knew her killer?"

He inhaled a sharp breath. "But who? And why?"

"I don't know. What could have been so important? Lorna wouldn't have even attempted to learn anything about the computer on her own. You know, come to think of it, she acted distracted right before we left the church on Sunday."

"Like something she saw or heard? At the party maybe?"

"Whatever it was, she had a couple of days to think things over." I sat up. "Or maybe she was puzzled that no one mentioned a gunshot through my window."

Josh shook his head. "Lorna would never drive in a pouring rainstorm to shoot at someone. She said she had to check out a few things before talking to you?"

"Yes, but what? Maybe she wanted to talk to someone else first."

"I wonder who she talked to in the last twenty-four hours?"

****

"I'll be fine," I assured Josh for the umpteenth time. "I'll keep the doors locked. And the only places I need to go are the police station, and then lunch at Gina's."

"Cancel it," he replied in a stubborn voice.

"Gina's is a quarter of a mile down the road. I refuse to hide in my own house."

It was barely six o'clock. Josh was about to leave for the newspaper. He'd been up late writing about Lorna's murder and arranging for a special edition with the printer. Mindy had agreed to come in early and cover the delivery. Neither of us slept well. For once I didn't have sex on my mind. All I needed was Josh cradling me in his arms and sharing his warmth.

"Oh, all right, but for God's sake keep your eyes open and don't walk to Gina's, drive. You promise?"

"I promise."

"And if you feel scared, call me."

"I will. What kind of special edition did you set up?"

"It won't be much—a banner headline, a photo or two from the archives, an obituary, and a long editorial about the crime spree in Wellington, just to bug the Chief of Police. I'll get reactions from people and their comments."

"Well, you can quote me as saying this shit I can get in Chicago."

"I also think I'll make a pest of myself at the police station. I want those reports about your mother."

"Good luck with that. I don't think the chief was too happy with you last night."

"I don't really give a rat's ass." He leaned down and kissed me. "I'll see you tonight. Want me to bring dinner?"

"Nope. Got it all planned."

"What are we having?"

I wagged a finger under his nose. "It's a surprise. Don't forget to go to the police station today."

He kissed me again. "I won't. And..."

"Be careful," I finished for him. "I will."

My good humor disappeared as soon as Josh left the house. Last night had been worse than awful. Why I didn't have a nightmare, I didn't know. I hadn't slept well. Lorna's body kept intruding every time I came close to dozing off.

I thought about the conversation Josh and I had last evening. What had Lorna wanted to tell me? Something about Mother? Daddy? Did she know who the other woman was? Had she remembered something that might be a clue as to her identity? *Assuming she even exists, of course.*

Could a twenty-five year old memory have led to her murder? If so, then that meant the killer had struck again—and that I was upsetting his nice, safe existence. Did that mean I could be next? I'd made no secret I'd begun to remember things from that night. A cold shiver crawled over my skin.

I jumped up and rechecked the doors. All were locked. Telling myself to calm down, I washed up the breakfast dishes before wandering onto the enclosed back porch. My eyes were drawn to a bare space on the wall. The hunting knife used to kill Mother was gone, probably in some long-lost box in an evidence room somewhere. The hook from which it had hung was still in place.

I let my gaze sweep around the enclosure. To the best of my knowledge, it had always been used as a dumping ground for what I called "stuff." Maybe this would be a good time to clear some of the mess out. The packers Aunt Dee and John Casey had hired wouldn't have bothered with this area. It was a back porch, generally open to all. Nothing of value would be kept here. Knowing my aunt, she likely hoped someone would break in and steal all the crap.

Aunt Dee had always said, "Begin at the beginning." Sounded like good advice. I grabbed a trash bag from the pantry and attacked on old desk set up in the corner.

The morning passed quickly. By the time eight-thirty rolled around, I'd created some order out of the chaos. I'd even discovered an old bookcase hidden under and behind boxes. It wasn't an antique or even well made, resembling the efforts of a high school workshop project. Had Daddy made it? Denny? Maybe some other ancestor? The shelves contained what appeared to be old ledgers. I carried them to Daddy's office with the intention of looking through them later. Might be fun to see how the farm had progressed over the generations.

After a quick shower, I slid into a pair of jeans and a sleeveless top. The cool rainy weather of the last few days had given way to bright sunshine with the promise of warmth ahead. Spring in Iowa—diverse and always a surprise. I looked forward to lunch with Gina, but first I had a date at the police station to give my statement concerning Lorna.

Chief Jackson was cordial, but kept going over details until I wanted to scream. I learned Josh had already been through this earlier.

Finally finished, I signed the damned statement and headed for Gina's. She greeted me at the door with a smile and a hug.

"Is it true? You discovered Lorna Bell's body?" she asked leading me toward the kitchen table.

I sat in the same chair I'd used years ago and nodded. "It was awful."

Gina shivered. "Kyle made me promise to keep all the doors locked and my cell handy. He's over in Benson today seeing to his parent's place. I don't know what's happening in this town. First you get robbed, and now this! I hope Chief Jackson finds this guy fast."

I was tempted to tell her about the gunshot, but held my tongue. No need to worry her further.

We chatted as she prepared the lunch. I let my gaze wander around the kitchen. It was pretty much as I remembered. New cabinets, countertops, and appliances added a modern touch, but the layout hadn't changed. How often had I sat and watched Gina's mother do what she did right now?

"I hope you don't mind soup and sandwiches. The soup is homemade last Tuesday."

"Sounds wonderful. So bring me up to date on the life and times of Gina Howell Anderson."

She laughed. "Let's see I dated Rory Hightower all through high school, then sampled the male population at the University of Iowa. Even hauled off and married one of them. That lasted five years. I caught him cheating, dumped his ass, and moved back home. I hooked up with Kyle a couple of years ago and the rest is history."

"No kids yet?"

"We're thinking about it. After all, my biological clock is ticking."

She set a steaming soup bowl in front of me along with a plate containing a large roast beef sandwich. The vegetable soup was chunky and had a tang to it. The beef was cooked medium and practically melted in my mouth. I was eating leftovers and loving every bite. I preferred it to the heavy meals at the Kozy and certainly to Ruth's pretentious spread a few days ago.

"How's everything?" she asked.

"Fabulous. Reminds me of when we were kids."

She reached across the table and squeezed my hand. "I'm just glad you're back. I was devastated when you left. I knew your mother had died, but not the circumstances. I was too young. For weeks after you were gone, I'd sit by my bedroom window and look down the road at the house. Sometimes, when the lights were on, I'd pretend you had come home. One day, I even sneaked over to the tenant house. I remember I got scared because someone came by while I was there. I hid in that closet under the stairs until they left again."

"Funny, I was in the tenant house not long ago. Remember how we used to play pioneers?"

She laughed. "And our dolls were our children. Do you remember the time I fell out of your hayloft and broke my arm?"

"We were playing Tarzan and you were going to use a rope or something to swing across the barn from one loft area to the other. You missed the rope."

"You know, that arm still hurts when it rains." She spooned some soup into her mouth. "So, tell me all about life in Chicago."

I filled her in on my life omitting the darker side of memory loss and dreams. We finished eating as I talked and Gina set a slice of apple pie on the table. Without hesitation, I scooped a bite into my mouth.

"This is wonderful. I'd say it rivals Miss Emma's," I said.

"It should. It's her recipe. When Kyle and I got married, her wedding gift was her recipes to apple, cherry, and lemon meringue pie. She refuses to part with the pumpkin. I imagine it'll go to the grave with her."

We talked for hours about the past as seen through the eyes of childhood. It was close to four o'clock before I returned home. The friendship had withstood the test of time. It was like I'd never left. So much so I'd almost forgotten the events of last evening. Almost. I wondered if the chief had any clues and if he'd share. I kind of doubted it after Josh's performance at Bell's.

I sat in my nook on the sectional and turned on the TV. *Judge Judy* was on. I have a weakness for reality shows.

Maybe it was the televised courtroom, or perhaps, the subject matter—vandalism—that made me think about something Gina had said. At the time, it had gone right over my head.

"I'd sit by my bedroom window and look down the road at the house. Sometimes, when the lights were on, I'd pretend you had come home."

Lights? What lights? I picked up my phone and called Gina.

"Gina, you said you used to see lights on in the house? When?"

"Can't remember for sure, but it wasn't long after your aunt took you and Denny away. Every once in a while the lights would be on in your parent's bedroom. Why?"

"Oh, no reason. Maybe people were cleaning or packing or something. Thanks for lunch. It was super. Let's do it again soon."

I hung up and stared at the TV, not seeing the judge or hearing the testimony.

If cleaners or packers had been here, it would have

been done during the day.

So, who had been in the house at night? *And why?*

Chapter Eighteen

Josh was in a surly mood. "I still don't have those reports," he grumbled when he came home. "I called the Chief to bitch about it. He promised them tomorrow morning. He'd better come through. If I don't have them by noon, I'm filing a court order."

"He'll stall as long as he can, but will eventually get them to us. How did the special edition go?"

"Decent, if sparse on information. The gossip grapevine has better news than I could print anyway. I'll have more details next week. Are you going to Phil's funeral?"

"Probably. When is it?"

"Tomorrow at two. How about dinner in Atwell afterward? I want to talk to the sheriff over there and take a look at the scene of the crime."

"All right, I'd like to see where it happened myself."

"Now, what's for dinner tonight?"

Pork chops smothered in cream of mushroom soup gravy, mashed potatoes, green beans, and a salad hit the spot. It was an oft used country recipe—easy to make and equally easy on the budget. Later, we tried to watch TV, but I found myself thinking about my mother's death, and if my memory would ever clear enough for me to remember. *If there's anything to remember.*

Josh was uncharacteristically quiet. He sat with a

frown on his face watching some network show.

I ran my finger down his cheek. "You look glum. Wanna talk about it?"

He sighed. "Murder and mayhem upset me."

"I'd think you'd be used to it from all the big city papers you worked on." I paused remembering our first date and Josh's comments about hiding out. "Why are you in Wellington? I Googled you when we first met. You only stayed on the job in St. Louis for six months."

He rattled the ice cubes in his empty glass of iced tea and frowned. "Have you ever done something out of arrogance or ambition that hurt someone else?"

I turned to face him, my arm stretched along the back of the sectional.

"Not that I recall. I didn't have much to be arrogant or ambitious about."

He drew a deep breath, and then slowly released it. "I was a staff reporter in St. Louis—just one of many people who contributed to various investigative stories. The lead reporter was a man named Jim Romanoff. Good guy, good reporter. My job was to gather information, verify, and give it to him and he would write the story. I was the bottom rung on a very tall ladder. Still, I was full of myself. This was my first experience in hard investigative news. My other jobs had been fluff and the occasional tornado damage articles."

He stopped talking and drained the melting ice into his mouth.

"So what happened?" I asked encouraging him to continue.

"A toddler was reported missing from a trailer park in one of the county suburbs. Her body was found in the woods a block away. The single mother was arrested and charged with the murder. The entire city was up in arms calling for this woman to spend a long time in jail. She was released for lack of evidence. Jim sent me out for any information I could find. We both were convinced she was guilty. Jim told me to prove it. I talked to a lot of people and turned what I had over to him. Only I didn't bother to verify. The ensuing stories were scathing in their assessment of the police methods used."

"And your information was wrong?"

He nodded. "I didn't talk to enough people to get an unbiased view. The woman's life was ruined. She couldn't get a job, got evicted from the trailer, lived on the streets, and eventually committed suicide. Two months after her death, the cops arrested a neighbor for the murder. He was one of the people I questioned. If I hadn't been so cock-sure of my theories and had bothered to check my facts, I might have seen the holes in his comments."

I touched his arm. "I'm sorry, Josh. You must have felt guilty as hell."

"That and then some. Her relatives sued the paper. I was fired. Jim never regained his reputation and eventually resigned. I heard a few years ago he was working on some tabloid out in Los Angeles."

"What did you do afterward?"

"I quit the business for a while, went down to Texas and worked construction whenever I could. Bussed tables in local diners during the off-season. Then one day, I realized I missed reporting. Only instead of the hustle and bustle of the big city, I decided to go for the peace and quiet of a small town. I searched for small market, weekly newspapers for sale, found this, and bought it. I vowed to never again be so sloppy with the facts or be so judgmental when writing a story. Opinions belong in an editorial, not a story. The *News-Sentinel* was safe, unexciting. Little happened to rile the citizens. Until a few weeks ago, I'd thought my investigative genes had withered and died."

"And now you're knee deep in helping me prove Daddy's innocence, and slap-bang in the middle of another murder."

"Looks that way." He set the glass on the end table. "I can't decide if I'm excited or dismayed."

I nestled my head into his shoulder. "You have the intelligence and the drive to right wrongs, be they human or social. Don't let the past get in the way. You made a mistake, paid for it, did your penance, and moved on. I, on the other hand, am stuck in the past."

He slipped his arm around my shoulder and pulled me close, kissing the top of my head.

"Thanks, Callie. You have no idea how badly I want to contribute to finding Lorna's killer and the clown that ran down poor Phil. And I'm more than convinced your father was framed."

Before I could reply, his cell rang.

"Hendricks. Good. When can I see them? All right, and thanks. Sorry if I've been a pain in the ass." He hung up and turned to me. "That was Bill Jackson. He found those reports and said he'll get them to me tomorrow morning."

"What do you think they'll say?"

"I don't know, but my guess is the sheriff at the time was in way over his head and botched the whole thing."

"Kind of like Daddy's defense," I added.

Josh rose, pulling me up with him. "Let's not talk murder and mayhem anymore tonight."

We turned out the lights and went upstairs where the night turned out to be slow and incredibly enjoyable.

****

Phil Carson's funeral had been packed. Mourners spilled out of the viewing room and into the foyer. Josh steered me onto the front porch and down the steps where we stopped next to Ruth who chatted with John and Jessica. All turned as we walked up.

Ruth spoke first. "I hear you found Lorna."

I nodded. "It was awful."

"I can't imagine what this town is coming to," Jessica said. "We need to put a stop to all these loitering farm hands. Planting is over, they should be told to leave."

"It's a free country, Jessica," Josh replied. "And there's no proof any one of them did it."

She sniffed and curled her lip. "Of course one of them did it. Who else? Why just last week your place was robbed, Callie. And the police have no clues."

"At least, none that they're sharing," John said.

"Well, I for one am going to keep a gun in the nightstand drawer. I'll be prepared," his wife declared, and then turned to me. "So, Callie, tell me what you saw at Lorna's."

I didn't want to talk about it, so gave her the bare minimum of an answer. "She was slumped over her desk. I saw the blood and ran."

"Where's Bob?" Josh asked Ruth.

I appreciated his attempt to change the subject.

"Oh, some client just had to see a property over in Sheridan. He's from out of town and looking for an investment. I guess he thinks a farm is it. Bob felt he couldn't say no."

"Well, at least you're here," Jessica said. "Phil was a nice guy." She glanced at the diamonds sparkling in Ruth's ears. "He sold you those, didn't he?"

"Yes, years ago."

"I'd have to say everybody in town bought from Carson's at some point in time," John added, glancing at his watch. "Are you all going to the cemetery?"

Josh shook his head. "Callie and I are going to Atwell. I want to talk to the sheriff over there and take a look at the crime scene where Phil died. I think we'll stay for dinner, too."

"Why on earth would you want to see that?" John asked with a frown.

Josh stared him down. "Because I'm a reporter. I like knowing. And I *like* uncovering the truth. You ready, Callie?"

I nodded. "I'll talk to you all later."

John's expression had turned grim and his gaze shifted away.

"Nice turn out," I said as we left the parking lot and headed north.

"Phil was one of those people who do their jobs, like what they're doing, and liked everyone. In turn everyone liked him."

"I can't imagine what information you'll find the police in Atwell haven't. I mean, won't they keep Fred up to date?"

"They should, but that doesn't always mean they will. Crime victims often find out about an arrest in the newspaper."

"Speaking of newspapers, did Bill Jackson get those reports to you?"

"Yeah, came by and dropped them off a little while before I left for here. Damn! They're still in the office. Meant to bring them along and read through everything tonight."

"Get them on the way back. I saw you talking to Fred at the funeral home. What did he have to say?"

"He wants answers. Can't say that I blame him, but I don't see how I can possibly find anything new."

We sat silently for a while as the scenery flashed by.

"Know what bugs me about the hit and run?" I asked in a puzzled tone. "Why was the driver in a residential area? Even if he was drunk and lost, wouldn't he have stuck to city streets?"

"That bothers me, too. Maybe the police will have more information by now. And maybe I can put a few things together from the crime scene. And another thing, why haven't they found the car?"

"Because the driver isn't from around here?"

"But why stop to get drunk in Atwell—a place where you don't know the streets or where they lead? Why not just get loaded in your own hometown? Doesn't make sense."

I saw his point. None of it made sense, and I could also understand why Fred was so adamant Josh find out the truth. Cold case files seldom got solved, especially in small towns. Not finding the car still bugged me. Perhaps someone was being ultra-careful and leaving it in a garage until the situation was pushed from the headlines.

But who can afford to leave a car in a garage that long? What excuse did he give his wife and friends? How did he get to and from work? I voiced my thoughts to Josh.

"Good questions. Maybe you should be a reporter. I intend to ask the same things of the sheriff."

It was close to three-thirty when we rolled into Atwell. The police station was our first stop. Inside, the Atwell Chief of Police met with us.

"All I can say is it's under investigation. Not much to go on really, but sooner or later that car has to show up if for no other reason than to get repaired."

"Don't suppose you'd be willing to share crime scene photos would you?" Josh asked politely.

"Can't do that. Like I said, it's still under investigation." He rose indicating our interview was over. "I can appreciate the concern of the Wellington citizens. Please reassure them we're on it and hope to have answers as soon as possible."

"Well, that was short and not so sweet," I said as we drove away.

"He knows more. He's just not telling at the moment. Let's go look at where Phil died."

"You have an address?"

"Fred told me. Man who hosted the poker night is Ben Logan. I'll talk to him. Might get enough for a follow up story."

A few minutes later we pulled up in front of a house, a nice Craftsman probably built in the 1920s or '30s. A man about Phil's age opened up when Josh knocked. He wore a dress shirt and tie. I spied his suit coat draped over the back of a chair in the living room beyond.

"Yes?"

"Hi, my name is Josh Hendricks. I own the *News-Sentinel* over in Wellington. This is Ms. Bryant, my assistant. Fred Carson gave me your name and address. Hope we're not intruding."

He motioned us inside. "Not at all. Talked to Fred at the funeral. He said you might drop by. Nice funeral. Just got home a while ago myself." He led us into the living room and indicated we have a seat. "Can't tell you how upset I am about Phil. Nothing like this has ever happened in this neighborhood. Can I get you something to drink?"

"No thanks," Josh said as we sat on the sofa.

Ben Logan sat in a recliner.

My gaze wandered around the room. It was neat with everything in its place. A large portrait over the fireplace caught my attention.

"What a lovely painting," I commented.

Ben looked up with a smile. "Thank you. That's my late wife and me. Had it done for our thirtieth wedding anniversary. She died five years ago."

"I'm so sorry. She was a beautiful woman."

"She was indeed. That's how the Monday night poker game came to life. Five of us, all widowers, got together once every two weeks for some fun. We'd play cards, shoot the bull, and during football season watch the Monday night game."

"Can you tell us what happened?" Josh asked.

"It was an ordinary night. We played, told a few off-color jokes, ate snacks, drank a couple of beers, and had a good time. Phil was the last to leave. I'd just walked out in to the kitchen when I heard what sounded like tires squealing, and then a scream followed by a loud thump. I ran out onto the front porch just in time to see a car blow the stop sign at the corner and keep on going down the street real fast. Didn't have any lights on that I could tell. Then I looked and saw something in the middle of the street. I ran out, saw it was Phil, and dialed nine-one-one. He died on the way to the hospital without ever regaining consciousness." He shuddered and shook his head. "Not a pleasant way to die. Finding a friend like that ain't nothing I ever want to do again."

"I understand," I said, not telling him exactly how much I could relate to his experience.

"Really wish I could be more help, but by the time I got outside, the car was too far away for me to see anything."

"What about the couple walking their dog?" Josh asked.

"They saw about the same as I did. The car raced through the stop sign and kept on going—no lights, no nothing. They noticed it was a dark-colored, mid-sized car of some sort as it passed under the streetlight."

"Tell me about Phil that night. Was he in his usual frame of mind?"

Ben frowned and thought for a moment. "You know, now that you mention it, he was kinda distracted."

"Distracted how?"

"Can't put my finger on it, but I could tell his mind wasn't on playing cards. When the others left, he stuck around for a minute or two. I asked if everything was all right, and he said yes, but that he hated getting old. Said he hated forgetting things and was glad Fred would be taking over the store soon. I told him he wasn't getting old. People our age often misplace and forget things."

"What did he say to that?" Josh asked.

"Not much. Just that there was something he should remember and couldn't. I told him to go home and sleep on it."

"And he didn't tell you any more than that?"

Ben shook his head. "Nope, although I did have the impression it had something to do with the store."

"You mean like a large unpaid bill or missing merchandise?" I prompted.

"Don't know. He kinda laughed at himself as he left. That's it."

Josh rose. "Thank you very much, Mr. Logan. I'll ask Fred about this. Could be he discussed it with his son earlier."

Ben also rose from his chair. "Thank you for stopping by. Hope the cops can find the driver. I'd like a few minutes alone with the bastard."

On the sidewalk, Josh looked toward the middle of the street. "According to Fred, his father had parked across the street and just down a bit from here." We walked down the street a ways and stopped. "My guess is here or close to it."

"Which direction was the car coming from?"

"From there," Josh indicated with his chin to the left.

"So he was hit from behind. Probably never saw what was coming until it was too late."

Josh walked toward the corner. If the car had taken the turn fast enough for people to hear tires squealing, then it stood to reason it had left some kind of skid mark. Nothing like that showed. We walked past the intersection. There, not far from the corner, were the faint remains of rubber on the road.

"Interesting," Josh murmured. "And there's no stop sign for this street on this corner."

"That is odd. Maybe the driver pulled over to get his bearings, and when he realized he didn't know where he was, got pissed and took off."

"Maybe." Josh looked at the distance from the skid marks to where Phil died, and shook his head. "Come on, let's go get something to eat. I have to think what I'm going to tell Fred."

"I'd ask if Phil had mentioned what had been bothering him."

"I will, but I'm not sure Fred knows or he'd have said something to me."

We went back to the car and got in.

"How about Morelli's?"

"That's fine, but it's awfully early to eat. Not even six yet."

"We could go back to the Kozy."

"I'll eat early."

Josh chuckled. "Thought you'd say that. The Kozy is good, but not fine dining. Need something special every once in a while."

Much to my surprise, Morelli's was busy. I'd forgotten it was Friday night. We were seated at the same table we'd had the last time. Josh and I both ordered red wine and spent several minutes looking over the menu. As before, the scents of garlic and Italian herbs made my stomach grumble.

When the waiter brought our drinks, we ordered— Italian sausage in a rich, red sauce for me, and lasagna for Josh.

We sipped our wine in silence. Josh stared into his

glass at the dark red Cabernet

"Josh?"

He looked up and sighed. "Sorry, I was thinking."

"Look, I'm sure the police will find this guy soon. It's only a matter of time."

"I know, but its stuff like this that makes me mad. Phil was a nice guy. He didn't deserve to be run down in the street like a stray dog. A stray dog doesn't deserve it either. You know, I thought I was content running a small town newspaper, but the past couple of weeks have shown me how much I miss the investigative end of things. First, your father's case, the letters, the phone calls, the gunshot, Phil's death, and now Lorna's murder. They've revived my instinct to dig, to probe. Not sure if that's a good thing or not." He drank a good portion from his glass. "Don't mind me. It's been a long day and an even longer week."

"I'll say. Do you think Bill Jackson is a good enough lawman to find Lorna's killer?"

"He'd better be or the citizens of Wellington won't vote for him next time around."

"Do you buy Jessica's belief it was some vagrant?"

"I don't know. On the surface, that makes the most sense, but I can't help but wonder if she knew her killer."

"Who'd want to kill Lorna? She was harmless."

"That's what makes it so odd. How did he get in?"

I shrugged and sipped my wine. "She left the front door unlocked for me. In spite of the closed sign, he tried the door, found it open, and walked in. When he discovered Lorna, he panicked and shot her."

"Yeah, but coming in the front door was ballsy. Suppose someone had seen him?"

"Maybe he went around back. I wonder if the back door was jimmied."

"If he broke in, then Lorna would have either run or called the sheriff. She'd have heard someone messing with the door. Plus there's a storage room between the back door and the hallway. The office is a good ten feet down that hall."

"So she could have had time to make a call, yet her hand position suggests she didn't even try until it was too late. And it's obvious she never attempted to run. She also must have heard the bell over the door if the killer came in that way."

"Maybe she thought it was you."

"Maybe." I rubbed my forehead. "This is getting confusing."

"I'd give a year's profits to know if that back door had been messed with," he muttered. "Perhaps the killer came in the front, and then left via the back door."

"That would be the answer if it wasn't jimmied. Just turn the deadbolt and leave in case someone heard the shot and decided to investigate. Think the chief will give you the information?"

"Probably not, but I could ask. I'll drop by tomorrow and make nice with him. Thank him for the reports and apologize for being so aggressive the other night. I'll tell him I was in shock over Lorna's death and worried about you. He might give me something. Election time isn't that far away. Even Bill Jackson understands the power of an endorsement."

Our food arrived, and while it was delicious, my mind kept reviewing the events of Wednesday night. Funny how just about every detail was sharp and clear. Other than that odd flashback, I remembered it all. So why couldn't I do the same for what happened twenty-five years ago? Because it had involved my mother? Or had my innocent mind refused to believe what I'd seen—if anything?

Josh also seemed to be deep in thought as he ate. *Guess tonight is not the night for casual conversation.*

We finished, paid, and left the restaurant walking slowly to where we'd parked. He paused beside the car, his hand in his pocket. The change jingled as he nervously jiggled it around.

"Josh?"

"Huh? Oh, sorry."

He unlocked the car and we got in. He still didn't start the car, but sat staring out the windshield, his fingers tapping on the steering wheel.

"Josh?" I asked again.

"I'm...I'm sorry, Callie, but I can't turn my mind off. It just keeps running in a hundred different directions at once."

"Maybe some hard work will help. I have several boxes up in the attic that can be brought down. We can refill the china cabinet in the dining room and go through some of the books. I swear there must be enough to start a bookstore."

"Okay, I can do that." He continued to stare at the car parked in front of us.

"Josh, what is it you're thinking now?"

"Maybe I have Lorna's and your mother's murders on my mind, but...you're gonna think I'm crazy, but..."

"But what?" I asked as he paused.

He turned to look at me with a worried expression. "Callie, what if Phil's death wasn't an accident?"

Chapter Nineteen

"What?" I exclaimed as my jaw dropped.

"I know, I know, it sounds far-fetched!"

"Who'd want to deliberately run down Phil Carson? And why?"

"Sorry, like I said, I've got murder on my mind." He started the car and drove away.

I couldn't tear my gaze away from his profile. It sounded crazy, but then I remembered the skid marks.

"You mean someone could have parked by the curb down the street, waited until Phil came out, took off, got up a head of steam and nailed him?"

"Could be, but I'm stumped as to why."

"Let's try to look at this logically." I thought for a moment and couldn't come up with a damned thing. "Okay, let's not look at it logically. Let's just guess. This was a poker party. One he and his buddies attended on a regular basis. Suppose it wasn't just nickel and dime stuff. Suppose it was for a lot of money?"

"Are you saying five old geezers got together every week or so to score big bucks?"

"Why not? Maybe Phil was a big loser and owed one of them money." When Josh remained silent, I went on. "Or maybe he gambled in other places with less reputable people and lost major dollars. They'd want it back ASAP."

"I've known Phil Carson ever since I moved here. I can't see him as a compulsive gambler."

"All right, maybe he didn't owe the money, but one of his friends did. The killer nailed the wrong guy. A case of mistaken identity."

"Now, that's a possibility. I wonder if Ben Logan would mind giving me the names of the rest of the group."

"Don't see why not. I mean, he wouldn't have had time to see Phil to the door, run get into his car, and mow him down."

"That makes sense. Ben's telling the truth and somewhere, someone knows Phil wasn't the intended victim. And in that case, then the car would have been stolen and dumped in the nearest river or lake. We may be on to something here. I'll call the chief in Atwell tomorrow and try to pry more info out of him." He stepped on the gas. "Let's get home."

Darkness had descended while we'd eaten and now we raced down the highway, the white stripes in the middle of the road flashing past in a never-ending blur. Twenty minutes later we neared the farm.

"Since we're in an investigative mode, I want to read those reports," he said.

"In that case, drop me off at the house. I want to get out of these funeral duds and into jeans."

"I don't like leaving you alone."

"The house is locked, the lights are on in the foyer, the living room and the kitchen, plus my car is in the drive. I'll be fine and it'll only take you fifteen minutes. The house is on the way into town anyhow."

He pulled into the drive and I exited the car. "See?" I said gesturing toward the warm glow emanating from the windows. "All safe and sound."

"I'll go inside with you," he insisted stubbornly.

He came in and scoped out the place, including the second story, and found nothing.

"There. Satisfied?"

"Yeah, I guess so. I'm overly cautious when it comes to you. I'll get those reports and be back in a few minutes."

"I'll be in the attic getting those boxes ready to come downstairs."

"I see major manual labor ahead."

I chuckled as he leaned down, gave me a toe-curling kiss, and left.

Shaking my head, I went upstairs to change. Peeling off the navy blue suit, I found a pair of jeans and pulled a t-shirt over my head, then headed for the attic.

Our speculation in the car ran through my mind. I didn't want to think Phil had been deliberately killed—even in a case of mistaken identity—but Josh had opened the door to my own imagination. If so, then the town of Wellington had a problem. Two of its citizens had been killed within a few days of each other. Granted, the two deaths weren't related, but for a town this size, the odds were enormous on it happening. Add my mother into the mix and things got even more bizarre.

I hesitated before opening the attic door. I wanted to read those reports, too, but I also wanted to get things back to normal in the house. The memories had been stored away in boxes for a quarter of a century. Time to bring them out. They might help me remember.

I jerked open the door, flipped on the light, and

trotted up the narrow steps. The open boxes of china and silver were where I'd left them. I turned left to drag the books over for Josh. Under the dim light, I noticed several of the containers had been opened and books removed. I moved closer for a better look. What the hell? I hadn't done this. A chill raced up my spine.

From behind me, footsteps charged. Before I could turn around something was flung over my head. My assailant pushed me. I fell over a box, hitting my head hard on the floor. I saw stars, and then blackness, but wasn't completely unconscious. The footsteps stumbled down the steps and through the hallway. A few seconds later, the back door slammed. Shortly after that, a car engine started and roared out of the driveway.

I struggled to get out of whatever had been thrown over me, but the harder I tried, the tighter the cloth bound itself around me. I was suffocating. Finally, I got an arm free and yanked it off. It was an old quilt.

I staggered to my feet, perhaps too fast. The room spun. I sank to my knees with a groan and toppled over once again hitting my head. Darkness closed in.

****

"Callie! Callie! Come on, honey, wake up!"

Josh's voice penetrated the fog in my brain. His arms wrapped me in a comforting cocoon of warmth. I groaned.

"Oh, thank God. What happened? Are you hurt? Can you sit up? Talk to me, sweetheart."

I struggled to sit up. My head hurt like hell and my stomach churned. I tried to remember what had happened.

"Say something!"

"Give…Give me a moment."

He helped me to my feet. The attic tilted and whirled. My legs sagged, but before I could fall, Josh swept me up into his arms and carried me down the narrow steps to the bedroom where he laid me gently on the bed.

"What happened? Did you trip and fall over those boxes?"

My encounter with the intruder came back in full detail. "Did...did you see him?" Nausea churned. "Oh, God, I think I'm going to throw up."

"See who?" he asked as he led me to the bathroom.

I stood for several long seconds over the toilet before my stomach finally settled down.

"See who, Callie? What happened?"

I made it back to the bed under my own power and flopped down.

"He was in the attic."

"Who?"

"I don't know. I went up to slide those boxes toward the stairs. The next thing I knew something was thrown over my head and I was pushed. I fell over the boxes and hit my head."

Josh jerked out his cell and dialed. "This is Josh Hendricks. I'm out at the Bryant farm with Callie. She was attacked a while ago by an intruder... I don't know, but she hit her head pretty hard. I'm taking her to the regional hospital in Atwell... I doubt there's much to find and no, I don't know how long she was out... In the attic... I have no idea and have to get her to a doctor. You can either meet us in Atwell or talk to her tomorrow." He hung up and turned back to me. "Come on, let's go."

I sat up. "I'm fine, Josh. I don't feel sick anymore

and the dizziness is gone."

"I don't care. You're going to get checked out. Head injuries shouldn't be ignored. People are fine one minute and dead the next. Now, can you walk or do I carry you?"

I walked. He slammed the car door and roared out of the drive.

"Talk to me, Callie. Don't fall asleep. What happened? Can you remember?"

As we raced through the night, I gave him the details.

"I checked out the house, but never thought to check any place else. I wonder where he parked."

"Behind the barn, next to the machinery shed? Who knows? We wouldn't have seen a car in the dark. And what the hell was he looking for in my attic?"

"Anything of value up there?"

"The silver, but that was in plain view by the steps. Maybe it was the same guy from last Saturday back to finish his search." I groaned. "God, my head hurts."

Josh stepped on the gas. We made the usual twenty-minute ride into Atwell in less than fifteen.

For a small town medical facility, the hospital was up to date. I was whisked away for a battery of tests including a CAT scan. Much to my annoyance, the doctor insisted I stay overnight.

"But I feel fine and the scan showed everything was normal. I just want to go home."

"Callie, it's just for a few hours. Let them monitor you until morning," Josh pleaded.

"Mr. Hendricks is right, Miss Bryant. You probably sustained a very mild concussion. Any concussion is a serious matter."

"There, you see, he agrees with me!"

I gave up. "Oh, all right, if you insist, but I want out of here by nine o'clock. Is that clear?"

Josh and the doctor both smiled.

"No problem," the doc told me. "By the way, there's a policeman in the waiting room. He wants to talk to you. You feel up to it?"

"Yeah, I guess so."

"I'll let him know. Now, if Mr. Hendricks will also leave, we'll get you into a room."

An hour later, I was settled into a bed in a semi-private room. Luckily, I had no roommate.

Josh and Officer Young entered followed by the doctor.

"Make it quick, gentlemen. She needs some rest," he said before leaving the room.

The policeman opened a small notebook and asked, "What happened, Ms. Bryant?"

I gave him the details. Five minutes later, I was finished.

"And you have no idea who the intruder was?"

"Not with that quilt over my head," I said in a dry tone. Did he think it was see-through?

"What about the footsteps? Were they heavy like a man's or lighter like a woman's?"

"They were footsteps." I paused and thought back. "Could have been wearing athletic shoes. I don't remember hearing clumps like from a work boot."

"And the car engine? How long after he left did you hear that?"

"I don't know. I whacked my head pretty hard when I fell. I was stunned and not sure of the time frame. I'm not even sure when Josh got there."

"I went to the office, got the files I needed and came right back. Couldn't have taken any more than fifteen minutes. I came inside, went upstairs to change out of my suit, saw the attic door open, called out a couple of times, and when Callie didn't answer, hurried up. Found her out cold in the middle of the floor. Scared me to death."

"Why were you in the attic, Ms. Bryant?"

I explained about bringing down the boxes for inspection.

After a few more inconsequential questions, Officer Young closed his notebook.

"I'll fingerprint the boxes and the doorknobs, but my guess is whoever broke in wore gloves. I'll be in touch."

"Yeah, right, like he was in touch after last week," I grumbled as he left.

"We need to talk about a lot of things, but not now. They'll wait until morning. Do you want me to stay? There's a free bed right next to you."

Of course I wanted him to stay, but I also knew the routine for concussion victims—being awakened and asked questions every few hours to make sure they didn't drift off into that big never-never land in the sky. Why should he have a lousy night's sleep, too?

"No, go on home. I'd feel better if someone was in the house." I yawned. "We'll talk in the morning. It's been a helluva night. I'm tired and want to get as much sleep as they'll allow. Don't worry, I'll be fine."

He leaned over and kissed me. "You'd better be. I'll be here bright and early to spring you."

Josh left and I settled into what I knew would not be a restful night.

****

"The bacon was limp, the scrambled eggs crappy, and the toast even crappier. I won't go into the coffee," I groused on the way home the following morning. It was after ten and I was happy to be out of medical purgatory. My sleep had been interrupted frequently during the night. I wanted the familiar.

"So, you're saying breakfast sucked?"

"I'm saying I want real food."

"Fast food all right with you?"

"Perfect."

Josh stopped at a well-known fast food eatery in Atwell where I ordered what was listed as "The Total Breakfast" consisting of pancakes, eggs, sausage, bacon, copious amounts of butter guaranteed to clog my arteries for life, and enough syrup to drown in. I ate it all and downed two cups of coffee. Josh had a more sensible meal.

"I take it you were hungry," he commented with a grin.

"I could probably eat more, but won't. How are things at the house?"

"Police were waiting there when I got back. They did their thing and left. Other than that, all was quiet."

"They'll never figure out who it was."

He finished his coffee and frowned. "Let's get back home where we can talk."

The first thing I did upon entering the house was change clothes. The t-shirt and jeans from last night were dirty from the dust of the attic floor. Back downstairs, I found Josh unpacking a box in the dining room. Several pieces of china were stacked on the table.

"When did you do this?" I asked.

"Last night. I couldn't sleep, so I thought I'd work. You'll find more boxes in the living room and foyer."

I unwrapped dishes and set them up in the china cupboard. The silver tea service had always been on the sideboard. I saw no reason to change it. Finally, I called a halt to work.

"You said we needed to talk, so let's talk."

Josh pulled out a chair and sat. I did the same.

"First of all, the car was parked next to the machinery shed. The gravel next to it showed recent signs of someone peeling out fast."

"I figured. And because the entire drive is gravel, there are no tracks to compare."

"Callie, the police also didn't find any signs of forced entry. Are you sure the house was locked?"

"After last weekend? Of course, I'm sure." I paused. "At least I am about the doors. Not sure about the windows."

"A couple of windows upstairs in the bedroom were cracked maybe two or three inches. Down here, the kitchen window was open and the two east facing windows in the living room, while closed, were not locked."

"I forgot about the kitchen window. It's always open, and I remember closing the windows in the living room before we left for the funeral. You think that's how the guy got in?"

He shrugged. "Your guess is as good as mine."

"Well, he'd have to be tall because the downstairs windows are a good six feet off the ground."

"Then that means someone had a key."

The implications made me catch my breath. "I meant to change the locks, but never got around to it.

Too much has happened."

"Who besides you would have a key?"

"I used Aunt Dee's when I first came here. And of course, John Casey had one. I'm not sure who else."

"John Casey, huh?"

"Why would John Casey be hiding in my attic? If there was something he wanted from there he had twenty-five years to look for it. I suppose Daddy could have one in his desk, although I don't remember seeing it. And an extra key somewhere on the back porch might come in handy, but no one bothers to lock doors in the country—at least, they never used to."

"They'd lock them if they were going away for an extended period—a weekend, a vacation. Something like that."

I sat back and thought. "Do you keep an extra key somewhere outside in case you need it?"

"On a little hook under the front porch steps. Not the most original of places, but I don't own a flowerpot."

We both rose and trotted through the foyer to the front door. A quick search of the steps revealed nothing.

"Of course, an extra key wouldn't be here. Not at a farmhouse," I said heading around toward the back.

The hook was two inches under the driveway side of the middle step. The key, however, was gone.

Back inside, I slapped together a couple of sandwiches while Josh paced the kitchen, muttering. "So whoever got in may have done so by using a key nobody remembered."

"But was savvy enough to look for it. But that still doesn't tell us *why*."

Josh paced faster, his movements beginning to fray my patience.

"Will you stop that? It's driving me nuts."

"What? Oh sorry, but I do that when I think." He stopped and sat at the table while I filled two glasses with iced tea and set lunch in front of him.

"Callie, this guy was in the attic for a reason. Maybe he was looking for something specific."

"Like what? Other than the silver and china, all that's up there are boxes of Hummels, a few old toys, and tons of books."

"What are Hummels?" he asked.

"Little porcelain figurines, usually of sweet-faced children. Personally, I find them kind of sappy, but my mother loved them."

"How much are they worth?"

"I suppose it depends on the age and condition. I wouldn't know by just looking. I'm sure a few might have been more popular than others. That could jack the price up among collectors."

"He could have been looking for those."

"How would a casual thief know about the Hummels and to look for them specifically?"

"He wouldn't," Josh said, and then paused. "That means we may not be dealing with a casual thief, but someone who knew your mother collected the damned things."

"Why wait until I come back to rummage for them? He had a long time to break in when the house was empty. I doubt John Casey or anyone else came by on a regular basis to check on the joint."

He ran a hand through his hair. "None of this is making sense."

"That's because we're over-thinking it. I come back and may have mentioned the Hummels packed away in the attic during casual conversation. The thief finds out, and takes a chance."

"Maybe. I don't know what to think. What about the books? Anything valuable in that line like a first edition?"

"I have no clue. Daddy was always reading. So was I. Same with Denny. Mother not so much, but I'm sure Daddy must have gotten the bug from someone, most likely his parents. There were bookcases all over the house."

During our discussion, we'd finished eating. I cleared the table and set the dishes in the sink.

Josh rose. "I suggest we take a look in those book boxes."

Three hours later, I had stacks of books all over the foyer floor and the tables in the living room. Most were paperbacks, but quite a few were hardcover complete with dust jackets in good condition.

"Some of these are old, but not old enough to warrant stealing," I said.

"You're right. Nothing here worth breaking in for."

I opened another box and started a new stack. This box contained hardcover editions, some dating back to the thirties. The garish jackets showed almost cartoon-like characters.

"Wow, someone really liked Hemingway," I commented. "*The Old Man and the Sea, A Farewell to Arms, The Sun Also Rises*, and *For Whom the Bell Tolls*, all with intact covers." Out of curiosity, I opened *For Whom the Bell Tolls*. The edges of the paper were yellowing, but not yet deteriorating. I turned a page and stared. "Holy crap, this one's autographed!"

"You're kidding." Josh looked over my shoulder at the name Ernest Hemingway emblazoned on the title page. "Is this a first edition?"

I turned to the copyright page. "I think it may be."

"Callie, this could be worth real money. Are the others signed, too?"

I quickly opened the other Hemingway books. "Yes! Where on earth did they come from?"

"Maybe someone in your family bought them at an estate sale or something."

"Or someone was a Hemingway fan, bought all his books and brought them to a book signing. Wasn't *The Old Man and the Sea* one of his last?" I flipped to the copyright page. "Says here 1951."

"Jeez, Callie, these could be worth a small fortune."

"I'll repack them and see if I can find a reputable bookseller. Is this what the thief was looking for?"

"Must be."

"But how would he know about them?"

"Maybe he thought they'd been shipped to Chicago when you moved."

"And when I came back, I mentioned to several people the attic had loads of boxes packed away," I added slowly.

"I don't know about you, but I'm beat. What time is it?"

"Close to five and I don't have a damned thing thawed for dinner."

"In that case, why don't we go out or get something in?"

"I don't want to go out. Just stop at the nearest

take-out joint and get something."

"That would be The Chicken Emporium."

"Works for me—fried chicken with all the accompaniments sounds as good as anything."

"Will you be all right here?"

"It's still light. I'll be fine, provided I don't go in the attic," I answered with a wry tone.

"No attics without me along," he said with a small smile. "I'll be back soon."

Josh left and I wandered around trying to decide what to do with all these books. While the farmhouse had had bookcases in every room, I'd sold most of them to Lorna not thinking I'd need that many.

I finally sat on the sofa, my mind going over the tangled and gruesome events of the last week—the shot, the break in, Phil's death, Lorna's murder, and now the attack on me. Everything had started when I returned. And I'd made no secret that I'd been asking questions about Mother and Daddy. But the happenings were random and my head hurt from trying to understand it all.

Then a thought so bizarre made me sit up and gasp.

Oh my God! What if what's happened isn't random? What if Mother's death and all the rest are related?

Had my return set the wheels of murder in motion again?

Chapter Twenty

I hit Josh with my theory when he arrived back with the food.

"I can't see how Lorna's murder, the break-ins, and Phil's death are related. Not likely."

"But they have to be," I insisted plopping mashed potatoes onto my plate. "This crime spree, as you called it, didn't begin until I came back to Wellington."

"Okay, let's start with Phil. How is he connected to your mother's death?"

I took a bite of crispy fried chicken and paused a moment to gather my thoughts.

"I met Phil Carson the Saturday after the party when I took Mom's bracelet in for repairs. He said it was an easy fix. We chatted for a minute or two and I asked him if he'd sold the bracelet to Daddy. He said he didn't remember. But when I picked it up on Monday, he said he did remember the bracelet, but not the circumstances, and then made a comment about memory and getting old. What was it his friend said along those lines?"

Josh forked some green beans into his mouth and chewed with a thoughtful expression.

"Ben Logan said Phil was distracted and spoke about getting old and not remembering things like he should. But what's your point?"

My shoulders slumped. "I'm not sure. However,

Lorna also said she wanted to talk to me about something important and that she needed to think about a few things first."

"I still don't see how the two are connected."

My theory was rapidly getting blown out of the water. I gave it one last shot. "Maybe Phil remembered something about Mother, too. When he told me how valuable it was, I couldn't help but think how Daddy could afford something like that." I paused pushing a green bean around my plate with my fork. "What if Daddy didn't buy it? What if Mother did?"

"You mean she just went in and bought it without telling your father? Would she have done that?"

"I've learned a lot about my mother in the past few weeks. She was used to the good life in Chicago, but had to make do here. She was unhappy and may have been about to leave. It could have been a kind of in-your-face type of thing."

Josh put his fork down and stared with a troubled expression. "Callie, what if she didn't buy it? What if she stole it? Would your father have made good on the bill?"

"Yes. He was that kind of person. If that was the case, you'd think Phil would have remembered those details."

"And here's something you may not want to hear, but what if your dad did buy the bracelet—for someone else? What if your mother found it, confronted him, and that's what the argument was about?"

I remembered the inscription on the bracelet, then inhaled a deep breath and blew it out. "I'm so confused."

"You said it earlier—we're over-thinking. Phil was

killed in an accident. That's all. We'll never know what Lorna wanted to tell you. The gunshot and the break-ins—well, okay, I don't have a good explanation for those other than you spoke about boxes being in the attic, someone heard, and took advantage." He paused with a frown. "But the thief who ransacked your bedroom apparently never went anywhere near the attic. Maybe he realized he didn't have the time and decided to come back later."

What he said made sense, or at least as much sense as anything else. Yet, I couldn't shake the notion all were connected in some way. I still had no clear memory of how I'd gotten the bracelet. Had Daddy bought it for a mistress? Had mother found it, hidden it in my jewelry box, and then confronted her husband with the knowledge?

I was about to give up asking myself questions when a curious thought popped into my head.

"You know, in all the hubbub of the attack, the hospital, the police and such, there's one thing that we forgot."

"What's that?"

"How did the thief know we weren't here? My car was parked in the driveway and the lights were on. That says someone's home."

He pushed his empty plate away and stared. "We told him," he finally said. "At the funeral home. We said we were going into Atwell for dinner."

"Oh my God, we were talking to Ruth, John and Jessica, and I recall seeing June Simpson with her husband standing nearby talking to Clovis. They could easily have overheard us. Maybe even passed the information along to someone else. But would any of them break in?"

"A lot of people were at the funeral. Could be someone else listened in, too."

"According to John, Ruth and Jessica helped the movers pack up mother's things after we'd left. Could one of the movers have noticed the signed books? With those two keeping an eye on things, the chance to grab them would have been slim."

"They packed things, but did they also take them up to the attic? After all, no one was certain if your move to Chicago was permanent. If not, one of the movers may have assumed the stuff had been shipped to Chicago."

"And found out otherwise via my big mouth. I need to talk to Ruth."

Josh cleared the table while I washed up. I was tired and my brain wasn't working in full logic mode. We had missed something, something important, and I had no clue what.

When we finished, Josh and I settled into our favorite sections of the sofa, the almost forgotten police reports in his hand.

"Guess it's time to read these since I made such a fuss over them. I'll start and hand off the pages to you."

The file was longer than I expected. The more I read, the angrier I got. Even I could see the old sheriff, Roy Wilson, had no clue how to conduct a murder investigation. He interviewed people, but made no follow-ups that I could see. Once the report came back that mother's blood was on Daddy's clothes, he ceased any effort. No wonder Bill Jackson didn't want us to read this. As a deputy, his biggest job had been to interview me, a seven-year-old, whom everybody assumed had been asleep. And my aunt's statement, provided by me, that Mother and Daddy had argued set the whole process in motion. In it, she stressed that Mother had been unhappy and was about to ask for a divorce. She also stated Daddy had been after the Conrad money from the get-go. I rejected that immediately. Daddy would never have married for money. True, it had been a whirlwind courtship, but I just didn't see dollar signs as a catalyst.

The end of the file included Daddy's arrest and questioning. Nowhere did it contain that he'd been Mirandized nor did it say whether he'd asked for an attorney. Exactly when and how had John Casey become involved?

Josh read the last page and returned it to the folder.

"Is that all? What's the last page?" I asked holding out my hand.

He shook his head. "It's the autopsy report. You don't need to see it."

"Yes, I do." My voice took on a hard edge.

"Callie…"

"I want to see it, Josh."

He reluctantly handed it over. I read with growing consternation.

"My God, she was stabbed six times in the back, five of them post-mortem. She also had cuts on her arms, neck, and face."

"Defensive wounds. Your mother fought back. She either fell or the killer pushed her to the floor, and then delivered the fatal wound."

I handed the pages back to Josh who tucked them into the folder. "I want this killer. I want him real bad."

"So do I, honey, so do I."

My head hurt, I was tired, and more confused than ever. Still, I couldn't shake the feeling that the answer to everything was right in front of us. We had way too much information and in sifting through it all had missed a major clue.

****

I arose the next morning not in the least rested. Dreams had dominated. They'd been disjointed as usual, but with a twist. I'd dreamed the familiar flashing red and white lights again, but the sound of flying gravel was added this time as a bonus—no doubt a by-product of my attic attack. I'd also had the floating above the foyer dream in which two people fought, only the combatants had been Phil and Lorna. Naturally, the sobbing and angry voices had been around, too.

"So, what's on your agenda today?" Josh asked.

"It's Sunday. I may go to church. After that, I'm not sure."

"I'm thinking I may try to find those witnesses mentioned in the police report. If they're still around, they'd be home today. Want to come?"

"No, I may try calling Ruth and Jessica later to ask about the packers. Today's going to be slow. I didn't sleep well."

Church was an eye-opener. Like on that first day, people stopped to stare at me. The news about the intruder must have spread fast. When I smiled and said hello to a parishioner, she grabbed her daughter and walked away. One woman was even blunter.

"I don't know what's going on in this town, but it all started when you showed up. Why don't go back to where you came from?"

Few people spoke to us at the social hour

295

afterward. I felt shunned, like an outsider. Was this what it had been like for Mother? While Josh gravitated toward a knot of people, I finally cornered June Simpson.

"I'm so sorry about Lorna. I know how close the two of you were."

She daubed at her eyes with a tissue. "I'd known Lorna all my life. I hope Bill Jackson catches the guy soon. I've never felt the need to lock my doors ever. Now, I do."

"I wish I'd gone to the store sooner. I was supposed to teach her some computer skills. Wanted to do it the night before, but she had a garden club meeting. Were you there?"

June shot me keen glance. "Yes. We discussed a few upcoming events. Very routine."

"She and Ruth suggested I join. Ruth's the president, isn't she?"

She sniffed and made a face. "For now. I was in charge several years ago. I may run again for the position. Lorna was one of my biggest supporters."

"At least you got to talk to her one last time at the meeting. How was she? I think the computer stuff may have scared her."

"She wasn't her usual self. Acted worried, like she had something on her mind. Didn't talk much to me. Spent most of her time talking to Ruth after the meeting." June suddenly stiffened her spine. "You're asking questions again. Why? Do you think I killed Lorna? Well, I didn't. Now, if you'll excuse me I have to get home."

I remembered our exchange on the street just thirty minutes before I found the body. And June had walked away in the direction of the store.

"Hello, Callie. Heard you had another break-in," John Casey said.

"Yes, and I'm getting tired of them. Where's Jessica this morning?"

"She's a little under the weather. Nothing serious. She should be fine by tomorrow."

"I wanted to ask about those people who packed up the house. Were they local?"

"I called a company out of Jessup, but they hire from all around the area, so I don't know. Good talking to you."

His abrupt departure told me he didn't want to discuss the packing. He hadn't even asked why I wanted to know.

"I think we can call it a day at the Presbyterian-After-Service-Coffee-Hour," Josh said as he rejoined me.

"I think you're right. I saw you talking to Bob and Ruth. What did they have to say?"

"Appalled at what happened. Bob suggested maybe you should consider selling out."

"Naturally. What about Ruth?"

"Shocked and hoped you were all right. Neither had much to say about anything."

I put my empty coffee cup on the serving table. "Let's get out of here."

"Good idea. I'll drop you off, change, and head for Sweet Daddy's to see if I can find some of those witnesses."

An hour later, Josh took off, leaving me with a long afternoon ahead. I decided to repack the books I didn't want to keep. Perhaps a nursing home or hospital would want them. The task didn't take long. I stopped for a glass of iced tea and gazed out the window in the door at the back porch. The empty bookcase reminded me of the ledgers I'd removed.

I wandered back into Daddy's office and raised the lid on the roll top. There were twelve, ranging in size from over a foot high to barely six inches. I guessed succeeding generations had kept books in whatever was available at the local store.

Settling in Daddy's creaky swivel chair, I found the oldest and opened it. The date told me my great-great-grandfather had written it. The slightly fading ink and spidery handwriting showed the farm making a profit. The information didn't make for scintillating reading, but gave me a glimmer of farm life in that era.

I moved on to another ledger, but more of the same had me leafing through it. Ditto with the next few. I sat back and stared at the ledgers. They were interesting from a historical standpoint. It was fun seeing my ancestors writing. It was almost as if they were telling me a story. But did I really want to keep them? *Why not? It's my heritage.* I'd replace them in the bookcase for future generations to ponder.

I began stacking them from tallest to shortest when a couple near the middle caught my eye. They didn't look like ledgers. I opened one, and then sat down with a thump.

Written in a feminine hand, the date told me the author had been my mother. These had nothing to do with farm accounts. These were diaries. I hurriedly shoved the ledgers back into the bookcase and took mother's musings into the living room. I set them on the coffee table, then sat on the sofa just staring. Did I want to read them? Did I *really* want to know the deepest secrets and thoughts of my long-dead, murdered, mother?

The answer was a resounding, yes!

Armed with iced tea and a bag of mini-candy bars, I took a deep breath and opened the first diary.

It's been six months since I married Eric. What began as an adventure has degenerated into a living hell. In my haste to spite Dee, I never considered where I'd be living. I hate this place. I'm expected to cook and clean, neither of which I've ever done before. And my husband has turned out to be a stick in the mud. All he does during the day is farm chores and at night he reads or watches TV. I'm so bored I could scream!

I paused to unwrap a candy bar and shove it into my mouth. So far, Mother's words didn't surprise me. Between what Aunt Dee had told me as she lay dying to the gossip from around town, I'd already deduced Mother was the old proverbial fish out of water. I read on.

I received a stern warning about spending last night. Seems we can't afford me indulging in a new dress or shoes every week. And now that the new year has begun, Eric has taken a job at the grain elevator to make ends meet. Thank God Daddy sends me a check once a month. Just wish it were for more.

I wondered how much he'd sent on a regular basis. On her deathbed, Aunt Dee had confessed that after my grandfather died, she'd chopped the payments. The Chicago family attorney had told me that my mother had received a small inheritance upon his death, but that the majority of his money had gone to my aunt. Apparently, Mother had blown through the money fast.

I pictured the shoes and clothes she never wore in the closet.

I continued reading. She'd used the diary to catalogue every gripe and moan from the barnyard smells to the weather to the lack of shopping opportunities, and finally to the people of Wellington.

Everyone looks at me like I was from another planet. My sense of style intimidates these bumpkins, and they laugh at what they assume is pretentiousness. What do they know about good grammar and fine dining manners? Lorna Bell comes close to being the silliest woman on the face of the earth. She giggles and makes eyes at Eric. June Simpson hates my guts even though she pretends to like me. She and Eric were an item in high school or something. She lost him to his first wife, and then again to me. Sorry Junie, tough luck. And don't get me started on that hack of a hair stylist, Clovis Fisher! Thank God my hair is long and she can't butcher it too badly. The only reason I go to her is that it gets me out of the house once a week. And my neighbors are more boring than my husband. At least Ruth and Bob Kendall show some signs of sophistication. Ruth is the closest thing I have to a friend in this town.

Then her tone changed. She discovered she was pregnant. Over the months, she had more or less ignored Denny except for the usual things one does for a toddler. Now, she had someone new to focus on—me. She described her pregnancy and my birth in detail, admitting she feigned frailty so Daddy would pay more attention to her.

But motherhood wasn't what she'd expected either. A baby in the house doubled the workload, yet she lived through colic, bottles, and potty training. All in all, she treated me not so much like a daughter, but more like a doll to be dressed up and cuddled.

When I became old enough to wander about on the farm or amuse myself inside, her boredom returned. Raising two children was hard work and cost money. Still, Mother seemed to enjoy being a mother and indeed, as reported by Ruth, doted on me.

Toward the end of the diary, the lack of money took its toll. From her tone, Mother never understood that she couldn't just buy whatever she wanted when she wanted. Her excuse was always, it's for Callie. And she became suspicious of Daddy's outside jobs. Arguments increased.

It was after midnight when he got home last night. He was supposed to be working in a supermarket in Atwell. His explanation was he was unloading the supply trucks. A likely story. The Simpson farm is near the highway to Atwell. Does he stop off there or maybe he's meeting her somewhere. After all, she does have a husband. And when he's in town, he spends a lot of time with Rich Bell. Rich—or that moron, Lorna?

This diary ended with a detailed description of my fifth birthday party. I finished just as Josh walked in the door.

"Hi babe, whatcha doing?"

"Reading one of Mother's diaries."

"Diaries? Where did you find it?"

I explained about the old bookcase on the back porch.

He frowned and sat next to me. "That's an odd place to keep them. What does she have to say?"

I sniffed and shoved another candy bar into my

mouth. "Nothing we didn't already know," I mumbled through chocolate and caramel. "She was bored, unhappy, and hated Wellington. She also suspected Daddy was having an affair. She just couldn't decide who with."

Josh hugged me. "I'm sorry, hon. I know you hoped the rumors were nothing but hot air."

I swallowed and shrugged. "What did you find out at Sweet Daddy's?"

He heaved a long sigh. "Not much. The bartender moved on about a year after your mother's death. Two of the witnesses died. Only one guy, Earl Bennett is still around, so I went out to his place to ask a few questions."

"What did he have to say?"

"Pretty much what the police report said. Your father came in for a couple of beers, but was definitely not drunk. Bennett recalls he seemed more sad than anything, and that he didn't say much. Just sat there real quiet watching the ball game like he was thinking."

"That last argument. You think he may have realized the marriage was over?"

"I don't know, but Bennett did say something interesting. He claims John Casey never even talked to him once the trial started. Never called him as a witness."

"What? But he could have corroborated when Daddy left and to his state of mind. He wasn't drunk or angry about anything!"

Daddy might not have been angry, but I sure was. John Casey had a lot to answer for and if nothing else came of this, I'd make sure he never saw that judgeship.

"It's the time frame thing. Remember? There's that

thirty-five minute gap from when he left the bar to when he called the cops. And people in bars don't pay all that much attention to the time. He could have left earlier than reported."

"Josh, are we at a dead end? We have a ton of information, but no answers."

"I don't know. When you get down to it, all we have are speculation, gossip, innuendo, and your dreams. We have no real evidence."

"We have letters, phone calls, two break-ins, and an attack on me. All of that says we've struck a chord with someone."

"The only thing we haven't done yet is see the appeal transcripts. There might have been something said during the trial we can latch onto. Tomorrow I'll go to Des Moines and see what I can dig up."

"That'll be a long drive. Will you stay overnight?"

He shook his head. "I'll drive down to Sioux City and grab a commuter flight. They run a couple of times a day to the capitol. I should be back tomorrow night sometime. Do you want to come?"

"Not really. I want to talk to Ruth about the house and read the other diary."

While Josh went online to make plane reservations, I sat back to think. So far, the diary had followed what I'd been told by others. Depression settled on my shoulders like a wet blanket. I'd been so hoping for a revelation of some sort. Nothing like that was forthcoming—yet. Perhaps the second diary would provide more insight.

And now I wasn't sure if Josh's trip would reveal anything we didn't already know.

Mother's murder, the break-ins, and the intruder

who attacked me all fit together. And I had the nagging feeling even Lorna and poor Phil were involved some way. I'd bet my life on it.

A shiver ran up my spine.

Maybe I already had.

Chapter Twenty-One

Josh was up and off at sunrise. He stuffed papers into his briefcase and unplugged his phone from the charger.

"My flight leaves at eight-fifteen and gets in around nine-thirty. That should put me at the court of appeals by ten. With any luck, I'll find what I need, grab the six-thirty flight back and be home around nine. Don't wait dinner. I'll get something at the airport." He leaned down to kiss me hard. "Are you going to be okay?"

I kissed him back, still tingling in the afterglow of making love early in the morning.

"I'll be fine. Bored without you, but I'll get over it. Have a safe trip and call me if you find something. I want to know why Daddy's appeal was denied. His version of the events leaves plenty of room for reasonable doubt."

He shook his head. "At that stage of the game, I don't think reasonable doubt enters the picture. They'd be looking for a technicality in the trial process."

"Like an incompetent attorney?"

"Maybe."

He kissed me again and left. I pulled a package of bacon from the fridge, and then put it back. Why not have breakfast at the Kozy? When I was finished, I'd drop by Ruth's and ask about the packing. When I got home, I'd read Mother's remaining diary.

I went upstairs, showered, and dressed, then headed to town. Breakfast at the Kozy wasn't as popular as lunch. Most of the patrons were men, which suggested this was the way many of the town merchants began their day.

I found a booth near the front door and slid in. A waitress appeared within a few seconds, slapped a menu in front of me, and asked if I wanted coffee. A minute later, she brought it.

"Know what you want yet?" she asked.

"I'm in no hurry. Give me a few minutes."

She nodded and left. I picked up the menu and pretended to read. I dared a quick glance around the room. Bob Kendall sat deep in a discussion across the room with the local insurance man. Fred Carson drank coffee with a man I'd seen before, but couldn't identify. Clovis shared a table with John Casey's receptionist, Serena, of all people. Clovis looked up, saw me and waved, her bangle bracelets jingling. Serena smiled and quickly averted her eyes.

"Well, you're up bright and early this morning," a voice said from beside me. I looked over and saw Emma standing next to me.

"Good morning, Emma, yes, I guess I am. Josh had some business to attend to out of town, so I thought I'd let someone else make breakfast for a change."

She chuckled. "Wise decision. Our breakfasts are killer."

I'd bet they were—on more than one level. Knowing the Kozy, they were probably loaded with fat and calories.

"Hear you had a problem the other night. Any idea

who the intruder was?"

"Not yet," I said shaking my head.

"You know, Callie, people are beginning to talk some pretty strange stuff."

"Like what?"

"Like maybe you should leave town. You're stirring up trouble. Things are happening and residents are uneasy."

"You mean that my questions about my mother, Daddy, and my memory are hitting home?"

"Could be. Be careful, honey. I'd hate to see anything else happen to you."

"So would I."

She smiled and patted my hand. "You enjoy your meal. Want a piece of pie to take home?"

I had to laugh. "At this hour?"

"My pies are good anytime of the day. Just took the first apple out of the oven."

Who could resist such salesmanship? I requested a slice to go.

When the waitress returned, I ordered—tomato juice, sausage links, eggs sunny side up, fruit, and a side of biscuits with sausage gravy. At least the fruit was healthy. She refilled my coffee and I sat sipping while watching Wellington wake up. Bob Kendall left and nodded at me through the window as he walked toward the real estate office. The awning out front shaded this side of the café from the sun that was now shining brightly.

As I waited for my food, I mulled over what Emma had said. Some people wanted me to pull up stakes. Bob Kendall had wanted that from the first day I'd hit town. Certainly, the letter writer and the caller were of the same mind. I found it odd that the notes and calls had ended. Since Lorna's death I'd received neither. Could she have been the culprit? Or was it someone else? Someone who just wanted me gone. Maybe whoever had done it decided harassing me wasn't worth the effort. I was still in Wellington. I supposed Lorna's murder had reminded the townsfolk of my mother's so long ago.

I liked living in Wellington. It represented home unlike the Conrad mansion in Chicago. It had been too formal, too cold to be called home. I wanted the citizens to like me. I wanted to reestablish the roots that had been so ruthlessly yanked out years before. And I wanted those roots to include Josh Hendricks.

I love him.

I finally thought the words I'd hidden from my mind for over a week. I wanted to live here with him and our children for the rest of my life. It was so simple, so strong a feeling I wanted to cry.

And regardless of what information he finds in Des Moines, we'll work it out. Somewhere, somebody will reopen the investigation about Mother. Daddy's name will be cleared and a killer will be finally brought to justice.

Just how this would come about was anybody's guess. I straightened my shoulders with a new resolve. I'd make it happen.

"Here you go," the waitress said jerking me out of my thoughts. She set the plates in front of me. "Anything else?"

"Uh, no thanks."

She moved on and I stared at the mammoth amount of food. The eggs stared back like two yellow eyes. The three sausages were twice the size of the kind I bought in the frozen food section. The juice came in a full eight-ounce glass, and the bowl of assorted melons, strawberries, and blueberries almost overflowed. But it was the biscuits and gravy that had me fascinated. I don't know why I ordered it. I'd only had the combination a couple of times at a chain restaurant specializing in breakfasts. It had had the consistency and taste of wallpaper paste.

Heaving a sigh, I picked up my fork and dug in. To my surprise, the wallpaper paste analogy never materialized. This was thick, to be sure, but creamy and with just enough pepper and sausage tang to make me want more. I took my time eating. An hour later I finished. The plate was clean.

I probably won't eat for the rest of the day.

I requested another cup of coffee and slowly savored the taste. The waitress brought not only my check, but also the pie. I vowed to only eat once a week at the Kozy Kafe. Any more and my next job would be as the fat lady in the circus. I needed to walk this off.

Since it was still too early to knock on Ruth's door, I strolled down the street to the city park. The bandstand stood in the center surrounded by oak trees, the leaves dappling the conical roof with bits of shade in the morning sun.

I paused to remember those Saturday nights in the summer. I'd played hide and seek with the other kids while Mother and Daddy would socialize. Just as I thought I couldn't recall anything specific, an image floated through my mind. Lorna walking past with a smile for Daddy and a nod for Mother.

"Bitch," my mother had said in a low tone.

"Gracie, don't say that. She just smiled," Daddy had replied.

"She's common and stupid in the bargain. She always wants something that belongs to someone else. And don't call me Gracie."

"I've told you, there's nothing going on between Lorna and me. Let's not argue."

Funny how that should pop up now. Had the conversation occurred the night of the murder or at some other time? I walked on, kicking acorns out of my way.

A quick glance at my watch showed it was almost nine. Josh should be about to land in Des Moines and I was another six blocks from the Kendall residence. *Might as well go the distance.*

I stood on the Kendall porch for a moment to organize my thoughts before ringing the doorbell. Ruth answered.

"Callie, my goodness you're up with the birds this morning. Come on in. Would you like a cup of coffee?" Her gaze swept the drive, empty but for her BMW. "Where's your car?"

"I had breakfast at the Kozy and wanted to walk it off, and thanks, but I don't need another cup of coffee," I answered as she led me toward the spacious kitchen.

She shot me a glance over her shoulder and rolled her eyes. "I can understand that. Big farm breakfasts never appealed to me. I'm a cereal or toast kind of woman. Have a seat."

I pulled out a chair and sat. "I know this is kind of early to be calling on someone, but when I realized how close I was to your house, I had to stop in and say thank you."

Her eyebrows rose as she sipped from a cup on the counter.

"Thank me? Whatever for?"

"John Casey told me you and Jessica helped pack up the house after Aunt Dee took us away. That must have been quite an undertaking."

"It was the least I could do. I owed it to Grace. After the trial, it seemed sensible. I knew no one was going to live there for a long time." She put the coffee cup down and frowned. "You have a strange look on your face."

"Do I? I was just thinking how sad it must have been to pack Mother's things away knowing she'd never touch them again."

"Heartbreaking, actually. She was a close friend."

"I found a couple of diaries she kept and read one last night. She said you were the only real friend she had in town."

She stared with wide eyes. "Diaries? I didn't know she wrote a diary."

"I think it was an outlet for how unhappy she was. You were right, she never felt like she fit in. I'm just glad she had a friend like you, and wanted to thank you and Jessica for all the work you put in."

Ruth sniffed. "Jessica... yeah, right. All she did was wander around getting underfoot and asking questions. She almost drove me nuts."

"What kind of questions?"

"Should she pack this, should she separate that? I finally remember sending her downstairs to supervise the movers while I took over upstairs. I'll say this, those men were good. They had everything packed away by late afternoon."

"Did they take it all to the attic?"

"Hmmm, no, I don't think so. I believe they left the boxes in various rooms. It wasn't until after your father's trial when your aunt informed—can't remember if it was John or Bob—that nobody would be returning. John was in charge of the estate, but Bob was dealing with the house hoping your aunt would sell. Well, anyway, word came from her to put everything in the attic. I hired a couple of local handymen to do it."

I sighed and stared out the window at a perfectly landscaped back yard.

"Are you sure you're all right?" she asked.

"I'm still upset about Lorna. I wouldn't wish finding her like that on my worst enemy."

Ruth gazed into her coffee cup. "Terrible. Just terrible."

"I wonder what she was going to tell me?"

"Tell you?"

I explained the conversation from Tuesday night.

"Did she seem all right at the Garden Club meeting?"

Ruth shrugged. "As far as I could tell. I didn't talk to her much. She chatted a lot with June. If I recall, she left as soon as the meeting ended. Knowing Lorna, she was probably trying to figure out a way of not learning something. New things scared her. She wasn't all that bright, you know."

I pushed away from the table and rose. "I'd better get back. Josh is gone for the day on business. He won't be home until late tonight. At any rate, I want to thank you again."

She waved a hand. "No problem."

I paused at the front door, then turned to face her.

"In spite of what you told me, you believe Daddy killed my mother, don't you?"

She sighed and captured her lower lip between her teeth. "Callie, I didn't want to think that. He was a kind, gentle man, but the evidence was there, and your aunt told me that when she last talked to Grace, she was upset about your father's affair and wanted a divorce. Passions run high in moments like those. It can happen to anyone. She was my closest friend. I still miss her. Please, for your sake, try to put it behind you."

I walked slowly back to town. Josh's suggestion that Aunt Dee had taken us away in order to protect me came to mind. The flashback I'd had after finding Lorna's body could be a sign that I did see more that fateful night than anyone knew. Perhaps my aunt had sensed that. Perhaps I'd said something that while inconsequential in my mind, allowed her to catch a glimmer of truth.

I hoped Josh got those transcripts of the trial from the appeals clerk. Perhaps they would open the locked door to my memory. And I needed to remember.

****

After leaving Ruth's, I walked around town window-shopping. The crime scene tape had been removed from Bell's. The dark interior looked cold and foreboding. I shivered and wondered what would happen to the store. As far as I knew, she and Rich had no children.

On a whim, I went to the bank and my safety deposit box where in the solitude of the little examination room I inspected Mother's bracelet again. The fluorescent lights bounced off the red and white stones, setting them ablaze, making it an almost living, breathing entity.

I gazed hard at the tiny inscription on one of the links again. *To my beloved.* This just didn't sound like something Daddy would say. But then what did I know? I didn't remember much about him. He could have had a wildly romantic side he showed only to Mother.

Phil Carson's face that Monday morning popped through my mind. He'd looked puzzled, just like Lorna. Even Josh had used the allusion to a jigsaw puzzle when we'd discussed clues. I remembered one of our theories that Mother had bought the bracelet on her own. If that was the case, then the inscription made no sense. If she'd stolen it, then the words were from and to someone else. *Perhaps* she'd been in the store one day. *Maybe* Phil had shown it to her and when his back was turned, she'd taken it. I wondered if the owner had perhaps sold it to Phil for some ready cash. *Anything's possible, I suppose, but why wouldn't Phil remember an incident like that?*

I snapped the bracelet on and twisted my wrist. Once again the stones shot fire, reminding me of the flashing lights in my dreams. I gasped and hurriedly unfastened it, then dropped it back into the box.

Oh my God, is that what the lights represent? Had Mother been wearing it that night? If so, then how did I end up with it in my jewelry box? Impossible. The police would have confiscated it and eventually turn it over to Aunt Dee. The one thing I did know was that my aunt would never have given it to a child as a keepsake. She knew and appreciated fine jewelry.

I returned the box to its cubbyhole and left with more questions spinning through my mind. Perhaps, I was wrong about when I'd seen Mother wearing the bracelet. I could have even taken it from her jewelry box to play dress up.

Damn, why can't I remember!

I drove home with the undeniable feeling something was about to happen. I wished Josh would come home. I needed him.

Back home, I piddled around doing little household chores. It was mid-afternoon before I settled down with Mother's last diary. I wasn't sure I wanted to read it. From the conversations I'd had with others, the portrait painted was that of a selfish, spoiled woman. The first diary had confirmed the impression. She'd married my father out of spite and to get out from under her sister's controlling thumb. Aunt Dee had told me the whole story as she lay dying.

I pushed my aunt from my mind. Heaving a strong sigh, I opened the book. The date showed that almost eighteen months had passed since the first diary ended with my fifth birthday. This put it just months before her death.

I don't know what occurred during that time span, but the tone of her writing had changed. She was happy, almost giddy.

Love is a wonderful thing. It took a while for me to find it, but now that I have, my life is perfect. I'm no longer jealous of Eric or the women who flirt with him. Last week, I caught June Simpson in full vamp mode. I laughed and told her she wasn't woman enough to turn his head. If Eric had been interested, he wouldn't have married me.

I wanted to laugh out loud. I'd bet June hadn't taken that with a smile. And it was good to know

Mother had finally come to appreciate Daddy's finer qualities. I read on.

The entries for the next few weeks described an intimate relationship with lots of kissing and touching.

His mere presence sets me on fire. His touch awakens my very soul. Why did it take so long for me to recognize this was the man for me?

I scanned the rest of the pages in this section. I didn't need to know about their love life. Kids never like to think about their parents having sex, even though that's how they got to be kids.

I paused to make a quick dinner. I wanted to get back to Mother in love—and hopefully to another clue as to who had killed her.

By the time I'd washed up the dishes, dusk had fallen. I snapped on the light behind the sofa and glanced at my watch. Josh would be home soon.

I settled in to finish the diary.

Jessica Casey is a royal pain in the ass. John asked for a separation last month. Ever since, she's been after every man in town, including mine. I told her to knock it off. He wasn't interested. And if she didn't cool it, another woman just might snatch John out from under her nose. I hinted that that might be the reason why he wanted some space. She told me to mind my own business. Bitch.

Interesting. John had wanted the separation. Did John have a wandering eye? Strange, but in a town like Wellington, why hadn't the rumor mill brought that up? I had the feeling Mother just tossed something out in a moment of anger at Jessica flirting with Daddy.

The last entry was written just three days before her death. The angry, bitter words shattered all that my perceptions.

How could he do this to me? How??? I caught him in a hot clinch, sucking face. And with that simpering, stupid bitch to boot! There they were in the office of the furniture store showing no shame!

Lorna? She'd caught Daddy and Lorna? I didn't want to believe it, but there it was in black and white. I forced myself to read on.

I gave him an ultimatum—it was her or me. And if he chose her, I'd make damned sure her husband would know about it. They both tried to weasel out of it, but I know what I saw. I cried all the way home. I'd given him my undying love and this was how he repaid me!

The next day he told me divorce was out of the question. I could accept him as he was and not try to change him. I fired back that a divorce was the only solution. I gave him twenty-four hours to make up his mind. Tomorrow is Saturday. I'll know by the end of the evening what my future holds. A part of me will love him forever, but at the moment, I hate him. Hate him!

I shut the diary and tossed it onto the coffee table, sick to my stomach. The rumors had been true. Daddy did have an affair. And with Lorna Bell, of all people. What had he been thinking? He professed to love Mother. And Mother had just rediscovered her love for him. Yet she caught him in Lorna's arms. How devastating.

I rose and paced the living room. What had happened after the concert that night? I remembered the argument in the car, but not the subject matter. And were the arguing voices of my dreams the two of them later after he'd returned from the bar?

Oh my God, Mother demanded a divorce again and

Daddy in a fit of rage, said no. Yet even as I thought it, my heart rejected it. Daddy wasn't violent.

Then another thought occurred—could Mother have told Rich Bell? Could Lorna, in a fury, come over to have it out with Mother? Or maybe she just *feared* that Mother would tell Rich. And could things have escalated into murder?

I shook my head. I didn't see Lorna as a killer.

My phone rang. It was Josh.

"I just landed in Sioux City. I should be home in about an hour. Sorry I didn't call sooner, but I was running late. Almost missed the plane."

"Did you get the transcripts?" Heavy silence followed my question. "Josh, are you there?"

"I'm here. No, I didn't get the transcripts. There were no transcripts to get."

"What do you mean?"

"I mean, John Casey didn't file an appeal."

Shock left me speechless for a moment. Then my voice rose in anger. "I…I don't understand. What kind of a defense attorney doesn't file an appeal in a murder case, especially with no eyewitnesses and circumstantial evidence?"

"*Strong* circumstantial evidence, and only John Casey can answer that. And don't go calling him tonight. Not while you're pissed off. I suggest we pay him a visit tomorrow morning. Okay?"

"Oh, all right."

"I'll see you in a little bit. We can talk more then."

I hung up. Anger chewed in my chest. I wanted to rip John Casey a new one in the worst way. No appeal? That coupled with Mother's diary was the last straw. The events of that night twenty-five years ago were locked in my head.

I needed to remember. Now!

Chapter Twenty-Two

Aunt Dee had always said to begin at the beginning. Dr. Halloran had told me to take it from the first thing I remembered. I inhaled a deep breath, and then let it out slowly.

First I had to set the stage. In my dreams, I was either at the top of the stairs or floating above the foyer. I closed my eyes and fixated on the top of the stairs for several minutes. Nothing happened. Since I couldn't float in mid-air, that meant I had to dig deeper.

The dream images were dimly lit and shadowy. I turned off all but one light in the living room and climbed to the top of the steps. Too dark. I returned downstairs and switched on the chandelier in the dining room plus the overhead in the kitchen, then resumed my position. Better, but still not right.

I stared into the foyer below. Had the light been on in the master bedroom? I flipped the switch. No, much too bright now. Besides, if I did witness something, how could the killer have missed seeing me silhouetted against the light? I closed the door to within a couple of inches of the latch. Yes, this was more like it.

I inhaled another shaky breath, walked down a few steps, and stared over the banister. The foyer stared back. No images appeared.

Sometimes, bars played a role in my vision. I knelt and gazed through the spindles. I swallowed hard and broke out in a cold sweat. A memory flashed across my mind. Shadows struggling, a loud crash, screams, and then someone sobbing. I had no idea if things were in the right sequence, and didn't bother to organize them. I hunched over to seven-year-old size gripping the spindles with my hands. The voices returned.

"No, no!"

"You deserve this!"

"He doesn't love you!"

Those last words made my eyes pop open. My father's mistress? Or was what I'd read in the diary intruding into my thoughts? Was I hearing the disjointed comments I'd read? I had no idea.

I leaned my forehead against the spindles, blinking tears from my eyes. Through the watery haze, I had a view of the space below, but it didn't match my dream image. I moved up to the hallway and knelt behind the barred barrier again. Two figures struggled. Screams ripped through the air. Suddenly, I saw a shadow crash into the table by the staircase, sending the vase toppling to the floor where it shattered. Lights glinted off something. A knife? More flashing lights entered the picture.

This was it! This is where I'd crouched that night. The same fear that had gripped me so many years ago gripped me now. Most of the foyer was in my line of sight. I heard the angry voices again. Another shadow—my mother?—turned for the front door. The other ran toward her. Then abruptly, all visions receded.

I rose on shaking legs. I'd remembered something, just not enough. Mother had tried to escape out the front door, but didn't make it. Was the unidentified shadow Daddy or his mistress? Perhaps reading the diary had been a mistake.

I wanted to throw up. I ran into the bathroom and waited until my stomach no longer churned before making my way back downstairs and into the kitchen. I poured a glass of wine and tried to get my trembling under control.

Dr. Halloran had warned me not to force things, but I could no longer wait. He wasn't the one finding dead bodies and getting whacked on the head. Tomorrow I'd locate a good shrink and have him hypnotize me. Maybe the events of the last few weeks would make me more receptive to remembering.

One thing tonight had been proven—I was now certain I'd witnessed Mother's murder.

I drank a sizable portion of the wine. My shaking had stopped, thank God. Lights flashed in the driveway and gravel crunched as a car swept in.

Josh! He's home. God, I need him.

The porch door opened and footsteps echoed across the porch. Through the glass in the door, I spied Ruth Kendall. My heart sank. I wanted Josh.

Damn, I can't talk to her now.

She smiled and knocked before entering.

"Callie, I hope I'm not intruding, but I have to talk to you about something. It's important." Her smile vanished. She rubbed her forehead and licked her lips.

"What is it, Ruth? I'm not feeling very well at the moment. Can this wait until tomorrow?"

She stared with hard brown eyes, her lips clenched into a thin line. "No, no it can't. I want it back."

I set the glass on the counter. "You want what back?"

"Please, let's not argue or play games. Just give it

to me and everything will be fine. And while we're at it, you might as well include those diaries. God only knows what that two-timing bitch wrote about her and Bob."

Confused, I stared back. "Ruth, what the hell are you talking about?"

Her nostrils flared and her lips parted into a snarl. "So, it's going to be that way, is it?"

The fear of a little while ago returned. I backed up several paces with the strangest feeling that I'd done this before.

"Ruth, I don't know what your problem is, but you'd better go. We'll talk in the morning."

"We'll talk now, dammit! Give it to me. Don't make me hurt you!" Her voice rose to a shout.

In my mind, I heard other shouting voices. The veil lifted. Women's voices. Mother and Daddy hadn't been arguing.

"Get out," I said in a fear choked tone.

"No can do, Callie. You're just like her. Stubborn to the bone. I warned her to stay away from him, but she laughed. Laughed at me. The bitch! I will not be laughed at or made a fool of. Are you going to give me that damned bracelet or not?"

No words formed. My hand clutched at my throat. The image of a few minutes ago crystallized. The shadowy figure crashing into the table was Ruth Kendall, my mother's killer.

"I guess you're not." She glanced at the knife set on the counter. "Still here after all these years."

As she pulled the large chef's knife from its slot, my paralysis lifted. I turned, crashed through the café doors, and ran for my life. Behind me, Ruth screamed and followed.

I was doing the same thing Mother had done, only I was faster and Ruth twenty-five years older. I flashed out of the dining room and into the living room, my assailant not far behind. I skirted around the coffee table and chairs, stopping to overturn one in front of her. She tripped and fell, the knife falling from her hand and skittering across the hardwood. She screamed something unintelligible, but I didn't stop to listen. I ran through the archway into the foyer. Unlike Mother, I didn't even try the front door. It was locked anyway. I'd never make it. I headed for the stairs and my gun in the bedroom.

The sudden strong scent of a man's aftershave or cologne stung my mental nostrils, just like it had all those years ago. I remembered it from my first day home. Bob Kendall!

Through the side window, a car raced up the drive, its headlights flashing brightly followed by the taillights glowing red as the driver braked.

Josh! I didn't have time to stop and scream for him to hurry. Ruth had regained her feet and the knife. I pounded up the stairs as she entered the foyer. Rage gave her strength and speed. I gained the hallway and whipped to my right and the bedroom. The bed with the equalizer was five or six steps away. Behind me, Ruth stumbled on the last step and ran into the wall. That small misstep gave me the time to reach under the pillow and pull out the gun.

From below, a voice shouted, "Ruth, no! Don't!" Footsteps hammered up the back staircase. Through the window more lights flashed as another car drove up. The lights of my dreams! I didn't have time to think.

Ruth was at the door.

I pulled the hammer back and pointed the gun.

"I'll shoot, Ruth. I swear I will!"

She paused for a fraction of a second, then raising the knife over her head, she shrieked and charged. I had no choice. I pulled the trigger. The report blasted my eardrums. From ten feet away I didn't miss.

Ruth stopped, her eyes wide with shock as a large red stain mushroomed in the middle of her yellow blouse. The knife fell from her fingers to the floor with a clatter. She sank to her knees, and then slowly onto her side before rolling over. Her glassy eyes stared at the ceiling, but I knew they saw nothing.

Bob raced into the room. He didn't bother looking at me, but gazed at his wife. He ran to her side and lifted her limp body into his arms.

"Ruth, Ruth," he sobbed.

Had Daddy done the same twenty-five years ago?

"Callie! Callie, are you all right? Answer me."

Josh! He burst into the bedroom as the gun slipped from my fingers. I collapsed onto the bed.

The room went dark and at that moment, I remembered.

****

I came to in my old bedroom. Josh sat by my side holding my hand. I gazed into those worried, frightened gray eyes and burst into tears. He quickly gathered me in his arms.

"It's all right, sweetheart, it's all right. You're safe," he crooned.

"I killed her, didn't I?"

"Yes, but don't think about it now."

"I had to, she was going to kill me, just like she did

Mother."

"I know." He kissed my forehead and tried to wipe the tears from my cheeks, then hugged me close again.

"Oh God, Josh. I remember everything. It all came crashing into my mind when Bob and you ran into the room."

"Later, we'll deal with it later."

Voices echoed from down the hallway. "Who's...Who's here?"

"I called the cops. They came immediately and the ambulance arrived a few minutes ago. Chief Jackson has already called in the state police to investigate, but I don't think there's much to look at."

I struggled to sit beside him on the edge of the bed.

"It was the bracelet, Josh. It wasn't Mother's, it was Ruth's." I buried my head in my hands. "I...I found it that night, and when my memory disappeared, I forgot about it."

Chief Jackson stood in the doorway. "How are you feeling, Miss Bryant?"

"Shaky, but better than a while ago. How long was I out?"

"Not long," Josh said. "Scared me to death when I couldn't wake you right away."

"Can you talk?"

I nodded and stood. Josh's arm snaked around my waist as I swayed slightly.

"Are you sure you're all right?" he asked in an anxious tone.

"I'm fine, really."

"Let's go downstairs," the chief suggested.

We used the backstairs and sat at the kitchen table. My half-finished glass of wine still sat on the counter. I got up, retrieved it, and drank the contents. My gaze traveled to the knife holder. How often in the past couple of weeks had I used the original murder weapon? I shuddered and looked away.

Chief Jackson pulled out his notebook. "Okay, Miss Bryant, what happened?"

I took a deep breath and told him the story from the beginning to me pulling the trigger.

He nodded and wrote quickly. "I've called in the state boys on this, but I'd say it's pretty evident this is a case of self-defense. Now, explain to me about this bracelet."

"Before I do, I need to tell you I remembered everything—or mostly everything—from the night my mother died. I guess the trauma of pulling the trigger with the intent to kill someone overrode the trauma of seeing Mother murdered."

"Makes sense, I suppose. Go on."

Josh rose, opened the refrigerator, and poured both of us a glass of wine. This time I sipped slowly while arranging my thoughts.

"We'd been at the Saturday night concert. On the drive back Mother and Daddy argued. I'm still not sure what about. When we got home, Mother put me to bed. Don't remember hearing Daddy leave again. I fell asleep and later on woke up to hear two people arguing. I assumed it was my parents. I was scared by the voices and remember walking down the hall. I must have thought that if I asked, they'd stop yelling."

I stopped to drink again as the memories flooded into my mind.

"Take your time, honey," Josh advised. "Let it come slowly."

"The bedroom door was closed to within an inch of the latch. I…I was at the top of the stairs when I heard someone scream. Mother and another woman ran into the foyer. It was Ruth. They struggled. Ruth was slashing at Mother and Mother was screaming. Then Mother pushed her away and Ruth fell against the table, knocking over the vase. I remember she held a knife. The lights from the living room flashed off of the blade. Mother turned for the door, but before she could escape, Ruth rushed forward and plunged the knife into her back. I remembered being so scared, I fell and curled up into a little ball."

"Thank God, she didn't think to look up," Josh muttered.

"Has…Has Bob said anything yet?" I asked.

"No, he's still in shock," the chief replied.

I nodded and stared into the glass. "I'm not surprised. I remember hearing Ruth breathing and sobbing. Then suddenly, Bob was there. He kept saying, 'Oh my God, what have you done?' over and over. Ruth kept yelling that it was all his fault. He finally told her he'd take care of things and to get the hell out and go home."

"So, Bob Kendall was an accomplice after the fact?" chief asked.

"I guess. Funny, after all these years I can still smell his cologne."

"How did he take care of it?" Josh wondered.

"They…They both left the room. I remember a car leaving, and then Bob returned to the foyer with a large knife—the hunting knife, I guess. He removed the one from Mother's back and…" My throat closed. I didn't sip this time, but gulped. "He stabbed her again and again, and then jammed the knife back into the original wound. When he was done, he walked away. I heard water running in the kitchen, and eventually a car driving off. I'm not sure how long I lay huddled at the base of the banister, but I finally got up and came downstairs. Mother didn't move. I don't think I equated her stillness to death. There was blood everywhere." A child's voice echoed in my mind. *Mama? Mama?*

"I lifted her arm. It was heavy and scared me. Her long blonde hair was fanned out around her shoulders and on the floor. Something sparkled from under it. It was the bracelet. I picked it up, but can't remember much after that. I must have put it in my jewelry box."

"And of course, when Ruth saw it that night at the party, she damn near had a heart attack," Josh added.

"Lorna recognized it, too. Only so much time had passed, and I'd told everyone it belonged to Mother, she didn't make the connection until it was too late. I'm sure you'll find Ruth killed Lorna," I said to Jackson. "I should have realized the significance of the pillow."

"What pillow?" Josh asked.

"The one I tripped over on the floor at Lorna's. The one the killer used to muffle the sound of the shot. That spells premeditation. No vagrant would come in and think to do that. I'll bet Ruth came right in the front door and Lorna thought it was me. May have even called out, 'I'm back here, Callie' or something like that. She grabbed the pillow jammed it around the gun and killed her."

Bill nodded. "It was the same caliber bullet that I dug out of your wall. I'm sure ballistics will show it was the same gun, too. From twelve feet away, she could hardly miss."

I shuddered remembering the blood dripping down the wall behind the desk. A forty-five caliber likely blew off the back of Lorna's head.

"And Lorna must have either seen the gun or Ruth said something to her before pulling the trigger. That explains why she reached for the phone. Can't believe neither of us caught the premeditation thing at the time," Josh added

"That's why you aren't detectives," Bill drawled. "We saw the significance of the pillow right away."

"And she obviously was the intruder. She came one day to search for the bracelet and again later in the attic," Josh said.

I rubbed my forehead and finished the wine. Something about that statement didn't make sense. I needed to tell Josh more, but for now, the chief had all he needed.

"Are we finished? I'm really tired."

Bill nodded and rose. "You can't stay here tonight. We still have work to do."

"We'll be at my place, Bill."

"Can I grab some clean clothes?"

"I'll get them," Josh said, rising from his chair.

It dawned on me that perhaps Ruth's body hadn't as yet been removed. I had no desire to see it.

The chief nodded. "All right, but don't touch anything with bare hands."

Josh grabbed the necessities and came back downstairs. He laid them on the table and took me into his arms.

I clung to him—my rock, my port in a storm—and when his lips found mine, I knew he and my love for him would live a long time.

Chapter Twenty-Three

The police allowed us back into the house the following afternoon. As the chief had said, it was obviously self-defense. Even the state police agreed. However, Bill Jackson was re-opening my mother's case.

That was two days ago. The *News-Sentinel* had covered the crimes in detail, including the one twenty-five years ago. The paper had blossomed from ten pages to sixteen along with the circulation. Naturally, the town was buzzing with the news. The gossip wires at Sweet Daddy's, the Kozy, and of course, the Elite Beauty Salon crackled with activity.

The police hadn't said much to us regarding Lorna, but Josh and I speculated.

"When I spoke with June, she said Lorna and Ruth had an intense discussion at the garden club meeting, yet Ruth told me she'd barely talked to Lorna and in fact, had said she'd talked more with June. I'll bet Lorna either confronted Ruth about the bracelet or asked questions about it," I said.

"Probably asked questions," Josh replied. "Remember, Lorna wasn't all that bright. And you said she looked puzzled when you saw her on Tuesday. I can just see Lorna saying, 'You know, that bracelet looks a lot like one you had years ago' to Ruth."

"Which would be enough to sign her death

warrant." I sighed. "After all those years with Ruth thinking she was safe, along I come asking questions. Must have shocked her beyond belief. Bob, too. No wonder he landed on my doorstep before I had a chance to unpack."

"He was in it up to his neck. He covered up your mother's murder." He paused. "I'm sure Ruth entered the furniture store that afternoon near closing, walked back to the office, shot Lorna, and exited through the back door."

"I'm wondering about Phil Carson. He must have recognized the bracelet, but like Lorna, couldn't remember why. Think Ruth also ran him down?"

"Maybe. She couldn't take a chance on him putting two and two together. It's a very nice piece of jewelry. He might not have sold it to the Kendalls, but maybe he repaired it at some time. And if Phil did remember, he'd go straight to Bill Jackson." Josh picked up my hand and kissed it. "Thank God you run fast. I pulled into the driveway and saw two cars parked near yours, one with the lights on, the engine still running, and driver's side door wide open. I had just gotten out when I heard the shot. Scared the hell out of me."

"I might have been more vigilant if I hadn't misinterpreted the diary. My father wasn't having an affair, my mother was. The eighteen-month gap fooled me into thinking she'd rediscovered her love for Daddy. In reality, she was crazy over Bob Kendall, and the passage about finding the 'love of her life' in a clinch with Lorna must have been a jolt."

"What a mess. I always said small towns have more secrets than large cities."

Bill Jackson stopped by the next morning as we

were having breakfast. He accepted a cup of coffee and sat at the kitchen table.

"What's going on?" Josh asked.

"We've arrested Bob Kendall as an accessory to your mother's murder. Once I informed him and his lawyer that your memory of the night your mother died had returned, he started talking. Seems your mother wasn't his only conquest over the years. He'd had brief flings with several women, often clients, but always out of town. Grace Bryant was unhappy in her marriage and on the prowl. Sorry, Miss Bryant, but those were his words."

I waved a hand. "I know that now. Go on. How did it evolve into murder?"

He sipped from his cup before continuing. "Apparently Ruth didn't mind his wandering eye, provided it didn't humiliate her or cause gossip, but him having an affair with her so-called best friend qualified as humiliating. As long as the women were from out of town, she didn't care. Ruth also hired private detectives to keep her up to date on each new squeeze. Starting up with Grace was an explosion waiting to happen. When she found out, she was livid. Demanded he break it off immediately."

"But he didn't," I said.

"Bob is a weak man. He couldn't scratch up the nerve to end it, so he finagled a way to have your mother find him and Lorna kissing. He hoped she'd be so angry, she'd do it for him."

"And instead, she gave him an ultimatum," Josh added.

The chief nodded. "She told him to get a divorce and she'd do the same."

"Only divorce wasn't an option," I said remembering the passage in the diary. "It all boiled down to money, didn't it?"

"Bob married a rich woman, but Ruth Kendall held the purse strings. Her money paid for Kendall Realty. It also paid for the house and the refurbishing. Bob danced to her tune. Everything was in her name."

I wondered if Lorna had known Bob and my mother were having an affair, or if Bob simply seized the moment and planted a kiss on her when he knew Mother would see it? Lorna being Lorna may have assumed Bob was overcome with her charms.

"So, how did Ruth come to be here that night?" Josh asked.

"According to Bob, Ruth had seen him and Grace talking at the concert. When they returned home later, she demanded to know if he'd told her to get lost. When he admitted he hadn't, she went ballistic. They argued, complete with his wife slapping and hitting him. He stormed out of the house to cool off. He says he was only gone for fifteen minutes, but when he returned, Ruth was gone. He was afraid she'd gone out to the farm and followed. By the time he got there, your mother was dead, Ruth hysterical, and his life about to go down the toilet."

"So, he framed my father for the murder. I wonder why neither of them thought to check on Denny and me."

"I brought that up. Bob said in their panic, they both forgot. It wasn't until later they thought about it. By then, however, the place was swarming with cops. Ruth missed the bracelet the next day, but there was no way to search for it at that time."

"No wonder she volunteered to help pack up the house. It gave her a chance to look for it. Obviously, she didn't find it. Why didn't she search sooner over the years?"

"Because John Casey had the keys. Your aunt must have told him to keep an eye on the place. Ruth had no legitimate reason for asking to be let in. And as time passed and no mention of the bracelet was made, she breathed easier," Josh speculated.

"Bob admits to coming close to panic again at your party when he saw you wearing the bracelet he'd given his wife years ago. He says they assumed she must have lost it somewhere else. He even put in an insurance claim."

"And Ruth returned to search for it while we were at the lake," Josh said.

The chief nodded as I refilled his coffee.

"You know, that day out at the lake, I had the feeling when we first arrived that someone was in the woods watching. Eventually, the feeling eased and I forgot about it."

"Bob was at the table next to us in the Kozy that morning," Josh said. "He'd have no problem overhearing our plans. He follows us to make sure we're going to be there for a while, and then ransacks the house looking for the bracelet."

"Or calls Ruth to do it. He said he had an appointment with an out of town client."

"And that shouldn't be hard to verify. Obviously, either he or Ruth was responsible for the letters and calls. I'll bet Ruth fired the shot, too, with the same gun she used to kill Lorna."

"That's about the size of it," the chief confirmed.

"And Phil Carson?" I asked in a soft voice.

"When she found out you'd taken it to him to fix the clasp, she knew that sooner or later the shit would hit the fan."

Josh stacked our long empty breakfast dishes in the sink, poured another cup of coffee, and returned to his seat.

"How did she know where to find him?" he asked.

"Phil's Monday night poker mania was well-known around town. Not a secret. She followed him to Atwell in her old Mercedes, waited until he left, and ran him down. Bob said he was horrified when she got home and told him what she'd done. Claims Ruth spoke as if she'd hit an animal in the road. They left before dawn the next morning, took the car to a junkyard down in Sioux City and had it destroyed. We're checking with the junk yard now to verify."

"And when I mentioned I'd been up in the attic, she thought perhaps..." I paused, realizing my logic didn't make sense. "What was she doing in the attic? I didn't mention the diaries to her until Monday morning. She seemed genuinely surprised about them."

"Your intruder was definitely not Ruth or Bob Kendall," the chief insisted. "They were out to dinner in Atwell with clients until after ten. The clients, the restaurant, and the credit card receipts confirm that."

I glanced at Josh who shrugged. For the life of me, I couldn't figure out who had been here or why. Maybe it was one of those things we'd never learn.

Bill drained the last of his coffee and rose. "That's all I can tell you at the moment. By the way, we found your jewelry box intact along with your wallet in the trunk of Ruth's BMW. You can pick it up at the station anytime."

I'd almost forgotten about it. Relief flooded through me that I'd have another portion of my childhood back, especially the photos.

"How much of this can I print?" Josh asked.

"Bob signed his statement late last night. Hold off on the details. He might demand a trial, but I doubt it. He's tired and heartbroken about Ruth."

"Heartbroken?" I echoed. "After what she did and all the women he boinked?"

The chief raised an eyebrow and had a sardonic look on his face. No doubt he found my language surprising.

"In spite of all his philandering, he loved her."

"And her money," Josh claimed.

"Maybe. Who are we to assume?" The chief rose. "Thanks for the coffee. I'll be in touch."

After he left, Josh encircled me with his arms. "I'm sorry your mother didn't turn out the way you hoped."

"I'm not really surprised. Aunt Dee told me things as she lay dying. One of them was that Mother was selfish, self-centered, and spoiled."

"I thought it was your father she hated."

"She hated them both." I paused. "When Daddy went to Chicago for that farm implement show, he met my grandfather and Aunt Dee. Aunt Dee was smitten. Then Mother walked in the door, sensed her older sister had eyes for Daddy, and snatched him right out from under her. My aunt resented that they ran off and left her to deal with my grandfather who was in the early stages of Alzheimer's. So resentful that after Daddy was arrested, she told Roy Wilson, the sheriff at the time, a whopping lie. She claimed Daddy physically abused Mother over the years. That Mother was afraid of him, and planned on getting a divorce. Aunt Dee called Wilson a dolt who never followed up on the information to verify."

"I don't remember seeing anything like that in the original police report. He must not have included it."

"She also spread the story to various people at the funeral."

"Including Ruth," Josh said. "Only after you left for Chicago, *she* modified it to include him having an affair to take the heat off of her husband."

"Wilson *did* give that bit of gossip to the prosecutors. They dropped it when no evidence turned up, but the rumor persisted. After Aunt Dee died, I decided to do what Denny had planned."

"What was that?"

"Coming back to the farm and proving Daddy's innocence. He told me about it just before he left for Afghanistan that last time. His plan was to stay in the Army until he could claim his twenty years, retire, and run the farm. He never visualized a roadside bomb. When Aunt Dee died, I decided to do it for him."

Josh lightly kissed my forehead. "I'm taking the day off. How about you? Want to go somewhere for a change of scenery?"

I nestled my head deeper into his shoulder. "I was thinking up the staircase to the bedroom."

He laughed as we made our way upstairs where we made love soft and slow. Later, satiated and at peace, he propped himself up on his elbow and smiled.

"Callie, you've become a very important part of my life. I've heard it sometimes happens fast."

"What happens fast?" I murmured in a drowsy

voice.

He leaned over to kiss me. "Love."

The drowsiness left me as I stared into those gray eyes. "Are you sure?"

"I'm sure." An anxious look crossed his face. "What about you?"

I traced my finger down his cheek. "I'm sure, too. Deep down, I knew you were something special the night I told you why I'd come to Wellington. Something connected between us. I have no idea what. All I know is that whenever you're around, I feel safe—secure—like nothing can ever harm me again."

"That's the way it's supposed to work." He took a deep breath. "So I guess the next logical step is marriage. Will you marry me, Callie?"

Happiness squeezed my chest. I never thought about love and marriage much. It was always something that happened to someone else or in novels. Now, here it was happening to me.

Tears welled in my eyes. "Oh God, yes. I love you, Josh Hendricks with more passion than I ever thought possible."

He leaned over to kiss me senseless, his hand stroking and caressing the lambent fires back into flames. The loving had just begun.

****

I awoke much later to the sound of the shower running in the bathroom. Heaving a satisfied sigh, I swung my legs over the side of the bed with the intention of joining him. My feet hit the bare floor reminding me of what wasn't there—the rug. The image of Ruth's body was still fresh in my mind. For once, I wanted to forget. Josh had assured me that I'd done what had to be done and the image would fade over time. I hoped it was true.

The shower stopped and through the closed door I heard Josh whistling off key, and then the sound of water running in the sink. Oh well, the communal shower would have to wait for another day. Besides, I had plans for this afternoon.

After my shower, I dressed in a skirt, a long-sleeved blouse, and a pair of flats. In the kitchen, Josh took one look at me and knew what I had in mind.

"You're going to go see John Casey, aren't you?"

"Yep. I want to know why he never filed an appeal. Perhaps this time, he'll come clean."

"Want me to come with you?"

I started to shake my head, and then nodded. "I'd like that. If for no other reason than to keep me from strangling the son of a bitch."

At Casey's office, I sailed up to Serena with Josh by my side. Her eyes got wide and she fumbled for some papers on the desk.

"Uh, hi, Callie. What can I do for you?"

So we were back to Callie. "I want to see John. Now!"

"Uh…"

"And don't tell me he isn't in. I saw his car out front."

She hesitated and licked her lips while shooting a glance toward the closed office door.

"Are you going to tell him I'm here or do I just barge in? Your choice, Serena."

She picked up the phone and announced our presence, then hung up.

"He says to come on in."

I nodded and turned to the door. John opened it. He didn't smile.

"Callie, Josh, how are you doing? Quite a turn of events, wasn't it?"

He closed the door behind us and waved toward the chairs in front of his desk.

"Quite a turn," Josh agreed as we sat.

John took his seat behind the desk. "What can I do for you?"

I plunged right in. "I think you know. Why didn't you file an appeal in Daddy's case? It was a murder trial for God's sake. It should have been automatic."

John inhaled a deep breath and refused to make eye contact. "Because I didn't see the need. The prosecution had strong circumstantial evidence."

"And what did Eric Bryant have to say about that?" Josh asked in a quiet tone. When John didn't answer, he continued. "You never told him you didn't file, did you? You just strung him along until finally telling him it had been denied. Am I right?"

I sucked in a startled breath. Josh had verbalized what I had suspected.

"You never filed because the only appeal could have been gross misrepresentation, or whatever they call an incompetent lawyer. And Daddy never questioned you because you were his friend," I argued through the anger clogging my throat.

"I never wanted the case," John muttered. "I was the only lawyer your father knew, so when he asked, I told him he needed someone with experience in criminal law. He was grief-stricken about your mother and desperate to get you and Denny back home. Your aunt had whisked the two of you off almost immediately after his arrest."

"So, why did you take the case?"

"Jessica saw it as a springboard for better things. We'd just reconciled after a long separation. I wanted to make her happy."

"You took on a client you knew you were unqualified to represent to please your wife?" I remembered the snippet of information from Mother's diary. "Did Jessica try to seduce Daddy while the two of you were separated?"

He nodded. "She tried. He wasn't interested. She also had an eye on Bob Kendall. He didn't take the bait either."

The last pieces of the puzzle snapped into place. "Jessica was in the attic the other night. She's the one who attacked me."

His face bore a frantic expression. "Callie, please, don't say anything. She was terrified when you came back."

"She wanted the diary," I said.

"During the separation, your mother warned her off."

Only Mother hadn't been talking about Daddy, but Bob.

"How did she know about the diary's existence?" Josh asked.

"Grace once mentioned at some bridge game or club meeting that she kept a diary. When the house was being packed up, Jessica tried to find it, but with Ruth around, it was next to impossible. Eventually, she figured it was in some forgotten box and not likely to see the light of day again."

My conversation with Gina popped into my head.

"Only she did come back several times at night before the packing up was done. She used the key under the back step to search. That's how she got in the other night, too."

John shrugged. "She searched earlier? She didn't tell me that. She had no idea what was in the diary and was afraid the damned thing might become public. An opponent could use it against me in any political undertakings. She was desperate to get it. That's why she took a chance to look for it when you were gone that night. Look, Callie, please let it be. Jess didn't mean to hurt you. She was scared to death and panicked when you actually came into the attic. Just...just let it go."

Let it go? John Casey botched my father's defense and rather than admit it had lied to his client about an appeal. And all to appease his ambitious wife. His bungling of the case and Daddy's conviction must have infuriated Jessica. Neither of them deserved any mercy or consideration.

Josh squeezed my hand. "We'll think about it."

He rose and I followed him out of the office too surprised by his words to argue.

On the sidewalk, I stopped to stare. "Why did you tell him we'd think it over? As far as I'm concerned Jessica should be in jail and John disbarred."

"He may have admitted the way it was to us just now, but if we press it, he'll deny everything. He'll say your father asked him not to appeal, and we don't have anything to suggest otherwise. And Jessica will also deny having been in the attic." He shook his head. "At least we know the truth."

The logic of his words burned a hole in my chest.

The two of them would go on as if nothing had happened.

"You can bet that tomorrow morning, I'm in Atwell looking for another lawyer to handle the estate and the trust."

He took my hand and kissed it. "That goes without saying. He loses my business, too. He does the legal work for the paper. Now, suppose we go home and celebrate our engagement again."

The wicked gleam in his eyes eased my anger and made me go all warm inside.

"And to think I have a train whistle to thank for finding you."

"What train whistle?" he asked.

"The midnight train." I explained how it was entwined in my childhood. "I heard it again that first night home. Gave me a sense of security—until I met you."

He cocked his head and stared. "What train? There's no train in Wellington."

"Of course there is, silly. The tracks and the depot are near the grain elevators south of town."

"Callie, there aren't any train tracks anymore. From what I heard, the railroad abandoned Wellington fifteen or twenty years ago. The depot burned to the ground shortly after I arrived. Not even the grain elevators operate now. The farmers haul everything into Atwell."

My hand went to my throat. "But…But I heard it on more than one occasion."

He shook his head. "Maybe you were remembering, honey. Remembering something soothing from your childhood."

I thought about what he said as we walked to the car. Perhaps he was right. I heard a train whistle because I *needed* to hear it—the past linking me to the present, and to the future.

On the short drive home, I mentally built a fantasy around what lay ahead. He loved me. I loved him. Now that everything was solved, I could put the past behind me where it belonged. When bad memories sneak in, as they sometimes can, I won't shy away from them. I'll remember and deal with it. With Josh beside me to help, I can do anything. I was no longer alone and knew the future was bright.

I sighed with happiness. It was all about the love.

A word from the author...

I was born in Indianapolis, Indiana, but lived for many years in Memphis, Tennessee, which I now consider home. I have two adult children and seven grandchildren. At present, I reside in Ft. Lauderdale, Florida, with my husband.

I belong to Romance Writers of America and River City Romance Writers. I'm also a member of Mystery Writers of America, along with the Florida chapter of that organization.

I love writing and hope readers enjoy the journey along with me.

Thank you for purchasing
this publication of The Wild Rose Press, Inc.

If you enjoyed the story, we would appreciate your
letting others know by leaving a review.

For other wonderful stories,
please visit our on-line bookstore at
www.thewildrosepress.com.

For questions or more information
contact us at
info@thewildrosepress.com.

The Wild Rose Press, Inc.
www.thewildrosepress.com

Stay current with The Wild Rose Press, Inc.

Like us on Facebook

https://www.facebook.com/TheWildRosePress

And Follow us on Twitter
https://twitter.com/WildRosePress